FISTFUL OF RAIN

Other Books by Baron R. Birtcher

FISTFUL OF RAIN

BARON R. BIRTCHER

THE PERMANENT PRESS
Sag Harbor, NY 11963

For information, address:
 The Permanent Press
 4170 Noyac Road
 Sag Harbor, NY 11963
 www.thepermanentpress.com

Library of Congress Cataloging-in-Publication Data

Birtcher, Baron R., author.
 Fistful of rain / Baron R. Birtcher.
 Sag Harbor, NY: Permanent Press, 2018.
 ISBN: 978-1-57962-518-4
  1. Ranchers—Oregon—Fiction. 2. Nineteen seventies—
Fiction. 3. Suspense fiction.

PS3552.I7573 F57 2018
813'.54—dc23   2017058040

Printed in the United States of America

For

My father, Ronald Birtcher
and
My uncle, Arthur Birtcher
and
My grandfather, F. E. Birtcher

Cowboys all, and keepers of the Code

"We are stardust
 We are golden
 And we've got to get ourselves
 Back to the garden . . ."

—Joni Mitchell
Woodstock

———

"And those who were seen dancing
 were thought to be insane
 by those who could not hear the music."

—Friedrich Nietzsche

1975

I HAVE ALWAYS considered myself a pragmatist, which has served me well as both a cowboy and a cattleman. I've heard it said that the opposite of love does not express itself as hate, but as indifference. If that is so, then the obverse of loyalty and duty is not manifested by faithlessness, but apathy. As the sheriff of Meriwether County, I have seen this to be true.

The story of Cronos—the father of the gods who gave his name to time itself—has its origins in ancient mythology. He ascended to the throne by murdering his father, thereafter taking his own sister as his wife, and siring half a dozen children with her. His fear of familial treachery, however, was so acute that he massacred all six of the daughters and sons he had fathered and consummated the deed by devouring their remains. So while our present generation had clearly not originated the notions of degeneracy, solipsism, greed, sloth, lust, or envy, it seemed to be increasingly dedicated to the perfection of their practice.

———∞———

I HAD been raised in simpler times, taking pride in the cattle we produced on the family ranch, which itself had been assembled from the sweat and blood and sacrifice of three generations. But the tenuous threads that held the world together back when I'd returned home from my service

11

in Korea had been tested to their breaking point since the dawning of Aquarius.

What had spontaneously begun as a summer of love in 1967 had been corrupted in its infancy by the perverse and senseless acts of violence provoked by an aspiring musician and self-proclaimed messiah named Charles Manson just two short years after it had begun, and was ultimately nailed to a cross of its own construction during a rock concert at a California speedway four short months later, in December of that very same year.

—∞—

AS HAD become our personal tradition, my wife, Jesse, and I acknowledged the arrival of the New Year by watching the ball drop in Times Square from the safe distance afforded by the television console in the living room at the ranch house. We sipped iced champagne from the same etched crystal flutes that we had used to toast our wedding vows more than twenty years before, hoping as we always did that the upcoming year would be an improvement on the last.

On this night, however, I wondered how things could get much worse. But I kept that misanthropic notion to myself.

1974 had been one of the most demoralizing that I could remember.

The nation had endured the humiliation of Watergate and the resignation of a sitting president, who was subsequently succeeded by a man named Gerald R. Ford. In assuming his role as our thirty-eighth president, Ford became the only man to assume that high office by political appointment; he had replaced the disgraced Spiro Agnew as vice president, who himself had pleaded no contest to federal income tax evasion in exchange for the dropping of charges of political corruption.

But that was only the beginning.

The long, slow withdrawal of troops that marked our defeat in Vietnam had not only cost the lives of tens of thousands of United States soldiers, but was made all the worse by welcoming the survivors home with antipathy and derision. The Pentagon admitted that at least one-third of returning veterans had used heroin while overseas, and the goal of the typical eighteen-year-old grunt had atrophied to a degree that all he wanted was to simply live to see one more birthday.

Those young people who did return alive faced levels of unemployment not experienced since the Great Depression, rampant double-digit inflation that was forcing businesses to fold, and an international petroleum crisis that quadrupled gasoline prices and forced rationing at the pump. The price of a house had also moved beyond their reach—mortgage interest rates having doubled in a single year—and the traditional bright colored lights of Christmas celebrations had been banned in several states in the name of oil conservation.

As citizens, we had grown not only to distrust our own government officials, but to distrust our neighbors too. Justice Department surveys informed us that one out of every four households in America had suffered a rape, assault, burglary, robbery, or auto theft in the preceding year alone.

The economic abundance that defined the Kennedy and Eisenhower eras had been a byproduct of confidence about our future, but by the end of 1974 the average citizen had lost all faith in an economy managed by poseurs, pundits, and politicians, and We The People learned the meanings of new terms like *stagflation* while we watched Harlem and the Bronx succumb to the flames of arsonists on the nightly news. Such was our assimilation into the dark and hallucinatory vocabulary of an incipient nightmare state.

In response, the disaffected youth who claimed they would no longer tolerate establishment hypocrisy invented a version of hypocrisy that they could call their own. The utopian dream of the overnight elimination of poverty and prejudice and hatred had proven to be a fantasy. But the spark of rebellion that had spawned it remained, and this time there was television and mass media to help shape the zeitgeist, not as a mirror, but as a tool.

Seemingly overnight, membership in traditional churches declined, only to be replaced by the search for the Self. One of the best-selling books of the year was titled *How to Be Your Own Best Friend.*

Which left me with one nagging question as I shared that cold December evening with my wife: Who manned the rope line between the new world and the old?

—⊗—

I WILL freely admit that I have known fear, and that I have witnessed evil in the form and affect of dangerous and misguided elitists who treat the blood, treasure, and sacrifice of their fellow citizens as currency. I had witnessed it firsthand while serving in my war, and I had seen it on the streets, embodied in the actions of edacious and manipulative demagogues who lie outright while they look you in the eye and stake a personal claim upon the truth.

—⊗—

NO, THE ones who set my town ablaze, both literally and figuratively, were not insane; I don't know with any certainty if they were even particularly angry, or bore any personal malice toward the innocents whom they harmed. It was simply something that they felt had to be done.

But what are you supposed to do when someone visits malevolence and brutality upon your life, or worse, inflicts defilement on those you love most? As for me, I will not abide the construction of victims. I am the sheriff of this county.

But I'm getting ahead of myself.

As with all things, it's best to begin at the beginning.

PART ONE

LO-FI TENNESSEE MOUNTAIN ANGEL

CHAPTER ONE

MILA KINSLOW
(Excerpted from interview #MC1803/D)

I REMEMBER spending my sweet sixteenth birthday watching the lights flash on the Ferris wheel far below us, and the long line of cars idling outside those gates, waiting to get inside the fairgrounds. We was sitting on the porch of the old house, Momma and me, and she was having a cigarette and drinking rye whiskey out of a Bell jar in the same rusted-out metal rocking chair that Granddad used to sit in. I would have given almost anything to join those folks down there, but me and Momma never had two nickels to spare. My birthday gift that year was that Mr. Seely down at the café let me off from my job as a waitress there a whole hour early.

It was pretty nice, really. They stuck a candle in some whipped cream that they squirted from a can onto a strawberry waffle. They sang me that Happy Birthday song, then tipped me out, and let me go home after I blew out the candle. I don't remember what I wished for, but I had pretty much gave up on wishes by then anyways.

———

MY MOMMA had been pretty once, I heard. Kinda funny that it never occurred to me before that she might have ever been young, or ever had any real dreams of her own. These days she spent most of her time smoking Viceroy cigarettes and staring out at the haze that would settle across the valley like a threadbare cotton blanket. I never knew what she was thinking about, and never had the thought to ask her, not that she would have answered me. It seemed like as time went along she just got soft around the middle, and real, real hard on the inside. Sometimes her eyes would sort of shine with this faraway expression, then go blank and she'd drift off to sleep.

———∞———

I WAS seventeen when she died. I guess she didn't really die so much as kind of fade out, you know, like that last star in the morning when the sun bleaches the dark away and turns everything to blue?

Anyways, I found her laying there on the couch that morning, so I called the doctor who drove all the way up from town just to pronounce her dead, which I had already told him she was, then he phoned the mortuary and asked them to come pick up her body. I hadn't had a chance to cry, didn't even feel like it yet, and later on I ended up feeling pretty bad about that. I asked the doctor what I was supposed to do next, and he said since I was underage, I was probably going to be moved into a foster home if I didn't have no relatives to stay with, which I didn't. My choices became pretty clear to me at that point.

I wasn't going to stick around there for no foster care. I'd heard enough about the sick shit that happened to girls my age.

I gathered up my favorite stuff and crammed it into a beat-up old American Tourister suitcase that was tucked in the back of Momma's closet, then I took out the grocery money we kept stashed inside a Hills Bros. coffee can in the fridge, and lit out for the bus station before the authorities could come and collect me up. I couldn't even risk sticking around for her funeral, not that anybody'd show up for it. I still feel kinda bad about that too. But there wasn't likely to be no casseroles waiting for me on the stoop afterward.

No, I didn't have no burning urge to run off and be a movie star or beauty queen or something. It was more like an animal instinct to protect myself, like if I stayed around Tennessee too long I would end up stuck right there forever just like Momma had been, slowly dying from a low-grade fever or an infection that would just swallow me up whole in a gray shadow or a cloud of cigarette smoke or a tangle of cheap, sweaty sheets.

I STUFFED fifteen bucks into the pocket of my jeans for later, and took the rest of what I'd grabbed from the coffee can and handed it over to the man at the ticket counter for the Continental Trailways. I asked him how far that cash would take me and he made a scrunched-up look with his face and checked the schedule. He had these weird purple veins on his cheeks that looked like a bunch of itty bitty bugs had crawled up under there and made a nest, and I tried not to stare at him while he studied on that schedule.

He looked down at me and counted out my money again, then told me I could get as far as Phoenix or Denver or LA.

I picked LA because I'd never seen the ocean before.

Kinda wish I'd picked Denver instead.

CHAPTER TWO

THE FIRST TIME Mila Kinslow finally broke down and cried was in Amarillo, Texas.

She had taken a seat alone at a picnic table underneath the eave of a rundown truck stop, listlessly chewing the crust off a stale bologna sandwich and counting what remained of the fifteen dollars she had set aside. Mila had tried hard not to think too much about her mother, especially how she hadn't even had the presence of mind or decency to kiss the poor dead woman on the forehead before she'd fled the house. Now she found she could no longer blink back the tears that had begun to well behind her eyes. Uncharitable thoughts about the doctor, the police, hell, the whole damned uncaring town lit off inside her head like electrical sparks. It made her feel as though she was shrinking down to nothing. Mila knew nobody would be looking for her, just like nobody would be there to stand graveside when her momma's body was finally lowered into that black valley soil.

The drone of Amarillo traffic hummed on the overpass and the evening air smelled of asphalt, overheated rubber, and car exhaust. Mila pulled the collar of her sweater tight around her neck, and shivered even though the night was warm. The sandwich tasted like chalk dust in her mouth, and she noticed that the creepy-looking man was staring at her again through the flyspecked cashiers' window. The horn-rimmed glasses that rested crookedly on his nose reflected blue and green neon from the menu board, the planes of his face a moonscape of scars from a childhood disease. His attention felt like unwashed fingers on her skin.

"What the hell you lookin' at, Bubba?" she called out, and he slid his eyes away.

She hadn't spoken ten words since the bus had pulled out of the terminal in Tennessee, and the sound of her own voice resonated strangely to her. Her heartbeat felt constricted, like it was squeezed inside a fist, and tiny pinpricks of darkness crowded the edges of her vision.

Mila hadn't been aware that she had begun to weep. She swiped her cheeks with the sleeve of a stretched-out sweater and threaded her way between the tables toward the restroom as the bus driver sounded a five-minute warning on the horn. Her chest ached when she breathed, her throat raw and swollen from crying. She stepped inside the women's room, ran cold water in a porcelain sink, and cupped her hands beneath the tepid water, splashing it on her face. She dried off with a paper towel, waiting for some kind of signal, any kind of hopeful sign, from the misshapen image that stared back from the mirror that was bolted to the wall.

She made a wish, and waited for her reflection to slide right off the glass.

———

SUNRISE ARRIVED in soft focus the next morning, composed of warm pastels and gentle edges, and painted elongated shadows of white fir and lodgepole pine across the highway. Mila had leaned her head against the window and fallen asleep somewhere outside of Glenrio, Texas, and hadn't awakened until she felt the bus pull off the interstate. She stretched the kinks out of her neck as the driver announced their imminent arrival in Flagstaff.

Her mouth was dry and tasted foul from the sandwich she had eaten hours earlier. She briefly considered getting off the bus to buy something to eat, but knew she couldn't really spare the cost. Instead she reached into the rucksack she carried and searched in vain for a stick of gum, or anything that might push the hunger pangs away. She was disappointed that the pastel sunrise had already disappeared. Never in her life had she felt so alone.

Mila turned her attention to the passengers who had been sitting across the aisle. She watched them as they stood and tugged backpacks and parcels wrapped in brown paper tied with twine out of the storage space overhead. A rush of cool morning desert air swept along the aisle as the pneumatic doors sighed open, and she pressed her palm against the window to gauge the temperature outside. A susurrus of muted conversation and the shuffling of feet filled in the empty spaces as new passengers filed aboard, and she allowed her mind to drift as a single line of lacy clouds was carried by the wind across a blanched dome of sky.

"Anybody sitting here?"

The voice that startled Mila belonged to a young woman.

Mila gave the girl a glance, shrugged, and moved the rucksack off the unoccupied seat and placed it on the floor. Except for the unexpected burst of emotion she'd succumbed to in Amarillo, the trip had mostly been a long, slow-moving picture of depressing nothingness. So, the truth was, a seatmate might be a welcome distraction.

"Name's Alexandra," the girl said, and pushed a lock of hair behind her ear.

"Okay," Mila said.

Mila judged that the girl named Alexandra couldn't be much older than twenty, and though the expression in her eyes was soft, she possessed an air of circumspection that hinted at experience beyond her years. She wore a look of kindness and compassion that put Mila in mind of the images of angels rendered in colored panes of glass inside the arched windows at the church that she and Momma sometimes attended back at home.

"This is the part where you tell me *your* name," Alexandra said, smiling.

"Mila?"

Without warning, Mila felt herself swept up again by a sudden sense of isolation. She felt herself floating away, abandoned and forsaken, though she knew it had nothing to do with Alexandra.

"Was that a question?" Alexandra said.

Heat rushed to Mila's face and she sensed herself on the brink of losing her composure. She felt certain that this girl must think she was insane. Mila felt like she was disappearing, her fingers clawing an empty space beside her heart.

"Aw, sweetheart, hush now. Don't cry," Alexandra whispered, and looked into Mila's eyes as though she had seen inside her mind. "You're not just a name badge pinned to your sweater."

CHAPTER THREE

MILA KINSLOW
(Excerpted from interview #MC1803/D)

LOS ANGELES WAS a huge disappointment.

I was expecting palm trees and sunny beaches and side-walks filled with pretty people waiting for their close-ups. But there wasn't any palm trees at the bus station and the sun looked like a soggy yellow cotton ball floating around behind a big gray curtain of smog. On top of that, at least a month went by before I even found out which direction the ocean was in, and another month after that before I ever laid my eyes on it.

I didn't complain or fuss about it though.

Alexandra and I talked the whole way out from Flagstaff, and by the time we got to California she knew my entire sorry drama. She told me that her friends called her Sandi, and that's what I should call her too.

"Sandi with an 'i'," she said, and I remember laughing.

She offered to let me stay with her and her two room-mates in a tiny house they all rented a few blocks over from the Sunset Strip, said I could make a bed out on the living room couch until I got my feet set on the ground. Sandi made a couple of calls and even got me a job—two jobs, really—answering phones at a bail bond place during the daytime, and waiting tables at a twenty-four-hour diner at night. Sandi and her roommates didn't ask me to pay rent for the first whole month after I got there, just asked me to pitch in when the groceries ran low.

All three of the girls were in their early twenties, but none of them seemed to care that I was so much younger. They treated me like a little sister, I guess, assuming sisters teach you how to drink beer and smoke marijuana. I never had no sisters, not even any cousins, so I don't really know. We laughed a lot, though, and cried sometimes if we got too drunk, but mostly it was nice, and on weekends they'd sneak me into the music clubs along the Strip, where nobody seemed to care at all how old I was.

That's where I met Jack McCall.

I should have known right away he was going to be bad news, him having the exact same name as the sonofabitch who murdered Wild Bill Hickok. I never did do all that well at school back home, but I always did pretty good in history because I liked it, and I especially liked hearing about cowboys, so some stuff kind of stuck in my head like that.

Anyways, the Jack McCall I'm talking about was a guitar player and singer in a band called Hammerhead that played at the Whisky a Go Go. Their music was sort of heavy blues, and I met him the night they opened up for Rory Gallagher. God, but Jack was pretty then; sweet, soulful blue eyes and long, curly blond hair that would hang down in front of his face when he got lost in a song. This was, what, two years ago, so it was 1973 at the time and I hadn't even turned eighteen yet.

Sandi got us in for free because she had a friend who played bass in the band, so we all hung out together when Hammerhead finished with their set, and she introduced me to the guys. Like I said before, Jack McCall was movie-star good looking, and he liked his girlfriends young, so within a couple of months I'd moved my stuff out of Sandi's rental house and started shacking-up with Jack.

Sandi's friend the bass player would crash with Jack and me from time to time, and he was real nice to me too. Never tried anything with me, always acted like an old-fashioned gentleman where I was concerned. His name was Peter Troy, but everyone knew him as Sweet Pete.

SEVENTY-THREE turned out not to be a very good year on the Strip. Record companies that used to send untested acts out on the road to gain experience couldn't afford to do it anymore, so clubs weren't putting on live shows as much as they had before. Some of them locked up their doors for good. It seemed like the whole country had fallen into a funk, and nobody had any money. Jack would go days sometimes without leaving the apartment; spent his time laying on the sofa and watching the guys on the news talk about oil embargoes and Watergate and the war, or plinking on his guitar with the amp turned way down low. I didn't know it at the time, but that's when Jack took up with the needle.

I was young and stupid then, and never saw the signs. Until I finally did.

One night we were all together at the Whisky to watch Hammerhead open up for Buddy Miles. I was drinking beers at the bar with Sandi that night—they never asked me for ID—when the whole room watched Jack McCall implode onstage. When it was over, I heard one of the bartenders say, "I'm not sure the lead singer's supposed to stagger around and weep into the microphone through the whole damn show, is he?"

I didn't want to go backstage during the break. I didn't know what I should do. A half hour later, Sweet Pete came out and plopped down in the barstool next to mine with a look on his face like somebody had just shot his dog.

"He's going to hurt you, Mila," he told me.

I told him that Jack wasn't a violent man.

"I didn't mean he would hurt you by his own hand," he said. "But he's circling the drain and he doesn't give a shit if he takes everybody with him."

I was so mad at Pete for saying something like that, I couldn't even look at his face.

"Grow up, goddamn it, Mila," Pete said. "Jack's a fucking junkie."

"Don't you say things like that," I finally said.

"I don't think I can do this much longer," Pete said while I peeled the label off my beer bottle and pretended to ignore him. "I've got a friend who knows this guy up in Oregon. He's got a big ass bunch of land with lots of groovy people living there."

I asked Pete what the hell he was talking about. I was still mad at him.

"You and I could drive there together, Mila," was all he said.

I SPENT the next three days at Sandi's house because I didn't want to go back home to Jack. It was kinda like old times at Sandi's place, except it also kinda wasn't. Hammerhead wasn't working anywhere, and the whole scene had started to get pretty depressing. My mind kept drifting back to Tennessee, even though I had no mind to ever go back. I guess that's what feeling homesick is. I had been raised going to church. Sunday school from the time I could walk. I even sang in the children's cherub choir. But lately I had found myself wondering if there was such a thing as God, or as a soul, and if there was, how could you explain a man like Jack McCall and what he was doing to all of us.

I finally decided to go back to our apartment after my shift at the diner, having stupidly convinced myself that I could be Jack's savior. I found him laying face down on the couch wearing nothing but those striped bell-bottomed pants he hadn't even bothered to zip up all the way. I shook him by the shoulder and he rolled onto the floor. His lips were crusted with flecks of vomit and dried blood, one of his eyes had swollen like an eggplant and one of his front teeth was busted off clear down to the gum. His torso was marbled with bruises and his breath smelled like spoiled dog food. He tried to smile at me, and when he did I felt exactly like I had that night back at the truck stop.

I couldn't help it, and I started crying, more for Jack than for myself.

I asked him what had happened to him and he told me it was a misunderstanding about a money thing.

"How much?" I asked him.

"More than either of us has got, darlin'."

I got so mad I could have hit him, but I didn't. For all the vain and weak and selfish things Jack was, he never laid a hand on me in anger, so I wasn't going to be the one to do it to him. Besides, there wasn't much of him that hadn't already been abused.

"You don't get to call me that anymore," I told him.

He began to shiver and I could see then that he was dope sick. The whites of his eyes had turned the color of worn-out old piano keys, and the veins stood out on his arms like night crawlers that had up and died in there.

"I need a favor from you, baby," he said. "Just this one time."

"I'm not buying smack for you," I said.

His mouth made a dry clicking sound when he tried to speak next and he could no longer look me in the eye.

"It's not that," he said. "There's two guys. You've seen them before at the Whisky."

"I told you I won't help you kill yourself, Jack. I mean it."

He was still seated on that filthy rug, propped up against the sofa cushion. He shook his head and looked up at me with his one good eye.

"They want you to join them for a party," he said. "They said they'll clear my debt if you go."

I heard the hiss of air brakes from a city bus outside on the street, and the dying-dog howl of a police siren from somewhere in the distance.

"Christ, Jack," I whispered.

"I need this from you, baby," he said. "You love me, don't you?"

I could only stare, couldn't have said anything if I wanted to.

"I love you."

"You love me?" I said. I wanted to scream then. I wanted to kick him. Mostly I wanted to curl up in a ball and disappear. "You want to pimp me out to two strangers for a fix."

"Baby—"

I never heard the rest of what he said.

All I remember is that it seemed like the walls were folding in and I was weightless, and pinwheels started spinning in my head. My heart was slamming and my blood felt like it was boiling inside, and my thoughts were nothing but a confused tangle of pitiful emotions. I had heard words like heartbreak and fury, and I thought I knew what they meant. Turns out I had no idea until that night. I knew that hell must have been left unattended in that moment because the devil and all his demons had surely been set loose in LA.

———∽∽∽———

I DON'T remember how I got there, but I ended up standing at Sweet Pete's door.

"Have you still got that friend in Oregon, Pete?"

CHAPTER FOUR

JESSE WAS STANDING outdoors on the porch when I came out to the kitchen that morning. She was steadying herself with one hip on the railing, her shoulder wedged against a vertical post, and a pair of field glasses pressed to her eyes. The percolator on the counter was still popping, so I stepped outside to join her while I waited. The slender curve of a waning crescent floated low in the violet predawn like a Cheshire smile. It was the change of the seasons, and while the atmosphere still carried the last remnants of the cool chill of spring, the breeze coming down from the mountain smelled like summer.

"What are you looking at?" I whispered.

"Caleb's up on his roof again," she whispered back without moving the binoculars from her face.

"What do you mean, *again?*"

"Third time in the last two weeks,"

Wyatt, our blue heeler, was curled up beside Jesse's feet and his tail swept the floor when he heard me come out through the screen door. He raised his head for a moment to acknowledge me, but didn't move from his warm spot on the floorboards.

"You spend a lot of time spying on our foreman?" I asked.

"It's not spying when he's living rent free on our ranch."

"Looks like a duck, walks like a duck . . ."

She screwed up her face and pushed the binoculars into my hands.

"Take a look for yourself, smart guy," she said.

Caleb Wheeler was perched on the ridge of the wood-shingled roof of the cabin we'd built for him down near the creek. His back was leaned into the river rock chimney, his wrists resting flat on his knees. His shoulders were hunched against the wind currents, cocooned in an old Indian blanket, and his Stetson was pushed back on his head. I could see the deep lines on his face and the shine of his eyes in the momentary glow as he drew on his cigarette and stared out into the distance.

"Looks like he's speaking to somebody," I said.

"That's what I thought. Or singing some kind of song to himself."

"Caleb doesn't sing."

The flight call of a pheasant rolled out of the long grass that grew wild beyond the fruit orchard.

"Maybe you should go talk to him," Jesse said. "Just to be sure he's okay."

I placed the binoculars on the table and encircled her waist with my arms. I leaned down and kissed the soft skin at the back of her neck. Her hair smelled of green apples and lavender.

"I know what you're thinking," I said as I pulled away. "Caleb is fine. He may be getting old, but he's not senile. I work with the man every day."

"Caleb's like family, Ty."

"Which is the reason I'm not going to tell him you've been spying on him from our front porch with a Canada Leica."

"I wasn't spying on him."

I kissed her once more, turned, and headed back to the kitchen.

"Quack, quack," I said.

⸺∞⸺

CRICKET WAS sipping black tea, scanning the pages of the local weekly newspaper she had spread out across the breakfast table when Jesse and I moved inside.

"Can I use the Bronco today, Dad?"

"Good morning," I said.

"Good morning," she smiled. "Can I use the Bronco today?"

Jesse kissed the crown of our daughter's head as she passed into the kitchen for our coffee. Cricket had recently flown out to spend her summer vacation with us after completing her junior year at Colorado State.

"Working today?" I asked.

"Shopping."

"For what?"

"I'm taking up jogging. I need a tracksuit and a pair of running shoes."

"You need a uniform to run? You used to do that in bare feet and cutoffs. Besides, I thought you were all about tennis."

She rolled her eyes at me.

"That's so 1972, Dad. Try to stay with-it, will you? You're becoming an embarrassment."

Jesse handed my mug to me and my heart sank a little bit more at the passage of time. The name on my little girl's birth certificate is Laura, but she had been Cricket to me from her very first awkward hops as a toddler.

"Pick up a mood ring for your mom while you're out," I said. "And you can use the Jeep."

Jesse took a seat at the table beside Cricket and they both stared at me.

"Where are you going?" Jesse asked me.

"I've got to drive up to Lewiston," I said. "County Council meeting this afternoon."

"Already?"

"Third Tuesday of every damned month."

"Honest to God, Ty, I still don't understand why you have to attend those things."

"I'm the sheriff in this county, ma'am. It's my sworn duty."

Both Jesse and Cricket were well aware that I hated these demonstrations of political Kabuki, but they giggled at me anyway. The construction of our local government was a holdover from its founding in the early 1800s. Since there are only two towns in the county, there are no separate mayors, only a County Council comprised of nine civic-minded citizens, elected for rolling terms of two years apiece. To complicate matters further, the council acted as the school board as well, and the monthly meetings often droned on so long and drifted into minutiae so esoteric it made me want to take a pair of tin snips and lop off my fingers just to have something to do. Regardless of my personal predispositions, as sheriff I was obligated to attend.

Lately, however, the tone of the gatherings had grown far more sententious and autocratic and had driven me to reconsider the character of those drawn to the trappings of elected office, and the motivations that drove their desires. I found myself stunned at the speed at which some well-intentioned and congenial people could devolve into patronage, pomposity, and self-admiration.

"Some people feel invisible unless they're pontificating," I said.

"Well," Jesse said. "Please don't be late. Snoose Corcoran is coming over for dinner. It gets awfully quiet if you're not around for him to speak to."

"This day just keeps getting better and better."

COUNCIL MEETINGS were held at the Grange Hall in Lewiston, at the northernmost end of our valley, a full two-hour drive from my cattle ranch over twisting, two-lane blacktop etched into the floor of a wooded canyon whose steep walls were still weeping the moisture of snowmelt at this time of year.

The Bronco's tires hummed as I passed from the pavement onto the trestle bridge that spanned the wide throat of the river. I watched a bald eagle making low passes over the rapids where the watercourse grew narrow. I rolled down the window and breathed in the sweet scents of sugar pine and wet stone, and pushed through the last handful of miles into town.

The pea-gravel parking lot that circled the Grange Hall was crowded more densely than usual, and the sight brought a sinking feeling to my gut. I pulled into a spot at the far corner, where a set of seesaws and swings sat idle inside a field of untended grass.

I stepped up the stairway, held the front door, and smiled politely for a group of elderly ladies who attended these damned meetings every month without fail, and followed them inside. The overheated stillness of the indoor air smelled of furniture polish, mildew, and dust. Faded tintypes of bearded, severe-looking men glared down from the walls that lined the vestibule, and I steeled myself as I did every month, by taking a moment to admire an old photo of my dad and grandfather breaking a claybank somewhere out near our ranch's stockyard, from a year that predated my birth.

"That you out there, Sheriff?" a voice bellowed out from inside the main chamber. "Step on in so we can get this thing started."

An elongated conference table with ten matching chairs occupied the front quarter of the room, the remainder being taken up by row after row of disused church pews and metal folding chairs. Every seat in the house had someone in it, except for the one at the far end of the council's table that had been reserved for me.

Nolan Brody, chairman of the council, gaveled the proceedings to order, but not before throwing a scowl that was meant to express his displeasure at my tardiness in my general direction. He was an attorney by trade—specializing in contracts and civil litigation—which meant that he made a living standing in between two people who were otherwise prepared to strike a deal, then complicating the hell out of it and charging them a fee. Brody was diminutive in stature and in possession of a distinctly flinty temperament. He was the kind of man my father would have referred to as "fryin' size." Like many small men I had known over the course of my life, Nolan Brody tried to compensate with the use of confrontational tones, and by carrying himself as though he wore underwear made of plywood.

It took more than an hour to suffer through the first item on the agenda, which involved a proposal to install coin-operated parking meters along both sides of Ashton Street, the commercial heart of Lewiston. The floor of the Grange Hall was a checkerboard of black and green silicate floor tiles, and I occupied my time counting the broken ones, and noting the places where they had worn through to the under-layment and substrate.

"Any thoughts on this matter, Sheriff Dawson?" the chairman finally asked.

"You've just spent a considerable amount of valuable time pearl-clutching over whether or not to pay dollars for dimes, is what I think. But my professional question is this: Who's supposed to write the tickets for the folks who choose not to pay for the privilege of parking? I've got a grand total of five men—including me—to cover this entire county, and not one of us signed on to be meter maids."

"I wish you had mentioned something to us earlier," Brody said.

"With due respect, Mr. Chairman, I believe this is the third time I have expressed exactly this same sentiment, both to you and to the rest of this fine council."

A ripple of laughter floated up from the rear of the room, where the older folks tended to gather. Nolan Brody squinted at me, then brought down his gavel and put the matter to a final vote, which went down in defeat with a count of seven against two.

"While we're on the topic of law and order," Brody said. "We have a request from Harper Emory who has something he wants to say about our growing hippie problem. Why don't you come on up here to the podium, Harper?"

It was the first I had heard there was a hippie *problem* in the county, though it was common knowledge that a few dozen young people had taken up residence on an abandoned sheep ranch in midvalley. The first group of them had come here a couple years earlier, and their numbers had ebbed and flowed somewhat since then. But as far as I knew, there hadn't been any significant trouble owing to their presence. In fact, they had opened a couple of small storefront businesses in the town of Meridian.

The room fell silent as Harper Emory limped his way up the aisle toward the lectern. Emory had operated as a local sheep rancher for almost twenty years, a solidly built man of above-average height, known both for his fractious disposition and as a notorious torturer of the truth. Notwithstanding my personal feelings about the man's veracity, there was no denying that someone had taken out their aggressions on him, and had left him with substantial injuries to his head and face, and put his right arm in a sling.

"You all know me," he said. "And you know my place butts up against that goddamn commune where the goddamn hippies live—"

Brody's gavel rapped the table.

"Mr. Emory, please try to refrain from using profanity."

Harper Emory peered at each of the councilmen in turn, his eyes resembling piss holes in a snowdrift.

"Two days ago, a couple of my animals went missing, so I set out to check the fence line and to try to get 'em back. Well, sure as hell, I found a cut in the wire that runs between my place and the one that belongs to the hippies, and I knew right away that they'd up and rustled my goddamn lambs. Then I did what anybody in this room woulda done in my place, and I ducked in through that fence hole and went after the thieves. I wasn't more than a hundred yards inside that filthy place before three long-haired boys ridin' motor-bikes come askin' *me* why I'm trespassing. 'Trespassing,' I say to 'em. 'You sonsabitches took my lambs and I want 'em back right goddamn now.' "

Brody pounded his gavel again, but the sound was over-whelmed by the scraping of chair legs and the uneasy mut-tering of the gallery.

"You gonna let me tell my damn story or not?" Emory asked, and continued without waiting for a reply. "Anyways, these boys said they didn't know a thing about no stolen live-stock and told me to get offa their land. I told them they could all go to hell, and a minute later they were on me like a pack of coyotes, beating the ashes out of me. Those boys might look like girls, but they can damn well throw punches like Frazier and Ali. Nearly put out my eye. You can ask Doc Brawley about that."

I could sense that the tone of the meeting was rapidly shifting to one of rancor and recrimination. I didn't care for the direction, nor did I like the fact—assuming Harper Emory was telling the truth—that he had waited two days to report either the sheep rustling or the beating, and I had to wonder why.

"I have to admit," I said. "I'm a little vexed that you didn't report this to me sooner."

"I'm reporting it to you now," Emory spat. "I want those people paid back in kind, Sheriff. With interest."

"You know that's not the way the law works, but I promise everybody I'll look into it."

"That ain't good enough, Ty. Those bastards beat holy hell out of me and stole my damn lambs."

I shot a glance over my shoulder at Chairman Nolan, and his expression appeared oddly impassive. While I had long been suspect with regard to his principles, this public and intentional cultivation of suspicion and hostility being directed toward the kids they referred to as hippies seemed not only callous and cruel, but unwise. He made no attempt to tamp down the bedlam, and I was left with the distinct impression that we were all being gaslighted somehow.

"That's not fair," a female voice shouted from out of the crowd. When she stood, I recognized her as one of Cricket's former teachers from high school, but couldn't recall her name. "You don't know for sure whether they stole anything from you!"

Harper Emory spun around and pinned her with a glare.

"A hole in my fence that leads right to their property says otherwise, young lady."

"She's right, Mr. Emory," I said. "We won't know who's done what until I check it out. Okay?"

"No," Emory said. "That's not okay. We shouldn't have to put up with these lawless longhairs for one more goddamn day."

The atmosphere of malevolence was growing more palpable, and when I slammed my open palm on the table, the shouting and pandemonium died slowly away. The teacher had remained standing through the entire outburst and I gestured for her to continue.

"The reason I came to this meeting was to ask for the school board's permission to take my students on a field trip to the commune for a tour," the teacher said. Her complexion was ashen, but for the angry flush that had risen on her cheeks. "But, after witnessing all of this, I have no intention to ask that of you. Instead I am informing you that my class and I shall, in fact, be visiting Rainbow Ranch. And we shall be doing so before the end of the school year. That's all I came for. I have now done what I came here to do, and I will be leaving. Good evening to you all."

She nodded to me as she gathered her purse and stormed down the aisle and through the double doors at the back of the room.

Harper Emory was still standing at the podium. It seemed that his good eye had begun to quiver with fantasies of revenge.

"If you don't do something about those hippies, Sheriff, I swear to God I will," Emory said.

"You do and I'll haul you in myself, Harper," I said. "That goes for all of you folks. Just settle down and let the law do what you hired us to do."

My statement was met with catcalls and hoots, and I turned toward Nolan Brody.

"You'd better do something, Nolan. Call for a ten-minute break so everyone can cool off. This meeting went off the rails in a hell of a hurry."

He paused for a few seconds before he brought down his gavel and called for a recess, then regarded me with an expression of self-satisfaction. It was a look that suggested he knew that this outcome had been as foregone as that of the Knights Templar at the hands of the Saracens.

"I WOULD appreciate a private word with you, Sheriff," Brody said as he followed me into the vestibule.

We stepped outdoors into the welcome freshness of the early evening breeze. Off to the west, the low angle of the sun cast the narrow stone canyons that centuries had carved into the side of the mountain in shades of deep violet shadow and pale yellow light. Brody came to a halt when we reached the corner of the building and turned to face me, to square off with me, and I studied the strange architecture of his features again. There was a vaguely asymmetrical set to his small, dark eyes and a perpetual sliver of whiskers nested in the cleft of his chin that his razor never managed to reach. His eyes were illuminated by vanity and animus, his visage and posture oddly puerile, as if a cruel and angry little child still lived somewhere inside his flesh.

"What can I do for you, Nolan?" I said.

"What in the hell is the matter with you?"

"An angry mob can be an unstable and explosive thing. I've witnessed it too many times."

"You're not the only one who has experienced the hazards of the battlefield, Mr. Dawson."

"My title is 'Sheriff,' and from what I understand, you were a JAG officer in the navy. I'm not sure that your military duty—assigned to a desk somewhere in Rhode Island—entitles you to opine on the horrors of war."

"I prosecuted deserters and cowards."

"You did no such thing," I said. "You prosecuted brawlers and drunks on shore leave. You have no frame of reference to speak to me about cowardice."

"You're an angry man, Sheriff. Perhaps even dangerous. I don't believe you deserve the office you hold."

"You're welcome to try for my badge anytime, Nolan. But you're going to have to take it from me."

"You listen to me," he hissed. A cluster of tiny blue veins throbbed at his temple. "If that schoolteacher actually takes students out to the commune, you are going to escort them, and you are going to report back to me everything that you see while you're there."

My ears filled with a sound like falling water and my fingernails dug into the palms of my hands.

"That is not the kind of phraseology you want to employ with me, sir," I said. "Have yourself a good night."

I touched my hat brim and picked my way across the loose gravel lot toward my truck.

"You're not leaving, Sheriff. We're not finished here."

"Stand there for a few more seconds, Brody, and my taillights will prove you wrong."

CHAPTER FIVE

IT WAS FULL dark by the time I passed through the lodge-pole entry to the Diamond D and into the driveway behind the main house. Amber light spilled from the windows and the cloud of smoke that trailed out of the chimney told me someone had recently freshened the logs in the fireplace.

I parked beside Snoose Corcoran's five-window flatbed, pulled open the back door to the mudroom, and followed the sound of surprisingly lively conversation to where Jesse, Cricket, and Snoose sat at the dining table with a fourth person I hadn't met before.

"Climb down and cool off your saddle," Snoose said. "Let me pour you a tipple."

I leaned in and kissed Jesse on the cheek, and felt the warm flush of her skin.

"Snoose and his nephew were kind enough to bring over cornbread and this jug of wine," she said.

"My mama, rest her soul, taught me never to show up empty-handed."

"Very civilized of you, Snoose," I said.

"Grab you a glass." He smiled at me, but it didn't make it all the way to his eyes. "And look here. They make wine bottles that's got handles on 'em now. Mighty clever, if you ask me. If you hook your fingers in there just right, you can carry 'em out of the store four or five at a time."

I took off my hat and hooked it on the coatrack in the corner beside Snoose's. Wyatt curled himself on the floor between Jesse and me and lifted his head for a scratch.

"You're a good boy, Wyatt," she said to the dog, but the rest of her message was meant for me. "Some people don't call to tell us when they're going to be late."

Cricket grinned and I saw that her cheeks were flushed pink like her mother's. I wondered how much wine they'd gotten into before I walked through the door.

"That's bad manners, isn't it, boy?" Jesse persisted.

I tried on an apologetic expression, but Jesse had passed beyond the peak of her perceptive abilities.

"Anyone care to introduce me to the extra hand at the table?" I asked, changing the subject.

"This here is my nephew," Snoose said. "His name's Tommy Jenkins, my sister's boy from down in California."

I reached across the table and received a limp, damp handshake from a boy I judged to be about sixteen or so. He wore the bored, sullen expression of a modern teenager, and his verbal greeting to me was little more than a grunt. His hair looked as though it had gone unattended for some time, and was just long enough that it reached down to his earlobes, one of which was decorated with a tiny silver hoop.

"You studyin' on becoming a pirate, Tommy?" I asked.

"Dad—" Cricket said.

I winked at her, and Snoose said, "It's okay, darlin', Tommy's aware that he's got a ring poked through his ear."

"No, sir, I ain't no pirate," Tommy mumbled and went back to work on what remained of his pot roast and peas.

"He don't go in much for razzin'," Snoose added. "Just like his mom. You might remember her, Ty. You remember Sallyanne."

"He favors her," I said, but I was lying. Snoose's sister had been fairly attractive in her youth, and this slouch-shouldered, horse-faced child of God did not resemble her in the slightest.

"She finally divorced that useless husband of hers," Snoose continued. "When they got married and moved down there to southern California, I swear it raised up the average IQ of both places."

"How long are you visiting for?" I asked the kid.

Tommy shrugged without raising his eyes from his plate, and shoveled a forkful of beef into his mouth.

"He's stayin' with me for the summer," Snoose answered for him. "Sallyanne thought it would be good for him to come up here to get him away from his friends."

The boy shot Snoose a look that could peel paint off the wall.

"He ain't much of a talker," Snoose said. "But I'm sure he'll make a fine hand by the time autumn rolls back around."

"I'm sure he will," I said, lying again.

"How about some dessert?" Jesse offered, and it seemed like her powers of perception might have returned. "I've got pineapple upside down cake in the fridge."

"I'll help you," I said.

———

"CHARMING KID," I said to Jesse as we plated dessert in the kitchen.

"It's an awkward age."

"If I had behaved that way, my father would've taken three layers of hide off my butt."

"That's not how it's done anymore, Ty."

"This new way seems to be working real well, doesn't it?"

"You're in a mood. Bad time in Lewiston?"

"I'm not the most popular man in Meriwether County tonight."

"Want to tell me about it?"

"Maybe tomorrow," I said. "Let's get this thing over with."

"That's the spirit."

———

MY FAMILY and the Corcorans had a long history together, sharing a border fence that separated our ranches since Snoose's father, Eli, and my granddad had carved out their first stakes as amicable competitors in a harsh and unforgiving business. Both had been young men at the time, raising families right here on this land. But the Great War claimed the life of Eli's eldest son and when the boom finally came at the end of it all, Corcoran missed it, and the calamity that came with the Great Depression nearly drove the last nail home. My grandfather helped keep Eli afloat through those times, but a combination of poor luck and even poorer decision-making had gradually eaten up the Corcoran ranch like a cancer.

Two years had now passed since Jesse and I had discovered old Eli lying dead in the long grass of a pasture at the far western boundary of our property. He had died peacefully in the saddle, exactly the way he had lived.

Snoose always had a contentious relationship with alcohol, but the death of his father had come hard to him, and it seemed he had crawled into a bottle that day two years ago with little intention of climbing back out.

"Why don't you and Snoose take your desserts and coffee outside on the gallery?" Jesse said. "I'm sure you'd both enjoy some man-talk."

I saw Cricket wince at Jesse's use of an expression that was never uttered in our home, but I knew it was Jesse's way of letting me know that Snoose had something weighing on his mind.

A slow, easy wind pushed through the last blossoms that still clung to the dogwood, and the sweet scent of wisteria hung in the air. The sounds of the stock horses settling in for the night drifted up from the corral a short distance away.

I showed Snoose to a willow chair in a quiet corner of the deck well out of earshot of the kitchen, while I took a seat in the matching one adjacent to his. I snapped a Vulcan match to life with my thumbnail and touched it to the wick of the lantern that rested on the table between us.

"How'd they treat you at the auction this year, Ty?" Snoose asked as he scooped up a forkful of Jesse's pineapple cake.

"About like everyone else, I suppose. It's been a rough couple years all around."

Snoose's face was half hidden in shadow, but I could see his eyes dart and twitch like a bird looking for a place to land.

"Your granddad was smart breeding them Purples," he said. "The bottom's damn near completely dropped out on my cows. No money at all for Herefords or Angus on the hoof or otherwise."

Crickets chirred from somewhere underneath the house, and I watched his eyes slide away again.

"I'm down to my last three breed bulls, Ty. Likely going to have to sell one of 'em just to pay the property tax bill."

He picked at the crumbs on his plate while he waited for me to say something. I could see that his hands had acquired a slight tremor, and imagined he had expended a great deal of effort trying to remain as sober as he could for his visit with us. I shook a cigarette loose from the pack in my pocket and offered him one.

"No thanks," he said. "But I surely could use a post-prandial."

I set my unlit cigarette in the tray and got up to retrieve a bottle of brandy from the cabinet inside. He waved his hand in the air and told me to sit.

"Don't bother," he said. "I'm packin' something of my own right here."

He drew a stainless-steel flask from the back pocket of his jeans and unscrewed the lid. He tipped it to the edge of his coffee cup, then offered the container to me.

"Thanks, but no, Snoose," I said and lit up my smoke. "I'm content with this here."

He nodded, tucked the flask away, and leaned forward out of the shadows. It was the first time he'd made eye contact with me since we'd taken our places on the porch.

"There's something else, Ty."

I made a go-ahead gesture, and drew on my cigarette. Snoose took a stiff draught from the china cup in his hand, then placed it carefully back onto its saucer and sighed.

"I got a big favor to ask you."

CHAPTER SIX

I WAS AWAKENED from a dreamscape of fire-blackened hardpan and frozen gray Asian skies. The viscous smoke of flaming oil poured from the shattered iron carcasses of tanks, and the ear-shattering roar of American artillery salvos cleaved the air.

I hold no personal illusions that the nightmares I brought home from Chipyong-ni are any worse, more intense, or more noble than those suffered by the veterans of any shooting war. Anyone who has ever been exposed to the screams of a fellow soldier clawing vainly for the remnants of a severed limb, or heard a grown man weeping out his fear inside a foxhole slick with human excrement, or endured the odor of putre-fying flesh on a week-old battlefield has earned his right to the fear and rage and terror inspired by these hallucinations.

My heart hammered at my rib cage as I came awake, and I pushed aside my sweat-soaked bedcovers as silently as I could. I showered and I dressed without waking Jesse from her sleep, and stepped out to the kitchen where Wyatt sat patiently beside the door to the mudroom. It was still dark outside, and the only sounds came from the wind chimes Jesse had fixed onto the branches of the maple that grew outside our back door.

It has been said that if one failed to properly execute a full and complete assessment of one's situation, terrible consequences almost surely will follow. I have found that statement to be true, not only as a soldier, but as a cowboy and a man. When I revisit my experiences, as I am sometimes forced to in my dreams, I can see with the near-perfect clarity of hindsight that my war was only the initial feint, a first act of belligerence that has resulted in what the politicians have decided to term a Cold War, one that possesses no front lines, no uniforms, and no end. Korea had marked the first time in modern history that both the Communist Chinese and Soviets had combined their forces in a joint effort against the West. I often ask myself what might have happened had our country failed to respond, and I arrive at the same conclusion every time: Turning a blind eye to overt acts of aggression only invites more of the same.

Though, in the time that has passed since becoming a husband and a father, I have begun to develop a private and ultimately delusive aspiration about humankind: that somehow man might overcome the instinct to draw blood as recompense, or that despotism and mendacity will no longer be forced upon us by the narcissistic and violent will of tyrants. I number these notions among those that I keep to myself.

——— ⦿ ———

WYATT LED the way down to the barn, working the edges of the pathway just beyond the illuminated cone thrown by the flashlight in my hand as he would have had we been herding cattle. In unsettled mornings such as this one, I found it calming to spend time working with my favorite stock horse, a handsome bay I named Drambuie. He had proved himself over the years to be not only an outstanding cow horse, but a very patient listener as well.

The iridescent blue of predawn began to show along the eastern quarter of the sky, and I couldn't help but notice Caleb Wheeler's silhouette up on his roof again. I pulled up short before entering the barn, clicked off my flashlight, and moved instead in the direction of Caleb's cabin.

He had nailed an old extension ladder to the wall beside his trellis, so I hooked my finger through the cup screwed to the top of my steel thermos bottle and carefully climbed up. The shingles made a cracking sound beneath my boots and Caleb turned toward me with a start.

"What the hell are you doing up here?" he asked me.

"What am *I* doing up here?" I said. "Word has it this isn't the first morning you've been spotted on your roof."

"Somebody spying on me?"

"My wife's an early riser."

I took a seat beside him, poured some coffee in the cup, and handed it to Caleb. He cradled it between his hands and warmed his palms.

"What are you gonna use?"

"I'll take mine straight from the jug," I said.

He nodded and went back to staring at the valley, and the heavy mist that blanketed the river bottoms.

"Heard you had a rough day yesterday," he said finally.

"Where did you hear that?"

"Nobody enjoys sharing unpleasant news more than Lankard Downing does."

"I was a topic of conversation at the Cottonwood Blossom?"

"You could say that."

"And?"

"Jury's still out," Caleb said, and sipped his coffee. "Let's face it, Ty. Every generation's got its share of idiots, but this one's surely got the numbers."

Electricity flickered in the clouds beyond the mountain and momentarily reflected in his eyes.

"See that?" he said. "Season's coming to an end. Spring's done. Summer's coming. It's likely to be a dry one."

I lit a cigarette to fill the silence, snapped my Zippo lighter shut, and watched the gray smoke tail away into the dark. If I was expecting Caleb to be abashed or embarrassed by our present whereabouts, I was wrong, but I still felt compelled to address it.

"Care to tell me what you're doing up here on the roof, Caleb?"

He tilted his face skyward and squinted at the stars. He waited so long to reply, I thought he had chosen to ignore me.

"I was married once," he said finally. "A long, long time ago. Did you know that?"

I did not speak, but shook my head instead, not wanting to intrude on the place that his memory had drifted.

"We had a baby for a minute, but we lost him," he continued. His voice was like a whisper to himself. "I lost her, too, not long after."

"She died?"

"No, not right away. Just a little at a time. She couldn't stand the sight of me after our boy died premature, so she sent me packing. I heard she passed away about two weeks ago."

I stubbed my cigarette on my boot sole, slid the spent filter into the pocket of my shirt, and looked at the stars. A meteorite caromed off the atmosphere and left a fleeting silver trail across the sky.

"Do you know how old I am, Ty? I am seventy-goddamn-four. That ain't no age anybody ever dreams about being, is it? A man gives some thought to being twenty, or thirty, or where he might be when he turns forty. But after that . . ."

He balanced the empty plastic thermos cup on the ridge planks of the roof, and I poured a little more inside it as he pulled the Indian blanket tighter around his shoulders.

"What are we doing up here, Caleb?" I asked softly.

He swiped at his gray mustache with the back of his hand and took his time collecting his thoughts.

"Studyin' on mortality, I s'pose," he said. "I've been beset by dreams lately, and I don't care to sleep much anymore."

He paused for a long moment and his expression hardened.

"I swear to Christ, I can't even watch the TV nowadays. Nothing but bad news, and pictures of smug college infants setting things afire and throwing tantrums in front of the cameras. They used to have *Bonanza* on, but they took that show off the air last month. Goddamn. Getting old is not for pussies, Ty; every birthday, every holiday, your world just keeps on getting smaller. Your friends get sick and die until one day there's nobody a'tall. I'll tell you something else: you're about the only family I got left."

"I know that," I said. "You know Jesse, me, and Cricket feel the same way about you."

He waved his hand as if to scatter that sentiment to the wind. He hadn't been seeking my pity, and it hadn't been my intention to offer any.

"I'm only sayin'," he went on. "You gotta keep an up-to-date list of what you're after in this life, cause if you don't, it just becomes a habit and you end up chasing things you used to think you wanted."

He looked at me to see if I understood him. He nodded then, having convinced himself that I had.

The night before, I had told Snoose I would need a night or two to think about the favor he had asked of me. I had originally intended to let Snoose know I couldn't take his nephew on as a summer hand. Now, having heard what was troubling Caleb, I made a snap decision and changed my mind. I explained the situation to my foreman, who took the news in pretty much the manner I had expected.

"I don't need no willful teenage pup getting underfoot," Caleb said, and tossed the cold dregs of his coffee across the shingles.

"I'm not sure if the kid's got any will at all," I said. "I haven't heard him speak more than three words in a row."

He muttered something under his breath and I wasn't sure if his comment was meant for me.

"What was that?" I asked.

"I said I hope to God that it ain't true that your life passes before you when you sack your last saddle."

CHAPTER SEVEN

AFTER BREAKFAST I placed a call to Harper Emory.

I was still troubled by the fact that he had waited two full days to report the beating he claimed to have suffered at the hands of his neighbors, and had chosen to make a public spectacle of his injuries instead. I remained more convinced than ever that it was part of some design that he or Nolan Brody had conceived to either bring embarrassment to me, or worse, to galvanize the citizens of the county against the residents of the Rainbow Ranch. I failed to grasp what either man's motivation might have been, though I had accumulated enough life experience to know that there are men who operate without a moral compass or a purpose any more virtuous than self-glorification and avarice.

My conversation with Emory was brief, and concluded with my agreement to meet him at his house later that morning. I tried to shake off mental images of range wars and the Pinkertons, took a deep breath, and dialed the number for Snoose Corcoran.

"Make sure your nephew is at the ranch office tomorrow morning by seven o'clock sharp," I told him. "Tell him to bring his best cutting horse, a bedroll, and his plunder bag. He'll be bedding down in the bunkhouse with the rest of the crew for as long as he's working here."

Snoose sounded relieved and thanked me almost too profusely, which only served to rekindle my reservations about the whole damn thing.

HARPER EMORY'S sheep farm was nearly an hour's drive, but the day had turned fine after the morning mist had burned away and I used the solitude and silence of the ride to collect my thoughts. I harbored no illusions that this meeting wouldn't conclude with one of two possible outcomes, and only one of them held the remotest chance of ramming the cork back in the bottle that he'd sprung.

I eased off the paved road where a hand-lettered sign bearing Emory's name had been nailed to a fencepost on top of which a rusted mailbox teetered at an awkward angle. Rugged mountain peaks gave way to lowland meadows and rolling rangeland. Streams and rivers were not in abundance down here, and the landscape bristled with the towers of Eclipse water wells.

Loose stones pinged off the undercarriage of my truck as I bounced over the ruts carved there by periodic monsoon rains that blew across the flats. A quarter mile up, the road split into a Y where a weather-corroded oil drum had been situated at the junction and served as a directional sign. The words *Rainbow Ranch* had been spray-painted on it in DayGlo colors that had no analog in the real world, together with a childlike rendering of a rainbow and an arrow that pointed to the left.

I bore right and continued on for several more minutes, then I crested a short rise and finally coasted to a stop in front of Harper Emory's place.

It was a two-story Victorian farmhouse clad in painted clapboard siding, with a wide wraparound porch and a pair of peaked dormers over each side of the broad entry. I parked beside a picket fence that bordered a finely tended garden that overflowed with herbs and flowers and a tiny square patch of lawn. One of the chiffon curtains covering the windows upstairs parted briefly as I stepped out of my truck. The light that reflected against the pane obscured all but a silhouette, though I could tell it was a woman who was watching me move toward the stairs.

The front door swung open before I had the chance to announce my arrival. Harper Emory eyed me for a long moment before inviting me inside. He was dressed in overalls made of blue denim, a plaid flannel shirt, and goose down vest. A fixed-blade skinning knife was nested inside a scabbard on his belt, and he didn't utter a word to me as he gestured toward a chair in a small sitting room just off the foyer. The ticking of a pendulum wall clock marked the time, and the air smelled of candle wax and dish soap and fresh-cut garden flowers.

Emory leaned his weight against a hickory walking cane as he limped into the room and sat down on a small velvet settee. I took a seat in a ladder-back chair beside a floor lamp that had tassels on the shade, crossed my legs, removed my hat, and hung it on the toe of my boot. The whole of the interior appeared strangely out of time, possessed of a wintry, somber sort of threadbare elegance that belonged to another age entirely. Orange flames glowed behind the feed door of an old Wehrle parlor stove and made the room feel overheated and confined.

"I'd like to know why you're taking the side of those hippies," he said without preamble.

"I'm not taking anyone's side, Mr. Emory. I was unaware that they had broken any laws until you saw fit to finally mention it."

"For all you know, they're growing opium poppies out there."

"Are they?"

"Hell, I don't know," he said. "But as I was tryin' to explain yesterday before you up and walked out of the meeting, they stole my damn lambs—I don't even know how many they got—and then they near beat me to death when I tried to ask 'em about it."

"I gave my word that I'll get to the bottom of all that," I said. "But we all need to be cautious that we don't begin to see Charles Manson every time somebody with long hair comes into view. You following me?"

He narrowed his eyes.

"You want to get the grits out of your mouth, Sheriff?"

I drew a breath to keep from uttering the first thing that entered my mind. Outside the window, a cloud of apple blossoms fluttered down from the tree growing in his yard.

"I'm saying I don't understand why you didn't come to me right away. A less charitable man could conclude that you've got some other agenda on your mind."

Red patches of discoloration appeared on his neck and he leaned back in his seat.

"I've got a seventeen-year-old son still living here at home," he said. "Have you heard that rock and roll song they play on the radio? *If it feels good, do it.* There ain't no barriers those freaks won't cross."

Footfalls squeaked on the stairway down the hall, and a few moments later the rattle of dishware echoed across the wood plank floor from inside the kitchen. Over Emory's shoulder, a triangular shadow box occupied the center of a bookshelf. Inside it, the familiar field of blue embroidered with white stars.

"There's things going on around you that you don't seem to understand," Emory said.

"Enlighten me."

"I understand you were a soldier once. You are, no doubt, familiar with the atrocities committed during wartime."

My eyes strayed to the bookshelf again.

"Forgive me if I don't see the connection."

"You keep looking at my son's interment flag," he said. "It's all that we have left of him."

Emory heaved himself out of his seat and limped across the room. He lifted the frame off the shelf and laid it in my lap. He stepped over to the window and stared outside as he next spoke.

"That flag was draped over an empty casket the army sent back home to us from Vietnam. We buried that box at Arlington with only his dog tags and medals inside of it. His grave marker is nearly three thousand miles from our home."

I lifted my eyes from the framed flag in my hands and saw that Emory's wife had appeared while he had been speaking and was now standing mutely in the doorway. She was carrying a silver tray with two glasses and a pitcher of iced tea, her face expressionless. Her salt-and-pepper hair was pulled up in a bun, but one long wisp had fallen out of it and lay across her cheek. I offered her a smile meant as both gratitude and condolence, but she seemed to look straight through me.

"Not now, mother," Emory said without turning.

"Thank you, ma'am," I said. "But perhaps it's best if your husband and I continue this conversation outside."

I held the front door open as Emory crossed the threshold to the porch. He leaned his cane against a newel post, sat down on the balustrade and gestured in the direction of the grove of aspens on the horizon.

"You see that gray smoke in the sky over yonder?" he asked, but didn't wait for my reply. "The hippies cook their food over the garbage they burn. Sometimes at night we can hear them singing when the wind blows just right."

He sucked on his teeth and his eyes glowed with new intensity. Inside them I'd swear I saw the images of black flags affixed to battle poles, the signal for no quarter.

"My leg's too gimpy to take you to the place you need to see," he said. He stuck a pair of fingers in his mouth and issued an ear-splitting whistle. "Must be working around back," he said to no one in particular.

He gathered up his cane and I followed him around the corner of the house to an open shed garage inside of which a teenage boy was hunched beneath the hood of a battered Ford pickup. Half a dozen tools were neatly fanned across a bed sheet he had placed on the ground beside his feet. A thin white wire trailed down from his ear to a transistor radio snugged inside the pocket of his shirt. He startled badly when Harper Emory balled up his fist and rapped the kid between his shoulder blades, grazing his head against the pickup's hood.

The boy squinted his eyes against the sun in the sky behind me and plucked the radio speaker from his ear.

"This here's Bryan," Emory said. "The other son."

He looked me in the eye and wiped his grease-stained hands along his pant legs.

"Nice to meet you, Sheriff," he said and offered me a firmer grip than I had expected. "I'm Bryan. The other son."

"Don't be a smartass," Emory said, and cuffed him on the back of the head. "Take the sheriff down to where the hippies cut the wire. Then come straight back here when he's all through looking around. You're working for two until my goddamn arm heals up."

I watched Harper limp back toward his house while Bryan made some final adjustments on the engine. When he had finished, he dropped the hood and motioned for me to climb into the passenger seat. In the airless confines of the pickup's cab, I could detect the faint, sweet pungent smell of marijuana coming from inside the folds of Bryan's work clothes.

"You're bleeding," I said, and handed him a handkerchief from the back pocket of my jeans.

He dabbed the blood off his forehead and placed the soiled hanky on the dashboard.

"Thanks."

We drove in silence for several minutes, over the surprisingly smooth dirt roads that crisscrossed the sheep meadow. Spring rains had turned the long grass a brilliant emerald green, where clusters of black-faced sheep grazed peacefully across the rolling hills.

"You don't like my dad much, do you?" Bryan asked.

"It's not my job to like your dad or not. But I have always been suspect of people who make unsolicited moral pronouncements."

"You're saying you're suspicious of me?"

"I'm explaining the reason for my silence on the matter," I said.

He opened his palm and played it against the wind currents rushing outside his open window as we drove.

"It's just up here," he said, and pulled to a stop.

I followed Bryan as he beat his way through a heavy overgrowth of blue bunch grass and wild rye to the spot where the sheep fence had been breached. It was strung with several strands of spiked wire stretched between slender metal stakes. The break had already been mended, but the lengths of rusted fencing that had been replaced were lying coiled in the weeds. I picked them up one by one and examined the bitter ends. They were still shiny where the repair cuts had been made, but covered with rust in the places where it had been vented. Whoever was responsible had done the work some time ago.

"Odd spot for a bust-out," I said. "All choked up with grass the way it is."

"I guess," Bryan said.

I hunkered down and worked my way along the property line, halting periodically to check the integrity of the remainder of the wire. All I found was a pile of wood knuckles and scrups, the tailings left behind after cordwood had been chopped.

"I don't see a sheep trail anywhere, do you?"

Bryan didn't answer, and I noticed he had wandered back toward the truck. He had one foot resting on the running board, dipping a wad of Skoal into his lip. I started back in his direction, still trying to get a handle on the reason Harper Emory would go to all this effort to concoct a story that seemed so obviously suspect, when I heard the high-pitched whine of a dirt bike heading in our direction.

I was still knee deep in the weeds when it emerged out of the copse of trees on the other side of the wire. The rider was a young male, early twenties, wearing a tie-dyed shirt and carrying a carbine on a sling across his back. He pulled to a stop and killed the engine and I saw him raise his chin in Bryan's direction.

"Help you with something?" he asked when he noticed me emerging from the tall grass. He carried himself with the bearing of a man who had spent time in the service.

"Checking the fence," I said. "How did you know we were out here?"

"Sound carries out here in the lowland. It's like a beacon, man."

"You know anything about your neighbor's missing sheep?"

He cocked his head and studied me, then looked across the empty space at Bryan.

"Is this guy the fuzz?"

Bryan nodded.

"This is Sheriff Dawson."

He raised both hands in mock surrender and locked eyes with me.

"No disrespect, Mr. Sheriff, sir," he said. "But I got nothing to say to the heat." He threw a leg across the motorcycle seat and turned to me again before he kicked the engine over. "Other than I don't know anything about no sheep. Have a groovy day."

"We done here?" Bryan asked me as the dirt bike disappeared into the foliage.

I nodded and climbed into the pickup. Bryan hadn't said a word the whole way back, so I asked him to pull over before we came into earshot of Emory's house. Afternoon heat shimmered off the hood as the truck idled unevenly.

"You and that young man seemed to know each other," I said. "Do you?"

"Why would you think that?"

"Because you smell like marijuana and that kid across the way nodded at you like he knew you."

I watched Bryan's eyes tick nervously inside his head. I gave him time to weigh his options, and was curious to see whether he would attempt to lie to me.

"Are you going to arrest me?" he asked finally.

"They didn't steal your sheep, did they?"

"No, sir, I don't think so."

I could see the skin on his hands going white as he squeezed the steering wheel.

"That opening in the fence was an old one," I said. "Who did the number on your dad?"

"I don't know."

"Don't know, or won't say?"

"Don't know."

"This would be the wrong time to start lying to me, Bryan."

I looked out at a shadow in a shallow fold between the hillocks of the meadow. High overhead a red-tailed hawk circled on the slipstream. It tucked its wings and descended like a missile. I turned and saw Bryan staring out the side window into nothing, and I could see the quick beat of his heart in the vein below his ear.

"Do you buy pot from them?"

He swallowed dryly and said, "Mostly for my mother."

"Maybe trade them for a lamb from time to time?"

He nodded.

"Your father doesn't have a clue about that, does he?"

"He'd beat both of us senseless if he did."

We sat a moment longer in the silence before I told him to start the truck and take us back.

Bryan dropped me at the front door and drove off down the dirt road in the direction of the highway. I stepped up the stairway to the Emorys' front door. As before, it opened in anticipation of my knock. Harper Emory gazed out from the dark with empty eyes. During the short time Bryan and I had been gone, he appeared to have shrunken into himself. His entire physiology gave the impression of a man who had been twisted on the rack.

"Anything you want to say to me, Sheriff Dawson?"

"I'm very sorry for the loss of your son, sir," I said. "This is not a life that's built on fair exchanges."

CHAPTER EIGHT

I LIT A cigarette to chase away the rumbling in my stomach, and craned my neck to look out through the windshield into a sky so clear and blue it reminded me of the old hand-tinted postcards that my parents used to send to me at boot camp. I took a hard right when I came to the Y that split the road and was almost immediately swallowed up inside a tangle of unmanaged wild berry bushes and sagebrush that grew up around the knotted trunks of whitebark pine and juniper. The low-hanging vines and limbs and tendrils clawed my truck and forced me to roll up the window, leaving only a small crack at the top to draw the smoke out.

It was a full three quarters of a mile before the overgrowth opened up and I could see that deep blue sky again. Not far ahead of me the dirt road fanned into a cul de sac that abruptly terminated where a twelve-foot chain-link fence with razor wire scrolled along the top had been erected to block the ingress. A hinged gate had been cut into it, but it was threaded through with a heavy chain and padlock and had a sign affixed to it that warned against hunting and trespassing.

I pulled to a stop, crushed out my cigarette, opened my door, and climbed down from the cab. The clatter of scrub jays drifted down from the high branches of the trees. I had made it only halfway to the fence when two scruffy young men stepped out of the foliage on the other side. A third one watched us from a short distance away, leaning his shoulder against the upright of a dilapidated pole shed someone had constructed in the shade of an ancient white oak. All three looked to be in their early twenties, outfitted similarly in faded dungarees and T-shirts. The one nearest to me wore a headband made from a strap of old leather, and open-toed sandals whose soles had been fabricated from a blown-out automobile tire. His associate had both of his arms thrown over the ends of an aluminum ball bat that he carried across his shoulders like the crossbar of a cruciform.

"You lost, old man?" Headband called at me through the wire.

"My name's Ty Dawson," I said, and peeled back my jacket so he could see the badge clipped to my gun belt. "Sheriff of Meriwether County. You mind swinging that gate open for me?"

"You mind showing me a warrant?"

"What kind of warrant would you like for me to show you?"

He shrugged and gave me an insouciant grin.

"How should I know?" he said. "You're the one who came here out of nowhere."

"I'd like to have a few words with whoever's in charge. I've received a complaint regarding stolen livestock. Your neighbor claims he was beaten and abused by men that he believes live here."

"Our neighbor is mistaken."

The third man stepped out from the shade beneath the lean-to and whispered words I couldn't hear into a walkie-talkie that was clipped onto a beaded belt around his narrow waist, and I tried to read his lips.

"What the fuck are you looking at?" Ball Bat asked me. He leaned the bat against his thigh, interlaced his fingers, and cracked his knuckles.

"I am looking the fuck at you," I said. "Is that a problem?"

"You're laying down a lot of aggression all of a sudden, man."

I moved my eyes along the barrier, then turned my attention back to him.

"I visited here less than a year ago," I said. "I was under the impression at the time that this was a communal residence of some sort. Imagine my present state of surprise at finding a steel wire fence with a guarded gate."

"The world is an unpredictable place, my man," Headband said. "We got tired of being hassled by rednecks and squares wandering out here from town."

"I'm only asking for a few minutes of your time, and I'm sure we can clear up this whole thing."

Headband threw a backward glance over his shoulder for guidance, and Walkie-Talkie stepped into the sunlight, shaded his eyes from the glare, and shook his head.

"Bummer for you," he said. "Looks like it's time for you to split, Piggy."

"That's not one of my favorite expressions."

I raised a fist and popped up two fingers out of it.

"Peace," I smiled. "That's what you all like to say, isn't it?"

"Hit the road, Jack," Headband said.

IT WAS nearly dusk by the time I arrived back home. The Diamond D was unusually void of activity and I wondered where everyone had gone. I walked down toward the office and found Caleb working a young colt inside of the corral a short distance away. One of our new horses was fighting at the rope my foreman had wrapped around the snubbing post, resisting being broken to the saddle. I rested my arms on the top rail and watched Caleb work his magic. He was the best horse breaker I had ever known.

"Where is everybody?"

"Moving the stock off the North Camp," he said, and wandered over to me, leaving the horse to faunch and blow himself out inside the cloud of powdery soil he'd kicked up. "The brush is so thick out there, the snakes have to climb up to see out."

A circle of sweat soaked through the felt beneath his hat-band. He pulled a bandana from his back pocket, shook it out, and wiped it along his brow.

"Snoose's nephew'll be here tomorrow morning at seven," I reminded him.

Caleb narrowed his eyes at me.

"You know I ain't overly tickled to be training up no shorthorn. Especially one Snoose Corcoran don't even want on his place."

"We've done favors for the Corcorans as long as either one of us can remember."

"A hard-luck outfit to be sure. Still, sometimes it's best to control your generosity when you're dealing with a chronic borrower."

The sun reflected off the ripples where a pair of green dragonflies dipped at the surface of a metal water trough. I dug at the dirt with the toe of my boot, suddenly fatigued to the core, and it must have shown on my face.

"How did it go with old man Emory?" Caleb asked.

"Like trying to rope a maverick from a unicycle."

He tilted his hat to the back of his head with a knuckle and looked me straight in the eye. It was plain that he was preparing to air out something he'd been gnawing on all day.

"About our conversation on my roof this morning—"

"Just two old cowboys jawboning," I interrupted.

He gave a quick nod, turned his head, and spat on the ground.

"I better get back to that colt."

———

THE HOUSE was silent and empty when I stepped inside to hang up my hat, holster, and coat. Even Wyatt wasn't any-where to be found. I picked up the phone and dialed Harper Emory, absently watching the hummingbirds at the feeder outside the kitchen window as we spoke.

"You need to be able to specifically identify the persons who assaulted you, Mr. Emory," I said. "Can you do that?"

"Hell no, I can't do that. Those hippies all look the damn same."

"I can't make charges stand if you can't identify your assailants."

"You're useless as tits on a boar hog, Dawson, you know that?"

"The law exists for everyone," I said.

"So what you're telling me is that you ain't going to lift a finger to help an upright citizen of this county while those unwashed animals just keep on living high on the hog."

"Must be a mighty small hog."

"You being smart with me?"

"Making an observation."

I thought I heard another voice on his end of the line, prompting.

"Has anybody commented about airplanes to you?"

"You're doing it again, Mr. Emory. This is the first I've heard about any planes. Why would you have neglected to mention them when I spoke with you this morning?"

"Goddamn it all," he said, and the line went dead.

THAT NIGHT after dinner, I sat in darkness on the gallery listening to the wind in the new growth on the cottonwoods. The sweet alluvial smell of wet stones and lichen drifted from the creek bed, together with the murmur of the high summer snowmelt flowing over pebbles that had been worn smooth by centuries of friction.

I turned to look behind me when I heard the screen door open, and saw Jesse in the doorway, outlined by the soft light of the living room. She carried a plate that held the last slice of pineapple cake and placed it on the table next to my chair.

"I scooped some vanilla ice cream on it for you," she said. "It's better if you eat it before it melts."

She crossed the floor and took a seat on the glider and rocked herself slowly back and forth. I felt the weight of her eyes on me, but couldn't bring myself to look at her.

"You want to talk about it?" she asked.

"Not at the moment."

I heard the sullenness in the tone of my own voice and was again confronted with regret for that component of my nature, though in truth I was unlikely to correct it. I have never taken comfort in airing out unfinished business, having found it to be as helpful to myself and those I cared for most as the sharing of a communicable disease. I had been raised with the philosophy that every quarrel is a private one, especially the ones that raged inside the confines of my own head.

I didn't believe the story Harper Emory was selling, but I knew something about the depth of his personal loss, and the grief he was directing outwardly to others. He, too, was a victim of his nature, turning his helplessness into anger and his desire to put a face on the unreachable target of his resentment.

Later on I lay in bed and stared up at the ceiling. I was consumed and humbled by the complete and utter sense of normalcy and peace that lived inside that room, and simultaneously suffused with guilt at the solitary ugliness I brought there and into my sleep most nights. My breathing began to race, and my gut felt as though I had swallowed a hot stone. I rolled over on my side, my back toward my wife, and my eyes began to water. I felt Jesse's body shift beneath the covers and the brush of her soft fingers on my neck.

"You're burning up," she whispered.

I don't believe she had any idea how much truth was contained within the simplicity of her statement.

CHAPTER NINE

"You're out of bed early," I said to Cricket when I stepped into the kitchen the next morning. She was standing over a cookpot, her forehead wrinkled in concentration as she gently stirred its contents with a long-handled wooden spoon.

"Paramount's shooting a movie up this way. Mom's got me scouting locations for them."

"Another western?"

"I doubt it," she said without looking up from her work. "Cowboy movies are on the way out."

"Excuse me?"

"Don't take it personally, Dad. Times change."

"That's what I've been hearing," I said.

My wife and I had met shortly after my return from Korea twenty-some-odd years ago. I had taken a job as a wrangler for the same Hollywood studio where Jesse was working as a location scout. Soon after we married and moved to Oregon, she formed her own company, and continued to operate as an independent consultant to the studios. As Cricket neared her college graduation date, she had begun to display greater interest in her mother's occupation, and now worked for Jesse whenever the opportunity arose.

"Is your mom going with you?" I asked.

"She's letting me do this one on my own."

"Big step for you," I said. I took a porcelain mug from the cupboard and waited for the coffee to percolate. "What in the hell is that smell?"

"Oatmeal."

I leaned over and sniffed at the steam cloud that rose from Cricket's pan.

"Did you scrape that stuff out of the barn?"

"I got it from the health food store." Her eyes flickered sideways at me. "I made extra, want some?"

"Thanks, but no. You can offer my share to the chickens, but I doubt they'd eat it."

She ladled her breakfast into a bowl and drizzled honey over the raisins and walnuts she sprinkled on top. I took a seat at the table with her while she ate.

"Have you ever had dealings with the kids who live out on the commune?" I asked.

"Not really," she said, shrugging as she spooned another mouthful from her bowl. "They run the sandwich shop and health food place where I bought this oatmeal though. I see them in there all the time."

"What do you make of them?"

She put down her spoon and cocked her head as she looked at me.

"Harmless, I guess," she said. "Kind of lost. Trying to find themselves."

"Find themselves," I repeated.

"That's not something your generation ever did, is it?"

I couldn't be sure from her tone whether or not she was mocking me.

"I suppose we thought we already knew where we were," I said.

"Did you?"

I studied my daughter in the pallid light that shone in through the window. She had Jesse's fine features and physical stature, but the way she employed her stiff-necked resolve was all me. It was increasingly difficult for me to reconcile this beautiful, strong-willed young woman with the little girl I had taught to ride horses, and how to tie the laces on her shoes.

"Why are you looking at me that way?"

"I did battle in a foreign war," I said. "I lost my grandfather and both my parents within a year of my return. This ranch got handed down to me lock, stock, and barrel, but I never felt more alone and scared than when I found out I was going to be a father."

"You weren't ready?"

"Nobody's ever ready," I said. "But when you were born, it was the best day of my life. And you've proven me right every day since."

My chair grazed the floorboards as I pushed myself back from the table. I stood and kissed Cricket on the forehead before I headed out the screen door.

———— ⚬⚬⚬ ————

CALEB WHEELER was hunched over his desk in the ranch office, studying a bound ledger where the breeding lines of our bulls and cattle had been meticulously recorded for the last eighty-plus years. He didn't look up when I pulled the door closed behind me.

"Calf weights are up," he said.

"That's good."

"Yes, it is. But spot prices are down."

"Not much we can do about that."

He looked up at me and ran his fingers over his mustache.

"No, there ain't," he agreed. "This economy don't make too much sense. A-rabs are drowning in oil, but we spent the last year waiting in line for it. I remember when bread cost a nickel for a loaf."

"How'd the colt do yesterday?" I asked, steering away from an old source of Caleb's complaints.

"Damn fine, if I do say so myself. So gentle you could snub him to a hairpin."

"S'pose he's ready for the remuda?"

"Gotta start him out sometime."

Through the pebbled jalousies, I could see the vague shape of a horse and rider coming up the dirt track that ran between the Diamond D and Snoose Corcoran's place. I glanced at my watch and saw that it read 7:10. Caleb followed me out and we waited for Snoose's nephew to rein to a stop outside the crowding pen.

"Swing down offa that cat-backed nag," Caleb said. "And step over here."

The kid slouched before both Caleb and me, not knowing whom to look at, or what to do with his hands. He wore the same sullen expression he had shown me at my dining table.

"You going to announce yourself, or do I have to do it?" I asked.

"Tommy Jenkins," he answered. "But people call me TJ."

Caleb took a step forward, intentionally crowding the kid's space.

"Let's get a couple things clear, straight out of the chute," Caleb said. "First one is, I ain't 'people,' I'm the goddamned range boss around here. Second, a cowboy gets a nickname as a sign of respect and acceptance, and both of those things is earned. I'll call you 'Tom,' or whatever the hell comes to mind, and you'll call me 'Mr. Wheeler,' or 'Boss,' either one suits me fine."

Tom Jenkins's face reddened and he shoved his hands into his pants pockets.

"You own a timepiece?" Caleb said.

The kid looked blankly into our faces for a few seconds before he said, "Yeah."

"Does yours say ten after seven like mine does?"

"I guess so."

"Let's be clear about something else while we're at it. If you're not early, you're late. Understand?"

"Makes sense," Jenkins said.

"Are you razzing me, son?"

"I ain't your son."

Caleb squinted and pulled the brim of his hat low over his eyes.

"Don't flatter yourself," he said. "I wasn't making no claim. Let's start off by having you empty out your war bag and let's see what kind of equipment your uncle sent you over here with."

I shot a quick grin at Caleb while the kid untied his pack from the back of his saddle. He lugged it back in our direction and shook the contents onto the ground. Caleb sorted through it like it was dirty laundry, making grim faces as he poked at various pieces of tack with his boot.

"I'm going to advance you some wages so you can pick up some proper gear. Get yourself a decent pair of spurs with Texas rowels and a goose neck. I'm surprised the ones you got on haven't gutted that horse you're riding. Then pick you up some boots while you're at it. You couldn't strike a match without burning your feet on them you got on there."

Caleb took up the boy's catch rope and tossed it at him.

"That critter you're riding is pet food on the hoof," he said. "I'm going to loan you a new colt from the remuda that I trained up myself. He's young, like you are, but he's saddle broke. We'll wait while you swap out your seat, then I want you to shake out a loop and take the pins out from one of those cows in the pen. You got all that?"

"Yeah."

"'Scuse me? I don't think I heard what you just said."

"Yes, Boss."

I watched in silence while the kid saddled up and rode in through the gate. Caleb shut it behind him and we both stood at the rail as Tom Jenkins cut a young cow from the small group that had clustered itself at the far end of the corral. The cow started off at a slow trot as Jenkins rode up behind it and threw the loop over its head. He dallied the string on the horn and backed the horse up to draw it tight. When he did, the young colt he was riding began to crowhop and spin, and dropped Tom Jenkins into the dirt.

"Looks like your horse decided to come un-broke," I said to my foreman.

Caleb shook his head and muttered a string of profanities under his breath.

CHAPTER TEN

MILA KINSLOW
(Excerpted from interview #MC1803/D)

SWEET PETE HAD a beater of a car and a little bread he'd set aside from playing with the band, so we took our time driving up the coast. We celebrated my eighteenth birthday at a seafood restaurant outside of Brookings, Oregon, and took a walk after dinner by the bay. We watched seagulls fuss over fish scraps that had been washed from the boat decks, and the otters and seals as they played inside the breakwater, the whole place smelling like decaying seaweed and old fish.

I knew that Pete had a thing for me that went all the way back to when we'd first met at the Whisky. But, like I told you before, he was always a gentleman, and set his feelings aside the whole time I was with Jack McCall.

Pete and I made love for the first time that night, on a squeaky spring mattress in a motel room with a long view down the coastline. Afterward we stood outside on the balcony in the cool wind, lit up a J, and watched the lights of the night fishermen move along the horizon. Earlier that day, I had picked up an inexpensive souvenir from one of the tourist shops we'd visited. It was a medal with the image of Saint Christopher sealed beneath a layer of blue enamel, hanging from a chain just like the pull-cord on a bedside lamp. That night on the balcony, after we'd made love, I slipped it from around my neck and gave it to Sweet Pete.

That drive was so peaceful I don't think either one of us wanted it to come to an end, but it did, and two days later we finally located the tiny turnoff that led off the paved road to the Rainbow Ranch. At first we thought we'd taken a wrong turn. Branches of wild berry bushes scratched against both sides of the car as we drove through the tall timber, but the road was so narrow we couldn't turn around even if we wanted to. It seemed like it took half an hour to break into the open, and get our first peek at the place.

I don't think that either of us really knew what to expect, and I admit to being a little bit freaked out as we drove past the gates. But the first person to greet us was a sweet little slip of a thing with big doe eyes and chestnut-colored hair that the sun had turned to gold down at the ends. The minute she spoke I could tell she was a Southern girl like me, except she had a Coppertone tan and the healthy orthodontics of someone whose daddy had money. She told us she'd been there six months. Her name had been CeCe—short for Celeste—when she first arrived, but the Deva had rechristened her "Aurora." Pete and me had no idea what a Deva was, but I knew we would figure it out.

The air smelled like pine trees and reminded me of the hill country back home, and I felt a stab of sadness in my stomach. I didn't have the time to think about it too long, though, because Aurora took hold of Sweet Pete and me just then, and practically skipped up the stairs to the house behind where we had parked.

She tugged us inside and introduced us to this burly guy with the longest, blackest hair I had ever seen on a man, and a beard that crawled all the way up past his cheekbones, almost to his eyes. He stared at us and didn't speak for so long that I thought something was wrong with him, but then he reached out and took one of my hands inside both of his and he smiled like he'd been expecting us all along.

Both me and Pete took to the guy right away, but you could tell there was something about him that he held back for himself, like a man who was hiding, but hiding right out in the open—a combination of a big friendly bear and a mountain man who had just wandered out of the wild. I don't know, cause it's hard to explain, but one part of you wanted to give yourself over to him, while another part wanted to run.

———

THERE WAS a circle of big army surplus tents where everybody crashed. There were probably nine or ten of them scattered around, and you just found a place inside one where you felt good and made up a soft mat on the floor for yourself. Outside, in the center of the tent village, was a huge fire pit that was encircled by stones. At night after supper, everyone gathered around it and sang songs, or smoked weed, and the Deva would assign chores for the following day.

The first few nights were strange, and I had a hard time falling asleep. I felt out of place, lonely, and homesick for Sandi and our friends in LA. Sweet Pete would hold me close to him, but I could not accustom myself to the sounds and the smells of lovemaking and bodily functions inside a tent we shared with so many strangers. I was embarrassed and conflicted, kind of mad at myself for the way that I felt. I had wanted to come here because I craved something that seemed like a family, which was weird because when I'd actually had one, I didn't think I had wanted or needed it at all. But, by the end of the first cycle—we did not use conventional calendars at Rainbow Ranch, we marked time by the phases of the moon—I felt like I finally fit in somewhere.

There was a ceremony of sorts that marked the occasion, at the campfire, where Sweet Pete and I were officially welcomed into the community. Nobody called it a "commune"; it was a "community," because it's not like we sat around talking about Chairman Mao or anything. It was about sharing, and living, and love. You contributed what you had and what you were good at, and shared in the fruits of what others did real well. Sweet Pete gave up his car for the use of the community, and I gave up most of the clothes I had packed inside the suitcase I'd carried with me since I split Tennessee. I even handed over that beat-up old American Tourister too.

As Deva says, "Who owns the daisy? Who owns the thistle?"

Thing is, we all felt like we were part of some beautiful outdoor palace, where all of us were royalty, but there was not a crown in sight.

I made friends with the girls I did chores with; the men and the women were separated for these. The men hunted for game or butchered the livestock, worked in the woods, or at building or repairing whatever was broken. We had a huge grove of old pines that they sawed down by hand, then cut up the logs for firewood with gas-fueled log splitters. There were a couple of guys who were really good with mechanical things who worked inside a big metal building on the far side of the forest where the generators and cars and motorcycles were stored. They didn't hang out with the rest of us too much, which was okay, cause both of them gave me the creeps, and I didn't want them even thinking about putting their hands on me.

The women tended the fruit trees and vegetable gardens, operated the record store and the sandwich shop in town, and took care of all the food preparation for the whole Rainbow Ranch community. Meal times were called by the ringing of an iron bell from the terrace of Deva Ravi's house. We took turns doing the cooking or cleaning up afterward, and there was always someone playing music of some kind. Those were the times I liked best because it gave us the chance to get to know one another, and to talk about where we were on our individual paths. Often the conversations would drift to the messages that Deva would share with us about the mystical threads of the Universal Mind.

Some of the other girls at the ranch had been runaways, angry at their parents, and angry at the world. They talked about parochial schools, having to dress exactly like everyone else, and being hovered over and hounded by gray-faced women wearing long, scary, black outfits. Their stories sounded sad to me, and I was grateful that we didn't have those kinds of schools where I came from. Of course, we also talked about sex.

It wasn't the feminist woman, hear-me-roar kind of thing that was popular at the time. We loved being female and being appreciated for what we were. It was empowering to have control over what we all knew men wanted. It's primal, you know? You can't pass rules or laws to make that go away. It wasn't about bra burning or marching or politics, either, it was all about pure freedom for us. The whole women's lib deal just seemed like some other old ladies' club. If you wanted to stay home and cook and do dishes and raise kids, that was cool. I can dig that. We figured if that's what you want to do, then do it. Bliss out on your own trip. It was impossible to imagine doing something you didn't *want* to do. But the whole sex thing is a natural deal. I mean, it would be a total drag to eat the same food for every meal, right?

—❦—

ONE AFTERNOON, I was called up to the main house for an aura check with Deva Ravi. It was the most beautiful afternoon of my life.

I had seen the effects that hard drugs had on people, had seen it up close with Jack McCall. It had never been my bag, so I stuck with pot, or maybe a hit of acid every once in a while. Truth is, I never dug acid too much; I've got strange enough thoughts in my head without adding chemicals, and I didn't need spiders or rats crawling under my skin, or to see someone's face melting off their skull.

Anyway, that afternoon was like magic.

Deva Ravi made a strong, bitter tea that he poured from a little Chinese pot, and we shared it together, alone in the Spirit Room, surrounded by the sweet fragrance of incense. It was what I imagined it would smell like up in heaven. He spoke to me of the universe and its plan for me, and that was the day that he renamed me 'Dawn,' because he said I had brought a new light, a new day, into the community.

My body began to feel as though it could no longer contain me, and reality and dreamtime moved together as one, showing me things that might or might not be true. I even thought I saw into the soul of the Deva, past that strange thing that always seemed present in him. I saw that he was a duality, both man and spirit, and that it was the part that was a man who concealed or was eclipsed; that he *enjoyed* hiding right there in plain sight.

I don't know for how long, or how many times we made love together. After a while it was as though we could do it without even touching.

———

WE THOUGHT of you all—the squares, I mean—as poor suckers who were just plodding through life to survive. I mean, to us, you all seemed like you were as afraid of living as you were of dying. And we thought we had a handle on all of it, man. It sounds arrogant or conceited now, but we had bought all the way in. There was no political or economic hustle at the Rainbow. We meant no harm to anyone, even though it was clear that most of the straights in town thought we were freaks, and barely considered us human. But for us, it was all about love and sharing and freedom and light.

For a while anyway.

CHAPTER ELEVEN

IT HAD BEEN several years since I'd had cause to meet with a teacher at Meridian High School.

The soft green buds of spring had given way to the leaves of early June along the branches in the groves of ash and poplar trees out front. A flag popped in the wind at the top of the flagpole, and the chain that held it aloft rang musically every time it struck the spar.

I checked in at the front office and inquired as to the whereabouts of the eleventh-grade social studies teacher named Molly Meadows. I was asked to take a seat inside the main office while I waited for the bell that signaled the end of the third period of the morning. I thumbed through the pages of a copy of *Time* magazine that was six months out of date. Joni Mitchell was on the cover, but the articles inside contained more depressing news than I had any interest in revisiting. When the bell finally sounded, a frazzled-looking woman behind the desk told me that I could proceed to Room 18 where Miss Meadows would be waiting for me.

I shouldered through a tidal current of teenagers rushing to their lockers, passed a clutch of cheerleaders in uniform holding court beside a trophy case, while the smell of cigarettes drifted out from underneath the door to the boys' bathroom. I found the classroom I was seeking and knocked before I stepped inside.

"Good morning, Sheriff Dawson."

"Miss Meadows," I said, removed my Stetson, and took a seat in the guest chair beside her desk.

"I have this period free, so we have about forty-five minutes."

She was conservatively dressed, a light-blue cotton blouse tucked into a knee-length skirt. She wore a pendant in the shape of what I took to be an astrological symbol on a simple silver chain encircling her neck.

"I never thanked you for your assistance at the council meeting," she said. "That was inconsiderate of me, and I apologize."

"It should never have been necessary. I don't claim much tolerance for a mob."

She smiled and suddenly appeared much younger than I recalled from that night at the Grange Hall, and seemed at odds with her slightly matronly demeanor. I judged her to be in her late twenties, with hair the color of a forest fawn and styled in a shag that brushed against the collar of her blouse.

"I remember your daughter from my class." She hesitated and her concentration focused inward for a moment. "Laura? Yes. Laura Dawson."

"That's right."

"A bright girl. Very sweet. I liked her very much."

"She felt the same way about you."

The room was a mélange of maps and presidential portraits, and a poster illustrating the three branches of our government. A framed copy of the Constitution had been hung at one side of the blackboard, together with the texts of all twenty-six amendments.

"Your daughter went by an unusual nickname," she said. "Cricket?"

"I've called her that since the day she started crawling."

"I couldn't bring myself to use it. It seemed too personal somehow," she said.

"I had expected to hear from you about the field trip you discussed," I said. "Are you still planning to go out there before the school year ends?"

"There was a disappointing lack of support from the parents of my students. Fewer than a dozen have agreed to let their young people participate."

"That's unfortunate. But perhaps it's for the best."

The contours of her cheekbones sharpened, and she snapped her head around to meet my eyes.

"Oh, I still plan to go," she said. "It's more important now than ever."

"Are you sure this is the hill you want to die on, Miss Meadows?"

She leaned her elbows on her desk and looked me over as if it were the first time she had seen me.

"This is America, Sheriff. We have a right to live the way we choose to, provided we do not impinge upon the rights of other citizens. The residents of the Rainbow Ranch have done no harm—"

"That we're aware of."

"Granted," she nodded. "Nevertheless they are the embodiment of freedom. Have you visited their shops in town? Have you really *seen* them? They remind me of Persephone, a child of the flowers."

"Persephone was forcibly abducted," I said. "Carried off to the underworld, and bound over as a concubine."

"You understand my meaning, though you pretend you don't."

"I cannot say I disagree with you, Miss Meadows. But I would feel better—as would the community at large—if you would allow me to escort you on your field trip. Think about your students; think about their parents. You're putting your career on the line if anything at all should happen."

She searched my face for signs of duplicity and found none.

"I like you, Sheriff," she said. "Please don't make me regret my trust in you."

⸎

I EXITED the breezeway and stepped into the sunshine. The school bell rang again announcing lunch. On a grassy hummock a short distance from the outdoor benches, a pair of younger boys had caught a garden snake and were tormenting it with sticks. I strode across the lawn in their direction just as one of them snatched up the snake and tied its body in a knot. Their laughter carried on the wind as I approached, and I saw them toss the writhing body into the branches of a walnut tree.

"You find it amusing to cause pain to animals?" I said.

The boys smirked at one another before turning to address me.

"It's just a fucking snake."

"So it deserves your mistreatment?" I asked.

"What?"

I crossed my arms and looked from one, then to the other.

"Give it some thought," I said. "It's a simple question."

"No."

"Now I want you to experience how it feels to rescue something," I said. "Climb your asses up that tree and set that creature loose."

"You've got to be shitting me."

I sat down in the grass and shade and stretched out my legs. I leaned back on my elbows and looked into the branches of the tree.

"Get that snake down from there right goddamn now," I said. "I'm not going anywhere until you do."

———— ⚬⚬⚬ ————

I ATE a cheeseburger and fries at the counter of Rowan Doyle's diner in Meridian while I perused a handbill for the upcoming upcoming rodeo and county fair. I bought a couple of bottles of grape soda to go, and left a dollar as a tip on the counter.

I took my time walking back to the substation, the warmth of the sun at my back. The sky overhead was empty of clouds, but crosshatched with the gracile lines of contrails.

Snippets of music caught my attention as the noise from a car's passing died away. A young man seated on an upturned milk crate played a steel-string guitar outside the health food store. A second one plucked the strings of a mandolin, while a barefooted girl danced in free form on the sidewalk wearing an organdy dress the color of pale yellow jessamine. They appeared neither to know or care that I watched them as they played, but the dancer slowed for a moment to smile at me before I continued on my way.

I stepped out of the fresh air and into the unventilated stillness inside the substation a few minutes later. We had repainted the dingy walls of the interior, but the place still retained a revenant odor that smelled like the husks of dead wood beetles. Two of my former cowboys—now sheriff's deputies—were occupied at their desks. Samuel Griffin was pecking out paperwork on his Smith Corona, while Jordan Powell busied himself scooping seeds from a pomegranate that looked as though it had exploded onto a square of butcher paper.

"Your desk blotter looks like a crime scene," I said as the door swung shut behind me.

"Afternoon, Sheriff," Samuel said without looking up from his work.

"You want a bite of this here, Captain?" Powell asked.

Powell was the only one I allowed to address me in that manner, primarily because it had become his habit. He was still one of my best cattle ropers, having been with the Diamond D for going on ten years. Early on, Powell had begun the practice of referring to me by my former military rank, though he and I had fought in entirely different wars. I knew he meant it as a sign of respect, not affectation, and I tolerated the eccentricity for what it was.

Griffin, too, was an extraordinary cowboy, and like Powell, had seen military combat in Vietnam, though Griffin had served as a marine. He had not been with the ranch nearly as long as Powell, but he rode for the brand, and had proven his loyalty to me beyond any question. The other hands had not made it easy on him at first, having not encountered too many black cowboys before Sam Griffin came along.

"Sam, I'm going to need you to come with me tomorrow," I said. "We're escorting a group of high school students and their teacher on a field trip."

He stopped typing and said, "Pardon me?"

"They're taking a tour of the Rainbow Ranch, and we're going along for the ride."

"I don't mean to second-guess you here, Sheriff. But does it really take both of us to do that?"

"I could use an extra pair of eyes," I said.

The sound of running water made a gurgling sound in the pipes inside the wall. This was followed by the thud of something heavy being dropped on the floor upstairs.

"You boys have someone in the holding cells?"

"Leon Quinn," Griffin said. "That's what I'm typing this paperwork for."

"What'd he do?"

"The usual."

"Anybody get hurt?"

"No, sir."

"Lankard Downing's feelings, maybe," Powell added.

Quinn was a frequent overnight occupant in our cages, a sad, ordinarily harmless alcoholic who sometimes caused a stir at the Cottonwood Blossom a couple of blocks away. He could grow boisterous and rude when he went on a bender, but was usually harmless, except to himself. The vicissitudes of his upbringing had been so detestable, his adult choices so debased, that the mere mention of his name had become an admonition in this town. The words "Leon Quinn" were all that a parent needed to say in order to haul in the reins on a contrary or difficult child.

I headed upstairs, and when I reached the landing at the top of the stairwell was confronted by the stale funk of body odor and whatever he had just flushed down the toilet.

"Are you doing all right, Leon?" I asked.

He was seated on the folding cot, wrestling with one of his boots.

"Sorry, Sheriff," he said. "I was pulling my boots on and I dropped one."

I could hear the muted mutterings of Griffin and Powell deep in conversation downstairs. I could not hear the words, but the tone had a familiar ring to it. The boys back at the ranch had taken to calling Sam Griffin "The Deacon," owing to his penchant for engaging in spontaneous conversations that were spiritual in nature.

"You ready for me to let you out of there, Leon?"

"I thought I was, but the ceiling keeps moving around."

"Stomp on the floor a few times when you want to go," I said. "Somebody will come up and get you."

Leon put his head down on the mattress and threw a forearm across his eyes. When I went back downstairs, my deputies' conversation came to an abrupt conclusion. Outside the front window, I saw Nolan Brody pull to the curb in his dark green MGB convertible. I moved quickly out the door to head him off before he had the chance to step into the office.

He slid his sunglasses onto the top of his head and rested an elbow on the unoccupied passenger seat.

"I understand you had a meeting with Miss Meadows at the high school this morning."

"You drove a long way just to share that tidbit of intel with me," I said.

"I was in town meeting with a client. Anyway I am happy to know that you're doing as I asked. I'll expect a report when you come back."

"Every man is entitled to his expectations," I said. "It's a beautiful day. Enjoy your drive home."

"I'm curious why you're allowing those kids up the block to panhandle."

"They're not panhandling; they're playing music. Nobody's complained to me about it."

"I'm complaining."

"Then go somewhere else. You don't make your home in Meridian, Mr. Brody."

He gazed into his rearview mirror and watched the young musicians up the block. Then he turned toward me and drew in a breath as if dealing with a petulant child.

"When I was a young boy," he said. "I used to visit my grandparents at their cabin outside of Whistler. Beautiful there, by the way, if you haven't been. At any rate, I befriended a young fawn, left food out for it every day. Eventually it ate right out of my hand. My grandfather warned me against doing that, told me the animal would fail to learn how to fend for itself, and never know the dangers posed to it from human interaction."

"Sounds like you enjoyed a lovely childhood. Have a nice afternoon," I said and turned toward the substation.

"I'm not finished yet, Sheriff. You see, as that young deer got older, he kept returning to the cabin. Over the years, he grew a fine rack on his head, and he continued to accept the food that I left out for him. One day he failed to return and even though I continued to leave things for him, he never came back. Needless to say, I was heartbroken.

"The following summer, my grandfather took me to a restaurant for dinner. Over the hearth was the mounted deer's head. I recognized those antlers right away."

"That's a very distressing story," I said. "I believe I have the business card of a clinical psychologist in the drawer of my desk. I'll get it for you. I believe you should give her a call."

"You know, the federal government has begun to post signs inside our national parks that warn against feeding the animals. It makes them dependent. I can see nothing wrong with those kids up the block that would prevent them from getting a proper job."

"Is there something you're trying to say?" I asked. "I never went to law school, so when you speak to me it sounds like nothing but word hash."

He slid his sunglasses back into place on the bridge of his nose and stared at me.

"Thank you again for accompanying Miss Meadows and her class."

"You can thank me by turning your car around."

SAM GRIFFIN was waiting by the door when I stepped back inside.

"I couldn't help but hear your conversation," Griffin said.

"You probably could have, but you obviously didn't."

"Do you mind if I say something, Sheriff Dawson?"

"Is this going to be a scriptural dialogue? I don't believe I'm in the proper frame of mind right now."

"No, sir," he said. "I'd like to drop a little Thomas Jefferson on you."

"Let 'er rip, then, Sam."

"Mr. Jefferson said, 'I prefer the dreams of the future to the history of the past.'"

"I take it you're referring to the kids playing their guitars up the street?"

Griffin shrugged.

"Woe awaits a country when she sees the tears of bearded men," I replied. "I believe it was Sir Walter Scott who said that."

CHAPTER TWELVE

THERE WAS NO sign whatsoever of armed guards, the steel gate at the entrance to the Rainbow Ranch thrown open wide and held in place by a length of hemp rope that had been threaded through the latch and knotted to a tree. Sam Griffin and I followed the tiny Blue Bird school bus past the gate, holding my pickup truck far enough behind to see beyond the cloud of dust the bus kicked into the dry June air. A quarter mile up the road we pulled into an unpaved roundabout and parked.

Sam and I stepped down from my truck and waited for the bus doors to slide open, then counted heads as the six boys and four girls whose parents had agreed to let them participate lined up outside and waited for Miss Meadows. Two Rainbow Ranch girls watched us cross the lot and make our way toward a sprawling prewar post-and-pier ranch house. We had assembled in the shade beneath a covered terrace at the top of a short stairway when one of them stepped forward and requested our attention.

"Welcome to the Rainbow Ranch, little brothers and sisters," the shorter of the commune girls said. She had a heart-shaped face framed by a nimbus of straw-colored curls that brushed along her shoulders, and eyes that turned up at their corners when she smiled. She introduced herself as Dawn, and told us that the taller girl beside her was named Summer, and that they would act as our Wayfinders during our visit, which I took to be the same thing as a tour guide.

Summer had eyes the shade of almonds, large and child-like, that put me in mind of paintings by Margaret Keane, and dark brown hair that had been parted down the middle of her head with razor-straight precision. While Dawn appeared to possess the disposition of a wood sprite, Summer's features and demeanor seemed as though they belonged to a woman twice her age. She seemed to be the bearer of some unspo-ken burden, as if something had been stolen from her and she had abandoned any hope of its retrieval.

From the elevated vantage point of the terrace, I took in the general layout of the compound. Next door to us was a newer, larger structure, rectangular in shape, and con-structed of split pine logs and roofed with corrugated metal. A hundred yards beyond, what appeared to be a small tent village sprouted up inside a grove of fruit trees and thick tangles of berry vines.

"Sir," Sam Griffin whispered as he nudged me with his elbow, and followed the students and their teacher through the door.

The anteroom inside was crowded, and it took a moment for our eyes to acclimate to the darkness. The windows facing outward had been draped with roman shades made from heavy velvet or velour that had been beaded with designs that represented stellar constellations. Pulsating shapes and shadows quivered along the walls, reflections of the dim light cast by clusters of beeswax candles.

"Deva Ravi asks that you please remove your shoes before we join him," Summer announced and waited quietly while the group complied. Griffin shot an uncomfortable glance in my direction as we wrestled off our boots and placed them in a line against the wall with all the others.

"When we step inside the Spirit Room," Summer added in a whisper, "we must all remain completely silent unless the Deva invites you to speak."

Dawn pulled gently on a slender cord that was suspended from the ceiling, and I could hear the tinkle of a temple bell on the other side of the door. After the briefest of hesitations, we passed inside and entered a room that had once functioned as a living room in a prior incarnation. The space felt like a cloister, devoid of furnishings of any kind. A fireplace faced with timber and red brick yawned unlit and cold along the far wall.

We took our places on the floor, facing an elevated dais where a broad-shouldered man sat cross-legged in placid silence, wrists balanced lightly on his folded knees, and chanting incantations that seemed to emanate from somewhere deep inside the hollow of his chest. He was flanked on either side by unadorned ceramic vases brimming with sand where bundles of fragrant incense glowed and suffused the atmosphere with silver haze that smelled of sandalwood and lotus.

"If the net you cast is made of beauty and intention, you will capture only beautiful things," he said, his voice resonating roundly off the walls, and startling the students with both its suddenness and the boldness of its tone. The scattering of nervous laughter that rippled through the room fell silent when he raised his chin off his chest and opened up his eyes.

He wore a dhoti wrapped and knotted at one side of his waist, the type that one might see in parts of India, his shirt a loose-fitting patchwork of brightly colored fabrics that had been stitched together in the manner of a quilt.

An enormous textile dosser spanned the entire length and breadth of the partition that rose behind him, a field of midnight blue strewn with the images of stars. The center was adorned with a bisected circular design, the top half of which depicted a full moon, the bottom half a golden sun that radiated shafts of copper-colored light.

"Each and every one of you is a godly being that has been placed with great intention upon this earth," he said.

A full black beard reached to his chest, and the hair on either side of his wide skull had been shaved down to the

skin. Along the crown of his head ran a broad swath of a
Mohawk, though this he had grown out long and it had been
woven into a braid that terminated at the center of his back.

"Your purpose is to seek the wisdom that is required to
transcend this flesh and be transformed into the essence of
who and what you truly are—billions of tiny particles and
waves of love and energy and light. Once you have attained
this level of awareness, you shall have gained the necessary
preparation to be beamed across the universe like Kohoutek."

He scanned the faces in the room with eyes so blue that
they appeared to be illuminated from within. His counte-
nance was wide and flat and olive toned, his features close
together, leaving the overall impression of an Aztec deity
carved from stone.

No one stirred during the time it took for him to catalog
the faces of his audience one by one. He locked his eyes on
mine for a long moment and I thought I saw a fleeting glint
of something not entirely benign.

Molly Meadows raised her hand and his gaze slipped
off me. His expression softened perceptibly as his attention
moved to her.

"You may speak," he said to her.

"Deva Ravi," she said, "do you mind sharing with us the
meaning of your name?"

"Dear sister," he answered, "everyone who comes to this
place does so because he or she has been summoned in
some way."

He paused to allow his message to find purchase.

"As we begin to learn the proper way to seek and take
counsel of the Universal Spirit, our infinite duty and true
identity are eventually affirmed. In my case, it was revealed
that I am 'Deva,' or the god-force. That is the role that the
universe defined for me, and did so long before the birth of
time itself."

He contemplated the gawping faces of his visitors again,
as though assessing that his meaning had been fully understood. I scanned the audience myself, and noted that the

faces of our tour guides, Dawn and Summer, had taken on expressions that were nearly rapturous.

"My earthly name," he continued, "is Ravi, which translates as 'benevolent.'"

"That is very beautiful," Molly Meadows whispered. "Would you object if my students asked some questions of you?"

For the next forty-five minutes, the man who called himself Deva Ravi listened to their inquiries, and answered with a dizzyingly convoluted admixture of astrology, astronomy, and eastern mysticism. He spoke of alien abduction and the Universal Mind; of OBEs, the Rigveda, and the Dhammapada. He enraptured them with stories of near-death experiences and resurrection, and the literal construction of Earth's own moon by the hands of ancient beings of an extraterrestrial nature. He concluded with a discourse on the virtues of good works, provided however that nothing must dissuade us from the path of personal enlightenment and the ultimate Divinity and Sanctity of Self.

The entire presentation had left me with a headache, but I had to admit that his aptitude with rhetoric and oratory was extraordinary. The modulation of his voice had held them captive; even Molly Meadows appeared to have been deeply engrossed by the time we were excused and guided to the bathrooms for a break.

Afterward Dawn and Summer introduced us to a third, rather hard-looking, girl who told us that her Universal name was Aurora. It was she who led us on a tour of the compound, a surprisingly well-organized arrangement of living quarters and agricultural utility. Several tapered peristyles made from castoff lumber housed the wellheads which fed holding ponds where herds of goats and sheep roamed aimlessly. Aurora told us that these herds were the source of much of the cheese and dairy products used at Mother Nature's, the health food store and sandwich shop they operated in downtown Meridian.

She strolled with us among outcroppings of igneous for-
mations that protruded from untilled acreage, reminders of
an era of prehistory when this region had been nothing but
a vast volcanic lake. The highlight, though, came near the
end when she guided us along the edges of the fruit orchard
where the ducks and chickens roamed freely among the shadows of the tree limbs. The male students seemed particularly
entranced by the appearance of a suntanned Rainbow girl
tending the vegetable garden, clad only in a wide-brimmed
hat made from handwoven straw.

Molly Meadows quickly shepherded her students back
toward the parking area, expressing gratitude to all three
of our hostesses as the kids climbed into the bus. Each had
been provided with a parting gift bag that contained dried
fruit and nuts, together with a tie-dyed T-shirt imprinted with
the logo of the sandwich shop. Griffin and I stood outside
the bus's door and counted heads again. Molly thanked Sam
and me as she followed them inside, and the two of us waited
by my pickup as we watched them drive away.

"I WOULD like to have a word with Ravi," I said to Dawn
once the bus passed out of sight.

She tilted her head, appraising me for a moment, then
asked me to wait while she went inside to check on his
availability.

Griffin wandered back in the direction of the orchard,
accompanied by Summer and Aurora. In the distance, a
column of white smoke and bits of ash from burning paper
rose beyond the grove of pines the commune grew for firewood, and I smelled the sweet tang of the blaze. I stepped
into the shade of a red cedar that had grown beside a dry
wash, and rested a boot heel on the remnants of a rotted
stump.

I turned when I heard footfalls moving in my direction.
Dawn waited on the terrace watching Deva Ravi walk toward

me, using the flat of her hand to shield her eyes against the glare.

Up close, the man who had designated himself a benevolent god was not as tall as I had expected, though he was broad across the chest and had probably participated on his high school wrestling team. The mystical light had vanished from his eyes, but what replaced it hinted at qualities both predatory and vulpine.

"So what did you think?" he asked me, squinting in the unaccustomed outdoor light.

"It sounded like a unicorn ride to the moon," I said. "I think you might be conflating science fiction with scriptural doctrines."

"Is there a difference? Narrow-mindedness is just another form of ignorance, Sheriff Dawson."

"My disagreement with your philosophy does not constitute ignorance on my part," I said. "I didn't come out here to pass judgment or harass you."

"You expect me to believe that you're any different from the chump turkeys who live in town? The same people who look down on us because of the way we look?"

He slid on a pair of sunglasses and the transformation was complete. He had transfigured from the guise of benign prophet to a swarthy, bearded enforcer for the Teamsters.

"I think that there's a part of you that enjoys the role of martyr," I said. "And that you cultivate it for purposes of your own."

He threw a glance over my shoulder, then returned his gaze to me.

"Santayana said that skepticism is the chastity of the intellect."

I smiled at him and put on my own sunglasses.

"Ironically," I said, "self-righteousness is like an echo chamber, and blinds you just as badly as it blinds the people you seem to hold in such low regard. Tell me something: If you're doing such virtuous work out here, why do you operate in secret, behind fences topped with razor wire?"

Something had begun to seep between the cracks of artifice he had constructed to protect his self-creation. I could not yet tell with any certainty if Rainbow Ranch was actually a commune or a cult, though I now believed this place was more like Asphodel, but putting on a masquerade as Elysian Fields.

"We built the barriers to protect ourselves from parochial reactionaries who are afraid of us because we don't live by the same rules as the straights. They see a man on the sidewalk with hair down to his shoulders and cross the street because they think he's dangerous or dirty. They speak publicly of mercy and forgiveness, but inside they're just bigots, man."

"I would advise caution throwing words like that around."

"Words like what?"

" 'Bigot,' " I said. "The preacher at my church speaks often about clemency and grace. I suspect you don't like hearing those subjects spoken of by a man who holds a bible in his hands. That makes you the bigot, son."

His attention drifted past me again.

"What is your deputy doing over there with Aurora?"

I turned around to see Griffin smiling broadly, in the midst of an animated conversation, though their words were lost to the distance.

"I suspect he enjoys chatting with an attractive young woman as much as the next man."

I was tired of discussing metaphysics and morality. Over near the trees, I saw the naked vegetable farmer giggling to herself and blowing iridescent soap bubbles into the wind.

"I'd be delinquent in my duties if I failed to ask you about your neighbor, Harper Emory," I said.

"What about him?"

Ravi shook his head dismissively, but his gaze remained locked in on my deputy.

"Mr. Emory claims that some young men who live here stole his sheep and physically abused him."

"Why would we do that?" he asked. "We've got a sheep herd of our own. Go look them over."

"I already did."

I heard Sam Griffin's boots crunching in the dirt behind me.

"Gimme some skin, my brother," Ravi said. He smiled broadly at Sam and offered the palm of his hand face up between them.

"I don't greet people that way," Sam said, and looked squarely into the lenses of Ravi's shades. "Do you act like that with everybody, or did you just pull that stunt because you see a black man standing here in front of you?"

"I meant no offense," he said and allowed his hand to fall to his side.

"No offense was taken," Sam said. "Consider this a learning opportunity. For you. *Brother.*"

Deva Ravi watched Sam and me as we moved toward my pickup, but I halted before we made it halfway there. I turned toward the bearded man and asked him one last question.

"By the way," I said. "What was your name before you turned yourself into a deity?"

He showed me a languid smile before he answered.

"You must not have been listening to me before," he said. "I am who I have always been."

———

THE AIR inside the truck cab was stifling, heat rising off the hood in somnolent waves as we passed through the gate. The scattering of clouds on the horizon were threadlike, as though they had been spun into the sky with a baking whisk. I took a left at the psychedelic oil barrel and pushed the truck along the bumpy road.

"Did you notice anything?" I asked Sam.

"Beside the obvious, you mean?"

"Yes, beside the obvious."

"Yes, sir. I believe we both did."

I slid a pack of Wrigley's Spearmint from my pocket, offered one to Sam, and took one for myself.

"Strange," I said.

He nodded then cut his gaze outside the window.

"Where are we going?" Sam asked.

"I have a question for Harper Emory."

Griffin nodded and adjusted the air vent in the dash, leaned back into his seat, and stared across the seared landscape, where the brown grass vibrated in the wind. As we approached Emory's Victorian house, I saw his son, Bryan's, truck silhouetted on a distant ridge, and a Country Squire station wagon parked beside the picket fence.

"I'll only be a minute," I said, and left the truck and the air-conditioning running as I stepped out into the heat.

Harper Emory was seated at a table on his porch, speaking with a man I had never seen before. They were busy unfolding sandwiches from waxed paper wrapping, and stopped talking as I stepped up the stairs into the shade. Emory looked as sclerotic as the last time I had seen him, but the other man was lean and tightly wired, like a man who was constantly spoiling for a fight. He turned sideways in his seat, threw an arm over the top rail of his chair, and glanced at Emory to gauge what he should do about me.

"Why'd you lie to me, Mr. Emory?" I asked.

"I swear you smell like the carrot juice and sandals crowd, Dawson. I can smell incense from all the way over here."

"I just had a visit with your neighbor."

"Tell me you finally did something right, and spare me from having to hire this fellow here."

A narrow smile stole across the thin man's face as he studied something lodged beneath his thumbnail. His skin was deeply lined and gave the appearance of leather that had been tanned by decades of exposure to the sun. His features were angular, eyes deeply set, lifeless and gray as a buffalo nickel. He wore a western style shirt, and a bolo tie of braided leather with a turquoise ornamental clasp and tipped with silver aiguillettes. His jet-black hair was slicked back with pomade, and a short-brimmed hat sat upside down at the edge of the table.

"If self-righteousness could be bottled, your neighbor would be a distillery," I said. "But I do not believe that Deva

Ravi and his people stole your sheep. Nor am I convinced that they assaulted you."

Something unspoken passed between the two men at the table, and I noted that Sam Griffin was watching every move we made from where he sat inside my idling truck.

"I'm sorry to hear you say that, Sheriff," Emory said and gestured across the table. "This here is Carl Spinell. He's a stock detective. They say he can track a bear through running water."

"This isn't 1890, and you are not standing in Johnson County, Wyoming," I said.

Carl Spinell leaned back, crossed his legs at the ankle, exposing Durango boots with zippers that went up the sides. He looked at me directly for the first time.

"I know my whereabouts," he said. "And I know my business."

He spoke with the peckerwood inflections common to sections of Bakersfield or the Texas oil patch.

"If Harper Emory elects to hire you on, Mr. Spinell, I will expect you to operate within the law. Am I making myself clear?"

"I already said I know my business, Sheriff."

"I'm pleased to hear that," I said. "I want you to remember how it ended up for old Tom Horn. I believe he was a stock detective like yourself."

Spinell pursed his lips and shot a look toward my truck.

"You seem a little—what do the kids say these days?—*uptight*. I hear there's a new bowling alley opened up in Lewiston. Maybe you and your colored friend ought to drive there and roll a few frames to relax. That's assuming that you hayseeds have caught up with the rest of the country, and that Negroes are allowed to go bowling with regular people."

"Perhaps you'd like to ask that question of my deputy yourself," I said. "He always enjoys a lively conversation with folks who express themselves the way you do. I imagine you'd find it instructional."

"I'll have to pass on that, Sheriff. Maybe another time. I haven't finished my sandwich yet, and I'm feeling kinda gut-shrunk."

"Just in case my earlier point regarding the law was lost on you, I will repeat it in simpler terms," I said. "Life is hard. It's even harder if you're stupid. Staple that to your forehead so you don't forget."

I climbed back into the coolness of the truck and backed out of Emory's parking lot.

"Did that discussion go as smoothly as it looked?" Sam asked.

"Like a mime at a blind school. When you get back to the office, I want you to look into the background of a man named Carl Spinell."

"Where's he from?"

"Can't tell exactly. Start with the agencies in Texas and California."

Sam shot a backward glance to the two men on the porch and pulled his hat down over his eyes.

—⚭⚭⚭—

WHEN I returned to my ranch that evening, I stripped off my clothes outdoors and left them in a pile on the concrete landing outside the mud room. I wanted no particle of anything to which I had been exposed that day to enter into my house. Jesse stared at me as I stepped into the kitchen wearing nothing but my boxer shorts and carrying my gun belt.

"I won't ask," she said.

"Good," I said. "I'll be in the shower with a can of lye and a wire brush."

Some of us grow up as kids believing that there might be monsters lurking inside the closet, or hiding in the dark beneath the bed. But that's not where you find monsters. You find them walking right straight in, directly through the front goddamned door.

CHAPTER THIRTEEN

I SADDLED DRAMBUIE in the early morning darkness, and set out in a northwesterly direction, through the whisperweed and foxtail, up the long winding trail that eventually opened onto the North Pasture. Two hours later, I was wandering through a clearing and stood beneath the outstretched branches of an old black oak. I leaned my back against the rough bark and lit a cigarette. I looked out across acres of rolling pasture that stretched all the way to the foothills that marked the far horizon. This ranch had sustained three generations of my family, so far. That was not the entire truth. The truth was that three generations of my family had shed blood and tears to flourish on this land.

I exhaled a smoke ring and watched it disappear on the breeze, thinking about a man I had last seen on this very spot, not all that long ago. He called himself Blackwood, though I remain uncertain as to whether that is his real name; he cautioned that I would not likely recognize this country thirty years from now. He assured me that his statement was not hyperbolic, though he was not speaking about my ranch in particular, but of the world as a whole, as he saw it. I did not want to believe him. Events of recent days had caused me to reconsider, which troubled me in ways that had reanimated his warning to me, and I had begun to recognize the truth of it hiding there like a shade.

Caleb Wheeler had told me that he felt the borders of his life shrinking in on him, and in that moment I knew exactly what he meant. Blackwood may end up proven to be right, but change purely for its own sake is not change at all, it's only corrosion. Thirty years from now, I intended to sit at the base of this same tree, watching my grandchildren rope, ride, and haze cattle, branding hides with superheated irons bearing the symbol of their legacy. I would very much like for Blackwood to be wrong.

———— ∞ ————

I HEADED southeastward, taking the long way home, following the course of the creek all the way to the ranch. As before, Wyatt ducked in and out of the low growth along the banks, cooling himself from time to time by rolling in the shallows and stone eddies.

Back at the barn, I unstrapped the cinch, racked the saddle and bridle, then took my time with the curry and comb before hooking Drambuie's hooves and leading him to his stall. I stepped outside into the sunlight with the intention of heading to the house for breakfast, but changed my mind at the last minute and walked down to the ranch office instead.

Young Tom Jenkins was snaking hay bales behind his new colt, while Paul Tucker, my wrangler, waited for him beside the stake bed truck. I looked across the empty corral and saw that Caleb had taken up a post beside an alder tree, rolling a matchstick across his teeth and watching the youngster and Tucker at their work.

I poured a cup of black coffee from the urn and scrolled through the Rolodex on my desk. I was looking for a number I had not had occasion to use in some time, the lawyer in Portland who handles my real estate and business transactions. I dialed Bill Kiefer's office and waited on hold while his secretary set off to locate him. Caleb had placed a copy of the handbill for the upcoming rodeo on my desk as a reminder that we had one of our breed bulls up for the judges' inspection, and ultimately for the auction that followed. Several of our hands had also signed up to compete in various rough stock events, so it was always a family occasion to spend a weekend at the fairgrounds. I fastened the poster to the wall with a thumbtack and paced back and forth down the length of the office.

Bill Kiefer's secretary returned to the line and asked if I'd mind waiting for another minute or two while he finished with another call. I agreed, and stepped to the window, tipped open the jalousies, and watched Caleb bawl out the Jenkins boy again. The kid's work shirt was soaked through with sweat from bucking bales onto the truck, but when he pushed back the brim of his hat I could see that his face was covered with red welts.

"What the hell is the matter with your face?" Caleb asked.

"There's clouds of mosquitoes out there."

"The cattle don't stop eating because there's mosquitoes. You look like every last one of 'em took a bite outta you. Goddamn it, boy, you gotta do what I tell you."

Tom Jenkins rubbed the palm of his hand across his cheek and stared at the ground, but Caleb wasn't quite through with him yet.

"I swear you don't have the sense to find a baseball in a tomato can," Caleb said. He reached into his shirt pocket, pulled out a cheroot, and waggled it in front of the kid's face. "This is the last one of these things I'm gonna give you."

"I don't like the taste of cigars."

"This time of year we get gnats over there by the river. Lots of 'em," Caleb said. "Any single one of 'em is only the size of a dust speck, but now you know they don't come in ones. The only surefire deterrent is cigar smoke. So pick your poison, youngblood, cigar smoke or gnat bites."

Tom Jenkins's eyes went watery with a combination of anger and humiliation. He wiped a sleeve across his nose and turned to stomp back to the truck.

"You only walk away from me once," Caleb said. "Set off in that direction before I finish talkin' to you again, you best keep right on going."

"I thought you were done."

"You'll know when I'm done when I tell you I'm done."

"Okay."

"Okay, *what?*"

"Okay, Boss."

Caleb shoved his hands into the back pockets of his jeans, leaned over, and spat on the ground.

"Now I'm done," Caleb said.

I returned to my chair and sat down when my attorney came on the line. Bill Kiefer asked after Jesse and Cricket, and we went through the rest of the ordinary pleasantries before we finally got down to the reason for my call.

"I need a favor from you," I said.

"Business or personal?"

"Law enforcement."

He was quiet for a long moment, and I could hear the clack of office typewriters and the ringing of telephones behind his silence.

"Not exactly my expertise."

"I need you to check on some real estate for me," I said. I described the location of Rainbow Ranch and waited while he wrote it down. "I'd like you to do a title search, or whatever you need to do, and tell me who owns the damn thing. As much of the chain of title as you can get."

"It may take awhile," Keifer said.

"I need you to keep this under your hat."

"You know I keep everything under my hat."

"That's why I called you."

⸙

THE KITCHEN smelled like bacon when I stepped inside the door. Jesse was hunched over the sink, washing the breakfast dishes, and Cricket was getting ready to drive out to the film set to meet with their client. I hung my hat and coat on the rack in the corner, and took a seat at the table. When I looked up, Jesse was staring at me.

"I woke up early this morning and you were already gone."

"Couldn't sleep," I said. "I rode Drambuie up to the North Pasture to clear my head and think."

"It was still dark."

"We know the way."

Cricket came out from her room and shrugged herself into a light jacket. She gave me a peck on the cheek as she swept past me and into the kitchen to grab a banana from the fruit basket.

"You missed a call while you were out," Cricket said as she plucked the key ring for the Bronco off a nail by the door.

"Who was it?"

"Mom took it." She smiled and breezed out the door.

I turned to Jesse, and her expression told me that she hadn't intended for this to come up right then and there.

"It was Nolan Brody," she said.

"I don't think I heard you correctly."

"He invited us to dinner tonight. At his house."

"And what did you say?"

"I accepted."

"Jesus Christ."

She folded her arms across her chest and leaned a hip on the edge of the counter. Her face was expressionless, but her eyes betrayed something else.

"I worry about you sometimes, Ty."

"I know you do."

She studied me for a few seconds longer and reached for the iron skillet that hung from a hook on the wall.

"Can I make you some breakfast?" she asked. "There's plenty of bacon left over."

"I would like that."

I watched her light the gas on the stove. The morning sunlight streamed through the window over the sink and highlighted the gold of her hair. Even though I was angry, I would have given anything to stall time in that moment.

"I worry about you, too, Jesse."

She stopped what she was doing and faced me. Her mouth turned up at one corner, her lips pressed together with the faintest trace of a smile.

"I know you do."

CHAPTER FOURTEEN

THE DRIVE TO Nolan Brody's house took the better part of an hour.

Jesse filled the silences with conversation about Cricket's work on the film production, and though I was grateful for her attempt at distraction, my mind kept returning to the Emory situation, gnawing at it like a feral dog. A lone cirrus cloud was suspended along the distant peaks of the Cascades, shot through with the colors of a ripened peach and illuminated from behind by the descending sun. I mentioned that I thought it looked like an airburst explosive, but Jesse said it resembled an angel.

A few minutes later, we turned off the highway and up the long, manicured driveway to Brody's home. It was a stately three-story affair that looked as if it had been transplanted from the banks of the Seine. I pulled in beside a late model AMC Hornet that was parked at an odd angle adjacent to one of the three garage doors. Jesse cradled a gift bottle of pinot noir in her arms. I judged that Brody's estate was not far from Postpile Falls, as the sweet scent of fast-moving water and newly mown grass laced the air. A soft breeze drifted in from the east and pressed the fabric of Jesse's dress against her thighs. I pushed the doorbell and she brushed something invisible from the lapel of my sport coat.

We were ushered inside by a middle-aged man dressed in the black suit, white shirt, and tie of a butler, who acknowledged us with only the slightest of nods. We followed him through the foyer and into a sitting room furnished in Chippendale and decorated in ornate rococo. Molly Meadows stood alone at the far end of the room with a flute of champagne in her hand, admiring a collection of paintings that resembled the style of Fragonard or Boucher or Antoine Watteau. The dour-faced doorman returned a few moments later carrying a serving tray and offered two crystal glasses to Jesse and me, and I introduced Jesse to the teacher.

"I'm pleased to see you again," I said to Molly. "I wasn't aware you would be here."

"Mr. Brody is the head of the school board," she said. "I can't very easily decline a command performance. What's your story?"

"I was under the impression he had some thoughts on improving my department's budgetary resources."

"So we've both been coerced," she said, and touched the rim of her glass to mine.

There was no sign of Nolan Brody as yet, so the ladies made small talk while I studied the artwork and tried to reconcile the appearance of this home with the Brody I had come to know. The overall effect was designed to intimidate, its component elements arranged to a point of fastidiousness that hinted at compulsion, yet was oddly bereft of personal touches, curios, or family photos. It was as if the decor and possessions displayed inside his home informed him of who he was; that his greatest personal fear was insignificance.

I found myself drawn to an oil painting depicting a well-muscled stallion rearing on its hind legs in a lush field of grass. The artist had infused the canvas with rich golden light, and a background that put me in mind of the Acropolis.

"Stunning, isn't it?" Molly said as she stepped up beside me.

I glanced at the brass plaque that had been fixed to the frame, then back into the wild eyes of the animal.

"This is a painting of Arion, from the Greek myth," I said.

I sipped from my glass and found that I could not look away.

"Poseidon, the god of the sea," I continued, "created the horse as a gift for Demeter, a woman of great beauty for whom he lusted. Legend has it that all of the world's horses are descended from Arion."

"You seem to know your mythology, Dawson," a male voice interjected from behind us.

Nolan Brody had somehow glided into the room unheard and unnoticed by any of us. He was dressed in gray slacks and bit loafers with a wide-collared shirt, its top button left unfastened, and a paisley foulard painstakingly knotted around his neck. His face had been recently shaved, vitric and glossy from a fresh application of scented lotion.

"I'm afraid I treated my early schoolwork as temporary knowledge," Brody said. "Retained it just long enough to pass the exams. Regrettably, most of whatever I might have learned about ancient myths has long since slipped away, replaced by subjects that I found to be of greater substance."

"You managed to make that sound like an insult, Mr. Brody," I said.

He stepped in close and smiled at Jesse. His eyes gleamed like black marbles, and his breath smelled of some sort of sweet aperitif.

"Is your husband always this thin-skinned, Mrs. Dawson?" he asked, and touched his lips to the back of her hand.

———◦◦◦———

DINNER WAS served in a dining room that matched the formal solemnity of the rest of the house, overcrowded with Queen Anne antiques, walls papered in damask and festooned with oils on canvas, and a long oval table surrounded by ribbonback chairs.

I had never claimed to know Nolan Brody, but nothing could have prepared me for the conspicuous excesses of his home. His manner and dress were far more foppish and effete when he was outside the view of the public, but his tone and deportment were as pugnacious and petulant as always. He was a man who was clearly at odds with himself, his east coast trust fund upbringing inconsonant with the image of self-made man-of-the-western-frontier that he endeavored to cultivate in his civic life.

Wine glasses had been refilled, and the second course served by Brody's manservant, when the conversation finally devolved into the inevitable. I had promised Jesse that I would endure this occasion as politely as was possible, but Brody had revealed himself as the chameleon and poseur I had always believed him to be. The evening had begun with his passive-aggressive civility, but after enduring one Brody homily too many, Molly Meadows was the first to give up on the game.

"Rainbow Ranch is a commune, not a cult," Molly replied to one of his pointed remarks.

"A distinction without a difference, Miss Meadows."

"I beg to differ. I found Deva Ravi to be a very polite and charming man."

"With due respect," I said. "A man can be polite and evil too."

Miss Meadows looked at me with surprise, though I couldn't tell whether the reason was my lack of support for her point, or the content of my statement.

"He seemed quite well educated. His responses to my students' questions were cogent and articulate."

"Ask a question, you'll get an answer," I said. "It doesn't mean it'll be the truth."

Nolan Brody appeared somehow titillated by the change in the chemistry of the discussion.

"I believe you're both underestimating the situation," he said. "I was in hopes you would recognize that when you visited that place."

"There is no 'situation,' Mr. Brody," I said. "I saw nothing out there that would require any further law enforcement involvement."

He threw his napkin on the table and glared at me.

"Did I hear you correctly, Sheriff Dawson? Harper Emory is the victim of a violent crime, and you still insist on doing *nothing*?"

I felt the heat climb up my neck, and Jesse must have seen the signs too. She squeezed my knee under the table. I ignored it.

"Doing nothing can be a valid form of action, Mr. Brody. You'd know that if you'd been paying attention back in Officer Candidate School."

"Sanctimoniousness is a very unattractive trait. It's not a good look on you, Sheriff."

I tipped my head toward the ceiling, scanned the frescoes of cherubs frolicking among the clouds.

"The difference between you and me is that I do not expect God's grace," I said. "I do, however, spend a great deal of time praying I'll be worthy of it."

Brody slid his eyes from my face and locked them on Molly Meadows.

"I'm shocked by the two of you," he said. "I think you have both been duped by those freaks and drug pushers."

"I'm no show pony, Brody," I said. "I don't think Emory *or* those kids have been forthcoming with me. Nevertheless there's no crime to prosecute. This subject is closed."

"Am I speaking Esperanto? Those hippies lied to you. They don't belong here."

"Why is it that cheaters always think they're being cheated, and liars always think they're being lied to?"

"Excuse me?" Brody said.

"You are way out of your weight class," I said. "If you keep stirring this pot, you'll have half this county mobilizing with pitchforks and torches. I told you before: the law applies to everyone. Not just you, or the people you approve of."

Jesse whispered something to me, but I couldn't hear it through a noise inside my head that rumbled like the collision of tectonic plates.

"I'm sorry," I said. "But this is like arguing over who saw the biggest pile of shit."

"Ty—" Jesse said.

"How colloquial." Brody smiled. "I think perhaps every-one involved has veered off script."

"Off script? I didn't know that there was one."

"Oh, come on, Dawson. You know what I mean. Harper Emory has been aggrieved."

He paused for a sip of his wine, then smiled, but his eyes reflected cold rage.

"Sheriff, you need to get this situation in hand. Encourage those young people to skedaddle off to San Francisco or wherever they came from, and leave us all in peace."

"You can't do that!" Molly Meadows said.

"I have no intention of doing anything of the sort," I assured her. "There's no reward for being wrong first, Brody."

"That is a faulty line of thinking, Sheriff. You had better act swiftly and decisively, and move that commune out of our county before something goes seriously wrong."

"Do you know something I don't?"

"They say you never hear the shot that kills you."

"Who in the hell says that?"

"It's a saying."

"It's a damn stupid one. Care to explain how anyone could experience a kill shot, then go on and tell anybody about it?"

He sighed, as if I were a slow child.

"As I said, it's a saying."

"Or is it some sort of veiled threat? Are you making a reference to Harper Emory's new employee?"

Jesse kicked me under the table this time.

"I've met him," Brody said. "He seems like an old-fashioned, no-nonsense sort to me."

I thought about Carl Spinell and those eyes the color of dull metal, void of expression or complexity.

"Carl Spinell is a dangerous man," I said. "If not to himself, to everyone around him."

"From what I understand, Mr. Spinell advocates the same use of force that I do in order to recover control of this situation," Brody said.

"I'd advocate being mindful of where you get your advice. Don't ask a barber if you need a haircut."

The blood had drained from Molly Meadows's face, and she had begun to look faint.

"The sheriff is right," Molly said softly. "Everyone needs to de-escalate."

Nolan Brody pinned her with his stare.

"Perhaps you've had a little too much sensitivity training, young lady," he said. "My god, 'madness' is now called 'mental illness'; 'laziness' is called 'unemployment.' Crime is being downgraded to 'delinquency' right here in my very own county. I swear, the shrinks that are redefining our language are going to get all of us killed."

"You have a tendency toward recklessness with other people's lives, Mr. Brody," I said.

"I haven't convinced you, have I? You're still planning to do nothing."

I nodded.

"T. E. Lawrence wrote about the 'Irrational Tenth.' Have you heard of it?" I asked.

"I have not."

"Lawrence said that nine-tenths of tactics could be taught in a classroom. But that final piece, the 'Irrational Tenth,' could only be accessed by intuition. I've learned to trust mine."

I stood up from the table, carefully refolded my linen napkin, and placed it on the seat of my chair.

"Good night, Miss Meadows," I said. "Thank you for dinner, Mr. Brody. It was very interesting."

Jesse's cheeks were flushed pink with embarrassment or anger, I couldn't tell which. Probably both. I offered my hand to help her get up from her seat. We were halfway to the door when I turned back around.

"One more thing, Nolan," I said. "Don't ever second-guess me, or insult me with bribery again. You can take your enhanced budget and new patrol cars and park them up your ass."

THERE WAS a wrinkle between Jesse's eyes as she stared unblinkingly through the windshield and straight out at the road.

In the end, it is our choices that define us.

There are lines of demarcation in our lives: events that define the boundary that separates the way that we felt before from everything that follows. It constructs the prism through which our perceptions will be filtered for the remainder of our lives, a mist that can never be entirely cleared away. We had no way of knowing that night, as Jesse and I made that long, silent drive home, that at that very moment, a line was being drawn that would forever scar Meriwether County and reshape the way that the people who lived there would thereafter view their own lives, and the way that we viewed one another.

CHAPTER FIFTEEN

I WOKE UP early the next morning, snuck outside, and clipped a fresh bouquet of irises from the garden, still dressed in my bathrobe and slippers. It was June 17, Jesse's and my wedding anniversary. It had always been a day of mixed emotions for my wife, as it also marked the date that Jesse's father had passed away after a long and painful illness. He had died several years before I met her, and she selected that date for our wedding with great intention, an attempt at achieving some kind of divine balance: to supplant a day that had previously been one marked by grief and loss with an occasion that represented love and new beginnings. In practice, though, it became both. I had always wished I had had the chance, if only to assure him of my devotion to his daughter. So, in the end, I always likened our day of celebration to one of blue sky rain.

I returned to the kitchen, placed the cut garden flowers into a vase and set them at the center of the table, together with a card I had picked up at the stationery store. The night before had not gone well, and I owed Jesse a special night out. I stepped out onto the porch to call the front desk at the Gold Hotel, whispered my reservation request for dinner that night in their restaurant. It was the nearest approximation to fine dining to be found in the valley, and the only establishment to feature white linen tablecloths, candlelight, silver flatware, and a respectable wine list. It was one of my wife's favorite places.

———

THE CALL came less than two hours later, with the morning sun barely cresting the peaks of the mountain range, as I was cooking french toast for my wife.

CHAPTER SIXTEEN

MILA KINSLOW
(Excerpted from interview #MC1803/D)

IT HAD ALL been so outta sight when it started.

In the beginning, one of the things I had dug the most was the vibe that the Deva radiated. He'd look at a tree, or a flower, or the body of a woman, and his face would totally transform, like a child's. I don't think I had ever seen an adult act that way before. His eyes would just sparkle like little stars. He used to say, "Nirvana is right here, right now." We felt like we already lived in heaven.

We had become a volunteer family, glued to each other by a universe of love and the power of the Deva, who was a father, a brother, a lover, and a spirit all at the same time. We gave up our given names, even gave up our birthdays; Deva remade us into something better, something more beautiful and connected.

"Together we make one completed body," he said to us. "Separately, you are the limbs, while I am the heart and the soul and the mind."

When I was a little girl, I remember when my mom would sometimes have friends over to our house. When it got late, she would tuck me into bed in my little room, but I could still hear the drone of conversation from wherever the adults were, in the living room or out on the porch. I remember that warm, safe feeling I'd get when I heard the grown-ups laughing. I couldn't hear what they were talking about, but that rhythm would lull me to sleep. That's what it felt like when we first came to the ranch. The patterns and pulse of the community became so familiar, made me feel safe and alive, like I was wrapped in a cocoon.

———◦◦◦◦———

I DON'T know if I was ever in love with Deva, but I loved him in a way that seemed to please him. I don't think that I knew what real love actually was at the time. Maybe I still don't. Either way, it makes me sad to think about it now, because sometimes when I would catch Sweet Pete stealing glances at me, I'm pretty sure I got a hint of what it was supposed to look like. Poor Pete.

Sweet Pete didn't have the same open-minded attitude where I was concerned. For most of us, it was a journey of sensual exploration. No big deal. Get it out and get it on, you know? For him it was different though. Pete and I had driven here together, trying to escape the craziness of LA, and to meet up with his friend. But his friend was long gone by the time we arrived at the ranch, and Sweet Pete felt alone and a little adrift because of that. Don't put me down for this or anything, but somewhere along the way I'm pretty sure that I kinda broke his heart.

———◦◦◦◦———

LITTLE BY little, I noticed that Deva began to separate the men from all the women, and he started getting super jakey. It was right after the high school kids came out to visit, and afterward Aurora was talking with that foxy, colored deputy. Deva Ravi fucking *hated* that. Excuse the language.

The topics of his nighttime bonfire talks gradually became these open-ended raps that could get pretty heavy and disturbing. Every once in a while you could still catch a little of that childlike glint in his eyes, but mostly it just seemed like some kind of cloud had drifted over him.

This one night after dinner, we were gathered by the fire singing songs and passing smoke around. One of the guys—I don't remember who, maybe it was Timberwolf or the guy we all called "Corncob" cause he had these big buck teeth, and looked like he could eat a corncob through a chain-link fence. Anyway, he started laughing at something. He wasn't laughing at Deva, he was just laughing and having a good time. But Deva Ravi had been spending more time with Larry and Mac from the mechanics shed. The three of them started doing more and more hallucinogenic stuff, like psilocybin and peyote and acid, and when they did, they'd all get super paranoid. So when that poor guy started laughing, Larry whipped out this buck knife that he carried and held the blade to that guy's throat. I was sure he was going to slice his neck open right then and there, right in front of us. Just for laughing. After that, we all called him Scary Larry. But never to his face.

Another time, Grand Funk Railroad was scheduled to play a concert up in Portland and bunch of us girls were all set to drive there and see them. Truth is, we all thought Mark Farner was pretty cute, and that hair . . . Anyway, at the last minute, Deva totally freaked out and wouldn't let us out of the gate. At first I was pretty pissed, but then I got embarrassed for him cause he was acting so crazy. I remember staring down at the ground while he screamed at us, just to have something to do, you know, so I wouldn't have to see his face.

From then on, it seemed like everything got way more uptight.

Deva's fireside talks about the Universal Mind gradually faded out completely, and the nighttime speeches became more about the rules we had to follow. Every few days, completely at random, we'd be called in one by one, to go up to the main house for an aura check. Deva would stare into our eyes, sometimes for minutes at a time, like he was peeling the skin right off our skulls; other times, he would circle us like a jungle cat, his palms inches away from our skin, feeling the waves and dimensions of our energy, making sure that we were still cosmically pure.

NOT LONG after the aura checks began, Deva Ravi had us gather in the Spirit Room, the men seated on one side, the women on the other. He went on and on about the differences between the genders, and how even the earliest of civilizations had relied on rituals to mark the passage into manhood. That was how the sojourns started.

Deva said the purpose was to demonstrate resourcefulness, courage, and loyalty, and in the end, the men would discover their Universal Purpose. Each man was expected to go off by himself, each one in a different direction. They weren't allowed to contact one another, and they couldn't carry money or food, only the clothing on their backs. They were to rely on the universe for the provision of their needs, and were forbidden to come back to the ranch until the next new moon. This was for the cleansing of their spirits, Deva said, and to prove their worthiness.

It all felt really sad, man. That same night, all the girls stood in a line and watched them walk out through the gate. The only men left behind at the ranch were Deva Ravi and the two guys he had really started to lean on, Larry and Mac. Both of those guys had turned super creepy, I thought, but that's a whole nuther story. The point is, that was the night that I remember feeling that sad and empty feeling for the first time, as we watched the men just walk away and disappear into the dark. Up until then I felt like I'd been living inside a magical world decorated with all these big, bold, fancy colors.

All of a sudden, it was like all those colors had turned to gray.

CHAPTER SEVENTEEN

JORDAN POWELL WAS standing on the elevated wooden sidewalk, leaning against one of the old steel tethering posts, scrawling something in his notebook. The yellow crime scene tape that he had strung across the entrance of Mother Nature's Sandwich Shop was fluttering in the wind, making a sound like a snake's rattle. Shards of shattered glass glinted in the sunlight across the width of the walkway, and crunched beneath my heels as I stepped up beside my deputy.

"Morning, Captain," Jordan said. "Hell of a way to start the day."

"Is there any damage inside, or did they just smash the front window?"

"They tipped over some tables, smashed up a few chairs, stuff like that."

"How about the cash register?"

Jordan shook his head side to side and looked up from his notebook.

"Either they got scared off before they could break into it—"

"Or it wasn't a burglary at all," I finished for him. "Anybody see anything?"

"Naw. The girls who work here said it was like this when they arrived this morning."

"Did you take photos of the scene?"

"Yes, sir."

I looked up the block, at the storefronts of small shops, and the bank, and the Richfield gas station on the corner, where the blue neon tubing still glowed along the parapet. The businesses hadn't opened at this hour, except for Rowan Boyle's diner a couple blocks up, and Mother Nature's, which had been vandalized, possibly burglarized, in the dark hours of the night or early morning.

"What time did the girls say that they came in this morning?"

He flipped a couple pages in his book.

"A little before six."

"Did you check with Rowan Boyle? Did he see or hear anything?"

"He said he didn't, said it was still dark when he opened up. He's two blocks away anyhow."

Two of the girls from the commune stepped out onto the sidewalk. The one I didn't recognize held a broom in her hand, and the other was Dawn, one of our Wayfinders from the field trip to the ranch. I touched my fingers to the brim of my Stetson in greeting.

"I forgot to get your last name," Jordan said to her. "For my report."

"Just 'Dawn.'"

"I need a full name."

"That is my full name," she said. "Once Deva Ravi reveals our Universal Identity to us, that's the only name we need."

Jordan looked at me with a question written across his face.

"Sheriff?" he said.

"It's okay. Just take her picture for the file. The Deva has no objection to that, I suppose?"

"I don't know," she said. "It's never come up."

I stood to the side while Jordan Powell snapped a few shots of both girls, then tucked the camera back into its case.

"Sorry about this," I said to Dawn. "Any idea who might have done it?"

Dawn looked up and down the empty street, and shrugged her shoulders when her eyes landed on me.

"Everyone?" she said.

"Have you got anybody to help you fix that window? Any men, I mean. It's going to be a bit of a job."

"No."

I recalled what Sam Griffin and I had both registered as odd when we had been out at the commune.

"Can you give a few of them a call?"

"They're gone. Out on sojourn," Dawn said. "There's no phone at the ranch anyway."

"What's a sojourn?"

"I don't know much about it. It's a guy thing. You'll have to talk to the Deva."

I looked across the intersection at the Gemini Record store, another of the commune's businesses. I wondered to myself why the sandwich shop had been targeted and not the record shop. I don't know if it mattered, but the question remained. If you wanted to punish the hippies, wouldn't you hit both places at once?

"Is it okay if we start sweeping up?" Dawn asked. "You fellas finished out here?"

"Sure, you go right ahead."

She turned to step inside and I called out to her.

"You don't happen to have a hammer and nails in there, do you?" I asked.

Dawn shook her head.

"What for?"

"Tell you what," I said. "I'm going to drive over to the hardware store and pick up some supplies to get this window boarded up. Maybe you can answer a couple of questions for me when I get back."

"That's mighty kind of you, Sheriff," she said. "I'll make you and your deputy a fried egg sandwich on whole wheat for your trouble."

"You don't need to do that."

"I insist. You want avocado and sprouts with that?"

She saw the expression on my face and laughed out loud.

"How about a couple slices of bacon instead?" she asked.

"That sounds fine."

"Don't look so surprised. We offer a few choices for the carnivores, Sheriff Dawson. If we didn't, we'd be out of business."

BY THE time I finished nailing the plywood over the hole where the plate-glass window had been, I saw Lankard Downing up the street, unlocking the front door to the Cottonwood Blossom. If anybody had an ear for scuttlebutt, it was Downing.

I walked a short distance up the block and ducked inside the bar, where Lankard was busy pulling the strings that lighted the decorative beer signs hanging on the walls. The room was stale from the night before, pungent with an odor like ambergris, and I took a seat at the bar while I waited for Lankard to finish.

"What can I do you for?" Downing asked, once he'd returned to the duckboards. It was a quip I had grown to detest, but was largely an accurate statement of intentions where Lankard Downing was concerned.

"Mother Nature's had their front window smashed in, and their restaurant vandalized during the night. You know anything about that?"

I studied his hatchet face as he listened to me, watched his septuagenarian eyes dance with delight at the news of fresh scandal.

"The hippie kids? First I've heard of it. Damned shame."

"What time did you close up last night?"

"Usual time. Around two, two thirty, I suppose."

"Anybody out of the ordinary come in here?"

"Like who?"

"How the hell should I know, Lankard? You know what passes for 'out of the ordinary' around here."

He appeared to consider my question for a few moments, even scratched at the three days' growth of gray whiskers that grew on his chin just to underscore how hard he was working at it.

"Can't think of nobody unusual."

"And you didn't hear anything? No windows breaking, or cars tearing off down the street?"

"No, sir. Not a thing."

I stood up from the barstool and readjusted the Colt Trooper in the holster at my waist.

"You call me right away if you hear anything," I said.

"Count on it, Sheriff."

It was one of the constants in this town that I knew for a fact I could count on. Downing *not* passing idle gossip quite possibly would be one of the signs of the End Times.

I WALKED the few blocks to the substation, the near-midday sun warming my back. The shops and businesses along Main Street had all opened by now, and I was certain that word of the damage to Mother Nature's had circulated all the way up one side and back down again.

I tucked my sunglasses into my shirt pocket as I stepped through the doorway into the station. Jordan Powell was hunched over the typewriter on his desk, pecking out his report with two fingers. Nolan Brody sat in one of the chairs in the waiting area, his legs crossed at the knee, thumbing through a back issue of *National Geographic.* He looked up as I crossed over the threshold and dropped the magazine on the table. The smile he showed me was both pernicious and smug.

"What are you doing in my office?"

"I won't state the obvious, that I warned you about something like this happening," Brody said.

"Then I'll extend you the same courtesy. Failure to report the foreknowledge of a crime could land you in hot water with the state bar."

"I have no idea what you're talking about. I came here to tell you that Harper Emory is of the opinion that the freaks caused that damage to themselves, to garner sympathy for their cause."

"Harper Emory ought not to involve himself with too much free-range thinking. Didn't I tell you to stay out of my business?"

Brody stood and picked up his briefcase from the floor beside him.

"I believe you suggested that I should not second-guess you. And something unintelligible regarding bribery. I'm still trying to figure out what you meant by that."

"You need to scrape the wax out of your ears, then, Nolan."

I stepped to the door and held it open for him.

"I thought I made myself pretty clear," I added. "Next time, call ahead."

CHAPTER EIGHTEEN

JESSE AND I strolled arm in arm along the sidewalk; the gas lamps that marked the hotel's entrance flickered like beacons a short distance away. The evening smelled of summer flowerbeds and lawn sprinklers and the sweet humidity of damp concrete. The sunset would not arrive until much later, so the atmosphere still radiated shades of turquoise and blue, with not a single star yet in sight.

The hotel was officially called The Portman, named for the family who had constructed it back in 1899. It was a relatively small establishment, only sixty rooms or so, but considered a most fine one by stockmen and their financiers, and had once been the center of gravity for business of every description before the interstate came through. In the few short years since that ribbon of asphalt had been carved across the flatlands thirty miles to the west, The Portman's status had gradually diminished to little more than a historic landmark, a tourist curiosity, and a temporary home for itinerant circuit cowboys. The annual rodeo was still ten days away, but business appeared to have picked up already in anticipation.

Those who lived in Meridian referred to it as the Gold Hotel, a reference to both the prices and the décor in its lavish dining room. Jesse and I stepped down the sweeping staircase at the far end of the lobby and into another time altogether. Original gas-fueled lanterns had been converted to electricity, and shone their muted light on walls covered in aureate blockwood, and velvet draperies tied in place with woven cords that were the thickness of my thumb.

I had requested a secluded booth in the corner, where the tall cathedral windows offered a view across the lawn of a tiered fountain sprouting from the center of a fish pond where water lilies bloomed. A waiter wearing a white jacket and black bow tie touched a matchstick to a tapered candle at the center of our table, and I saw its flame reflected in the shine of Jesse's eyes.

Our waiter reappeared carrying a silver bucket on a stand, with the slender neck of a champagne bottle jutting from a nest of chipped ice. He withdrew the bottle and displayed the label for my inspection, something French and unpronounceable and profligate in price.

"A gift from the gentleman at the bar," the waiter said.

I peered across the room and recognized Carl Spinell standing with two others. The crystal tumbler in his hand glimmered with amber liquid and he extended it in a toast in Jesse's and my direction.

"Please send it back," I said.

Our waiter's expression turned from professional aloofness to mild alarm and he cocked his head as if he had not understood.

"I'm sorry, sir, I can't do that."

"Then hand it to me, and I'll do it."

"Sir—"

"Please return it to the man who purchased it, and let him do what he wants with it."

"But—"

"Do it now, please."

The waiter slid the unopened bottle back into the ice and weaved a path between the tables toward the bar.

"What was that about?" Jesse said.

"An act of hubris from a man who does not deserve to breathe the same air that you do."

"He's coming over here."

My brain went on full combat alert. A moment later, Carl Spinell and his two companions were standing beside our table. I didn't want to give them the illusion of respect by getting to my feet myself, so I shifted sideways in my chair, leaned back, and crossed the tooled shank of my Paul Bond custom boot across my knee.

"I'm sorry you saw fit to refuse my gift," Spinell said.

"I didn't view it as a courtesy," I said. "You intended it as confrontation."

He cast his eyes on Jesse then slowly shook his head.

"Why would such a lovely woman involve herself with such a mistrustful man, I wonder," Spinell said to Jesse.

Spinell's two companions grinned at his wit and I took my time looking them over. I could tell that they were uncomfortable in an establishment such as this one, and they stood out like canker sores. Both men were younger than Spinell, but in possession of a familiarity with one another that left the impression they had spent considerable time in each other's company. The taller of the two had a head shaped like a bullet, shaved down to the skin, a face as flat and featureless as a coal scuttle, and a spider web tattooed across the back of his hand. He was bull-necked and barrel-chested, puffed up with the swell of yard iron. The briny funk of testosterone wafted off him like it was pressed into the fabric of his shirt, and it appeared that he had not been on the outside very long.

The other one had the look of an adult delinquent, the kind of kid who grew up slicing the valve stems off cars belonging to strangers purely for his own amusement. He wore his greasy hair combed back into a ducktail that was twenty years out of style, and his dark eyes vibrated with a kind of intensity that hinted at psychological disorder.

In an earlier era, these men would have willingly acted as bearers of the lash, riding horseback among rows of antebellum cotton fields or the terebinth groves at Parchman Farm. I recognized all three as the kinds of men who conceal their fear and weakness behind acts of outrage or petty cruelty.

"How long has your compadre been out of the joint," I asked Spinell.

"I beg your pardon?"

I looked at the bald-headed one again.

"He might as well have his inmate number hanging on a string around his neck," I said.

"You're saying I look like a criminal?"

"I'm saying that from where I sit, you look like the third man on a match."

Spinell ran his eyes across Jesse again, wearing an expression that was intentionally lascivious.

"Such a waste," he said.

"One more remark about my wife and you'll have one foot on a shovel."

"Don't mistake my common courtesy as weakness. If we were somewhere else right now, I'd drop you, Dawson."

"Given that there's three of you and only one of me, I do believe you'd try," I said. "I hold no illusions as to who you are. I'm sure I'll see you down the line."

I repositioned my chair beneath the table and, in my peripheral vision, watched the three men stalk away. I drew a breath, prepared to apologize to Jesse for spoiling our dinner, but even after more than twenty years of marriage she remained in full possession of the capacity to surprise me. Instead of being upset or angry with me, her manner was one of calmness and resolve.

"Those are the men who work for Harper Emory?"

"Yes, ma'am."

"Watch yourself with them, Ty. They don't belong here."

"Men like that don't belong anywhere."

The corner of Jesse's mouth tipped up on one side, the suggestion of a smile in her eyes. She reached across the table and touched my hand.

"You know, my father would have loved you."

—❧—

WE SKIPPED dessert of Baked Alaska at the Gold Hotel and headed home instead. We spent the rest of that night dancing to Chet Baker records in our living room, attended only by our candlelight shadows.

Sometime in the small hours of the morning I awakened with a start. I reached across the bed and felt Jesse's warm body curled up beneath the sheets and breathing softly. I rolled onto my side and watched the night sky in the narrow parting of the bedroom curtains. Somewhere above the ridgeline, chain lightning rippled through a cloud.

CHAPTER NINETEEN

THE RINGING OF the telephone bled through the edges of my sleep. Our phone was mounted on the kitchen wall, and the sound seemed not only distant, but disjointed from the context of my dream. Jesse stirred beside me, and I hauled myself from underneath the covers and moved as quickly as I could to get the phone.

I glanced up at the clock above the sink as I lifted the handset and pressed it to my ear. It was a little after two o'clock in the morning.

"There's a fire at the record store," Lankard Downing said. "Somebody'd better get down here quick."

"Tell me that you called the fire department before you dialed me."

"I may be getting old, but I'm not stupid, Dawson."

"Have they arrived on scene yet?"

"They're rolling out the hoses now, but there's only a handful of them."

The wail of sirens and commotion from the street outside his bar echoed down the line at me. Meridian's fire department was a volunteer affair, and their good intentions far outstretched their staffing.

"I'll be right there."

I raced into the bedroom, dressed, and jumped into my pickup. I leaned on the horn as I skidded to a stop outside the bunkhouse. Caleb Wheeler and seven sleepy cowhands staggered out into the dark, blinking their eyes against the headlights of my truck.

"In three minutes, I want you geared up and sitting in the back of this truck," I said. "Bring canvas jackets, leather gloves, and anything else you think you'll need to fight a fire."

I wound my way between the bunks as the men threw on their clothes, located Sam Griffin in the chaos, dragging his boots from underneath his cot. His eyes were bright from the rush of adrenaline, and I could see the combat soldier that still lived inside his skin. He unhooked his gun belt from the bedpost, but hesitated for a moment before he strapped it on.

"Bring it," I said. "We're gonna go back to being cops once this fire's snuffed out."

THE SKY above Meridian glowed like a prairie fire, shadows and light reflecting on the grim faces of the cowboys in my rearview mirror. I could hear no conversation whatsoever as we sped toward town, none of the dark humor or derisive banter that typically accompanied the beginning of a work day for my crew. Each man's thoughts appeared to have folded in upon themselves. Even Snoose's teenage nephew, Tom Jenkins, was stitched with an expression that reminded me of the one I wore before my first encounter with an armed enemy battalion, a look that registered somewhere on the scale between anticipation of the unknown and the certainty of death.

The Gemini Record Store occupied a building that had once been a Phillips 66 gas station. It was situated on a corner midway through town. I pulled onto Meridian's main street, and immediately felt the wave of heat that channeled from the flaming building more than four blocks farther on.

My men jumped down from the pickup's bed as I was braking to a stop. The town's two fire trucks were parked at diagonals near the entrance to the record store, aiming their deluge guns toward the flames that licked the shattered edges of the display window. A black column of oily smoke billowed from beyond the tall facade, somewhere near the center of the roof, where the header beams had failed and had collapsed upon themselves. The groan of superheated concrete and steel reverberated behind the curtain of heat and flame and smoke, and smelled of petrochemicals and steam. I waded through the bedlam, finally identifying the fire captain as he directed the operation of the water cannon, and short minutes later, I and all of my cowboys had been deployed.

SOMEWHERE IN the hours of predawn I stumbled, literally, across my deputy, Jordan Powell. It had taken us nearly three hours to bring the blaze under control, and in the aftermath, Powell was sipping coffee as he perched himself on the elevated sidewalk, stretching his legs into the street. He was barely recognizable, his face and all of his clothing having been blackened by the smoke, only the white of his smile visible beneath the angle of his hat brim.

"Morning, Captain," Powell said.

"When did you get here?"

"I was sleeping at the substation when the fire bell went off," he said. "Been here ever since." He took off his hat and examined it in the meager morning light. "Ruined my Resistol too."

I looked up the street where Rowan Boyle had opened the front door to his diner, and was wheeling a cart he'd stacked with pastries and an urn of coffee to the men who had fought the fire. The last few stars still shone inside the dome of pale blue sky, but the atmosphere down on the ground was shot through with the naphthous stench of charred gypsum and rubber.

"Lucky this place was out on the corner by itself," he said. "Any closer to them old wood buildings, this whole block might have went up."

I dipped into my pocket for my cigarettes, shook one out of the pack, and lit it. I squinted my eyes against a ball of smoke and steam that roiled over from the smoldering storefront.

"I feel like I been stomped on by a herd of Angus bulls," I said.

"I know what you mean," Powell said. "But we're both better off than that kid inside the record store."

"What kid?"

"I guess they didn't tell you yet. We found a boy who musta been sleeping in the back room."

"Alive?"

"Barely," he said. "He looked pretty crispy, Captain."

"Goddamn it," I said, and crushed the cigarette under my boot heel. "If that kid dies, it's murder."

"What are you talking about?"

I turned my head and looked back toward the wreckage. All that was left of the old Phillips station was a hollow, smoke-blackened plaster carcass. The stacks of vinyl records inside had fueled a fire that might as well have been raw petroleum. The flames had burned so hot they left scorch marks across the intersection, and cauterized the glass inside the streetlights.

"You think it's a coincidence that this happened one day after the sandwich place was vandalized?" I asked. "Record stores don't light themselves on fire."

❦

I SHOWERED in the locker room at the substation, then got dressed in one of the fresh sets of clothes I kept inside my locker. Sam Griffin did the same as me once I was finished, while Jordan Powell drove my Diamond D cowboys back to the ranch.

Outside on the street, I could hear the sounds of Meridian getting its day under way, and the snippets of conversation from passersby as they took in their first glimpses of the damage that had been done to the record store. The odor of smoke and waterlogged lumber lingered in the air, together with a nearly corporeal sense of suspicion and mistrust.

Sam Griffin came out from the locker room and sat down heavily in his desk chair. Beads of moisture shone in his hair under the fluorescent overhead lights as he shook out a pocket handkerchief and began wiping the grit off his boots.

"Did you get any information back regarding Carl Spinell?"

He picked up a file folder from his desk and tossed it to me.

"That's from California," he said. "You were right."

"I'm sorry to hear that."

"You'll be sorrier after you read it."

Spinell had worked as a brand inspector for California's department of agriculture before being abruptly terminated for reasons not mentioned in the report. He subsequently took a job as a livestock investigator for a private consortium of ranchers whose operations spread across three western states. Over a period of seven years in their employ, Spinell experienced a number of run-ins with various branches of jurisdictional law enforcement before being discharged— again for reasons not provided—and set out on his own. Since that time, he had operated independently in California's central valley. He had been arraigned on charges ranging from harassment to assault to aggravated battery in towns with names like Ballico, Gustine, and Ingomar, but had never drawn lockup time in any one of them. The most recent allegation stemmed from an arrest for his part in a violent uprising that sprung up between a property owner and a small group of agricultural workers and union organizers. The arresting officer's report stated that Spinell and several accomplices had used wooden clubs and bicycle chains in the dispensation of their duties against the unarmed migrants, scoring flesh, crushing bones, and leaving one without an eye. The charges were summarily dropped without explanation, making it clear to me that Spinell's compensation package included prosecutorial immunity to be supplied by his employers. And, thus far, he had received it.

"The man is a walking colostomy bag," I said, and tossed the file folder back on Sam Griffin's desk.

"What do you want to do now, Boss?"

"Take a walk with me."

—ᴑᴄᴇᴏ—

A SMALL crowd had assembled at the corner across from where the store had just been incinerated. The fire captain and someone else whom I did not recognize were wading through the rubble in search of the source of the fire, while the rest of the crew rolled hoses and packed up the last of the gear. I had intended for Sam to shadow them in their investigation, but stopped short when I recognized Carl Spinell's two acquaintances standing among the onlookers.

"Sam, run to the office and bring back the Polaroid camera, pronto."

Spinell's men stood close together, in the shade of a canvas awning that bore the logo of the bank against whose exterior wall they now leaned. The large, bullet-headed one took a swig from a soda can and whispered something to ducktail, who responded by laughing loud enough for me to hear them halfway up the block. I watched Sam lock the door as he stepped out of the office, the Polaroid hanging from a strap he had slid over his shoulder. I pushed my way through the crowd until I stood dead center of the two men's sightline.

"Good morning, Sheriff," Ducktail said.

The smell of dried sweat and stale alcohol bloomed off them in waves, enveloping the pair like a sandwich bag.

"You've got a rind on you," I said. "When was the last time you had a shower?"

"We had a late night," Ducktail shrugged.

"Doing what?"

"This and that."

They both grinned as if this was a special part of their morning routine.

"I'd like to see your identification," I said. "Reach for your wallet with your left hand. Very slowly."

Ducktail shook his head. His eyes had reclaimed the hint of mania that I had first noticed at dinner with Jesse at the Gold Hotel.

"I don't believe I wish to comply," he said.

"Is that a fact," I said. "Where are you staying while you're in town?"

"I don't wish to answer that question either."

I looked at Bullet Head.

"How about you?" I asked. "I'll bet you can understand simple questions."

He said nothing, only locked eyes with me and picked at something lodged between his teeth with the edge of a matchbook cover.

"You know, Sheriff," Ducktail said. "I am beginning to think you were born a quart low. Or maybe the best part of you ran down your mother's leg."

"I asked you to show me your ID."

"I refused your request the first time. I am exercising my right to remain silent."

"I must admit I am surprised," I said. "You must have paid attention in civics class." I held out my hand in Sam Griffin's direction. "Sam, hand me the Polaroid, please."

"What the hell are you doing?" Ducktail asked. He no longer found the situation amusing.

"I am exercising *my* right to conduct a lawful field interview. You and your buddy, Ox Baker over here, are standing in a public place, and I intend to snap your picture. If either of you refuse, I will handcuff you where you stand, and you'll spend the rest of the month eating wax beans and cheese sandwiches in my jail cell."

I snapped a shot of each man separately, and one of the two men standing together. The first two photos I passed to

Sam Griffin, the last one I slid into my shirt pocket, careful to handle it only by the edges.

THE FIRE captain confirmed my suspicion of arson, having found evidence that at least two or three road flares had been slipped through the record store's mail slot sometime between one and one thirty in the morning. I left Sam to man the substation while I made the drive out to the Rainbow Ranch for a word with Deva Ravi.

Carl Spinell, a known thug and strikebreaker, had slithered into my county, the reasons given for his presence abstruse and at odds with every aspect of Meriwether County's agrarian existence. He had a history of employment by protectionist business concerns which also had provided him immunity from the law. I wondered how Harper Emory fit into the profile.

I braked at the intersection and took another long look at the hollowed-out husk of a building that had stood at the center of town for the previous three decades. In one direction lay winding streets lined with shade trees, where early morning milk deliveries still waited on porch stoops at this hour, and kids riding on bicycles threw newspapers tied up with string. I turned and went the other way, and headed out toward the state road, past rolling hills dotted with cattle and sheep, and across a steel bridge that spanned the width of Cash River, where fishermen in McKenzie boats wrestled catches of wild salmon and cutthroat and redsides from the icy current that ran down from the mountains.

I had no desire to assist in the furtherance of the interests of corrupt malcontents or the men who directed their actions from Chesterfield armchairs at the club, where they engaged in egalitarian discourse, but treated the rest of the world like a controlled burn. Nor had I any greater patience for predatory ideologues wearing bell-bottoms and fringe, preaching tolerance, love, and equality, while at the same

time treating women as sexual objects and advocating violence in their protests ironically aimed at the condemnation
of warfare. Both sides represented a debauched and tattered
substitute form of spirituality, a system inherently rigged
against the stalwarts who dogged steers and pulled range
wire in exchange for a day's pay—families who sent their kids
to school or drove them to Sunday church services in station
wagons, all the while instructing them as to the merit and
importance derived from coloring inside the lines.

CHAPTER TWENTY

THE CHAIN-LINK gate blocked the entrance to Rainbow Ranch, strung through with heavy bindings and fastened with a Schlage padlock. I slipped a pair of riding gloves on my hands and grabbed a bolt cutter from the toolbox in the truck bed.

Deva Ravi was sitting cross-legged in a patch of sunshine on his porch when I drove up. The girl he had rechristened as Aurora sat behind him, fashioning his long ponytail into a braid. She was wearing shorts that had been snipped from a faded pair of jeans, and a Mexican-style blouse with tiny flowers embroidered on the yoke. He stood and dismissed Aurora back into the house, then strode across the parking lot to meet me as I climbed out of my truck.

"I could have sworn I locked the gate," he said.

The length of fabric that encircled his waist was printed in some sort of Polynesian design, and the muscles of his barrel chest stretched the seams of a V-neck T-shirt.

"I cut the chain," I said.

"You did what? Do you have a warrant?"

The ranch was quiet, no sign of activity that I could see. I cocked my head and looked at him in puzzlement.

"Why is it that every time I come to visit here someone asks me if I have a warrant?"

"Cause you're the fuzz, maybe?"

"You really need to stop it with the epithets," I said. "Exigent circumstances supersede a warrant, by the way."

142

I studied his face as he processed what I had just told him, and saw no sign of surprise or alarm; no sign of anything at all.

"What 'exigent circumstances' would those be?"

Aurora stepped back outside, leaned a shoulder on a post, and peeled the skin off of an orange while she watched us.

"You weren't aware that your record store burned down this morning? Or that someone was inside when it was torched?"

He looked off in the direction of Meridian. The distant sky was still suspended with a pale gray pall that veiled the sunlight.

"I was concerned that some harm may have come to your ranch as well," I added.

"No, I wasn't aware of that. I don't have a phone."

"Then you understand my situation. Exigent circumstances."

I reached into my shirt pocket and extended the Polaroid to Deva Ravi. He hesitated for a moment before he glanced at it.

"Do you know these two men?" I asked.

"No."

"I'd feel better about your answer if you had a closer look."

I dangled the photo between us until he took it in his hands.

"Why are you wearing gloves?" he asked.

"I burned my hands while fighting your fire."

A crease formed on his brow as he studied the image, but his eyes did not give up secrets easily.

"I don't know these guys," he said, and passed it back to me.

"First the health food shop and now your record store? As I said, one of your people was inside. You don't look overly upset."

I heard the whistle of the wind as it passed between the blades of a water well, and the bleating of a goat inside the orchard.

"We don't live in fear, man. We live in preparation."

"Preparation for what?"

He looked away toward the forest and shook his head.

"You're not the only heavy cat I've had up in my ears lately," he said. "You don't want to have this conversation with me."

"Try me."

"Look, humans are aspirational, man, they're acquisitive. If they weren't, nothing would ever get built, nothing invented; nothing would ever be stolen. Hell, nobody would ever get laid for that matter. Everything runs on friction, my man."

"I thought you repudiated conquest and war."

"I don't love your tone, Sheriff. It sounds like an argumentative brain-fuck to me."

"I'm trying to understand your logic."

He studied me, eager to detect deception, appearing almost disappointed when he found none.

"It's a paradox," he said. "Humans are acquisitive beings, but, in truth, they really don't want to acquire everything they dream of. If they did, they'd die. We all need somebody to be better than, something to aspire to. What could be worse than being devoid of purpose?"

"You're telling me that you don't care that somebody's trying to run you out of town."

"I'm saying that we don't live in fear about it. They want something; we want something. Everybody wants something."

"What do you want?"

"Mostly to be left alone to do our own thing."

"Why don't I believe you?"

"Cause you're a cop and you don't believe anybody?"

I had to hand it to him, he had his rap down cold. But in spite of his tranquil demeanor, an undercurrent of repressed hostility continued to emanate from this place. He cloaked himself inside an aura of hippie mystic ennui, but inside I could see that he was seething. I maintained no illusions regarding his capacity to have assaulted Harper Emory, but I was relatively certain that if, in fact, it had happened at all, it had nothing whatsoever to do with sheep.

"I think we're finished here, Sheriff," he said.

I took a couple steps toward my truck and pulled up short.

"One other thing," I said. "Where is everybody?"

"Working."

"I haven't seen a single man here at the ranch in quite some time."

He crossed his arms along his chest and looked into the sky.

"They're on sojourn."

"What does that mean?"

"What does it sound like it means? Good-bye, Sheriff."

"Care to tell me about the airplanes?"

"I don't know what you're talking about. Good-bye, Sheriff."

And now I knew without a doubt he was lying.

———

I PAUSED at the fork in the road outside the gate, took a minute to slip the Polaroid Deva had handled into an evidence bag, then turned left in the direction of the Emory place. The wind was blowing harder across this part of the valley, the well fans rotating furiously where they stood out in relief against the clouds that scudded along the jet stream. Ranching had never been an easy life, but between the stagnant economy and the long absence of rain, I wondered whether Harper Emory had properly prepared himself, and whether he could hold out through another dry season.

There were no automobiles parked in the driveway when I pulled to a stop in front of the old Victorian. Mrs. Emory's zinnias and irises were heeled over in the garden, and the magnolia in the side yard seemed to sigh in the wind.

I rang Emory's doorbell and waited on the porch. The sun had scorched the acreage beyond the yard the color of desiccated chaff, and I saw Harper's son, Bryan, pushing feed bales off the bed of his truck onto a patch of pasture that had been nubbed down to the topsoil. I was about to ring the bell again when the door finally sighed open.

Harper Emory's wife took a step backward into the foyer, cast her eyes down to the floor, and crossed her arms over her chest as if to form a barrier I could not pass through. I removed my hat and remained on my side of the threshold.

"I'm sorry to interrupt you, ma'am. I came to speak to your husband. Is he home?"

She shook her head slowly, as if it induced pain to do so. Her hair was pulled back in a bun, loose tendrils dangling, framing her face. The hem of a flannel nightgown drooped beneath the housecoat she wore tied tightly across her waist. It appeared as though she had been sleeping, the shadow of a bruise beginning to show through the heavy makeup where her cheek had rested on her pillow.

"Tea?" she asked. Her voice was thin and childlike, so hushed that I almost missed the question.

"Mrs. Emory," I said. "Are you all right?"

"Tea?" she whispered again, oblivious to my question, and I had to look away.

"I'll be leaving, ma'am," I said and tucked my business card into the pocket of her robe. "But if I can be of any assistance to you at all, please call me. Anytime."

She turned and shuffled toward the stairway in the narrow hall. She hadn't bothered closing the door, so I reached for the handle and shut it behind me as I left.

In my grandfather's time, any man who physically abused a woman would have been bullwhipped and chain dragged by his neighbors. He would have shared the squalid social standing of a pedophile or a zooerast. What did it say about a society that seemed to have gone both blind and deaf to civil accountability, but demanded post factum reparations in its place? I did not want to believe that the codes I had spent a lifetime being loyal to had grown outmoded or, worse yet, irrelevant.

I drove up the same narrow track I had taken once before, when Bryan and I had set off to examine the alleged break in the fence.

He wore scuffed work boots and old Levi jeans, his work shirt sweated through along his backbone and a collar of fresh sunburn on his neck. He slipped off his work gloves and knocked the dust off his pant legs as he stepped up to the door of my truck.

"My dad isn't here," he said.

"I gathered."

"I don't want to talk to you."

He swatted at a cloud of gnats as they passed between us.

"What's going on around here, Bryan?"

"I don't know what you mean by that."

"I can't help you or your mom if you won't let me."

His eyes narrowed into slits, his knuckles white. Dust devils swirled down through the folds in the foothills, the grit that carried on the hot wind ticking against my windshield.

I reached into the glove box and drew out the cellophane evidence bag that had the photograph inside.

"Do you know the names of these two men?"

"No," he said and backed away.

"How about your dad and Carl Spinell? Do you know where I can find them?"

His eyes slid off my face and he began working his fingers into his gloves.

"I really don't want to talk about any of this," he said. He had turned away from me, so I could barely make out his words. "You can tell my old man about the grass if you have to. I don't think I care anymore."

———— ⬦ ————

IT TOOK the remainder of the day to drive all the way to Salem and back, but there was no other way to obtain the information I needed. Over the past couple of years, I had developed a friendly acquaintance with a man named Christopher Rose, the captain of the Criminal Investigation

Division of the Oregon State Police. He was athletic, person-
able, exceptionally bright, and particularly fond of his home
town of Stinnett, Texas, which was a stone's throw from the
famed Adobe Walls. I knew this because one could rarely
engage in a conversation with Chris Rose without the subject
somehow being shoehorned into it. This was especially true
after a couple of drinks.

His assistant guided me into his office after a short wait
in the lobby. I shook one of the captain's heavily calloused
hands, accepted the offer of a cold Shasta Cola and sat down
in the guest chair that fronted his desk. He rested his elbows
on the blotter and leaned into the space between us.

I took the evidence bag containing the photo of Carl Spinell's two associates from the inside pocket of my canvas vest
and showed it to him.

"This is a picture of two idiots who just drifted into my
town. I don't know their names yet, but that's not why I'm
here."

Captain Rose ran a hand through his hair and eyed the
Polaroid through the clear plastic.

"Okay."

"A commune has sprung up at the south end of the county,
out in sheep country. Its leader is a man who calls himself
Deva Ravi. He and his people have been on the receiving end
of some dangerous acts of vandalism, which I believe to be
aimed at driving them out."

"And you think these two fuck knuckles are a part of it?"

"Maybe," I said. "But, again, they're not my immediate
concern. I have reason to believe that this Deva Ravi character may be involved in something that may have brought this
situation onto himself. But I can't do much of an investigation because I have no idea what his real name is, where he's
from, or anything about his history."

The captain nodded in the direction of the photo.

"So what's with the picture?"

"I believe it's got Deva Ravi's fingerprints on it; a thumb-
print on the front, and two, maybe three of his others on the

back. I'd like CID to pull the prints and tell me who the hell this guy is."

Rose rocked back in his chair and eyed the evidence bag.

"Let me make sure I heard you right," he said. "You don't know one single thing about this ass clown, including where he came from before he showed up in your town out of the blue. Is that it?"

"That's about it."

"Well, Ty, I gotta tell you: In the absence of anything to narrow the search—"

"I know how it works, Chris, but these prints are all I've got. Probably all I'm going to get."

"How old is this person? Wait. Don't tell me. You don't know."

I shook my head.

"How about a guess."

"Between twenty-five and thirty."

"Well, at least that's something," he said. "If this kid ever entered the service, or registered for the draft, the Feds *might* have a record of him. Even if they do, they've got at least a forty-five-to-sixty-day backlog."

"I understand."

He picked up the evidence bag with the picture inside and handed me a form that would accompany it through the system. I took a pen from the holder on his desk set and filled in the blanks while he eyeballed me.

"This is a Billy Dixon-scale long shot, Ty. You're aware of that, right?"

"Like I said, it's all I've got."

"I'll put it on top of the stack," he said.

———

SAM GRIFFIN was preparing to lock up the substation by the time I returned to Meridian. The carillon on the clock tower at the top of the three-story office building up the block tolled six o'clock, but the summer sun hadn't yet fallen behind the ridge.

"Any word about the kid from the fire?" I asked.

"No," Sam said. "But you got a call from a lawyer named . . ." He picked through the pile on his desk until he located the pink sheet of paper he'd written the message on. "Bill Kiefer. His number's right here."

"You can go ahead and break range," I said. "I'll take it from here."

"You sure?"

"It's been a long day."

Sam seated his hat on his head and headed for the back door while I dialed the number for Bill Kiefer's office. Sam was almost to his truck when I remembered something.

"Before you go," I said. "Can you Xerox a copy of those photos we took this morning."

"Sure thing."

Bill Kiefer's receptionist came on the line and told me he'd left for the weekend. Whatever he had wanted to tell me would have to wait until Monday. I set the receiver into the cradle, squeezed my eyes shut, and pinched the bridge of my nose. My head felt like it had been wrapped in a strand of range wire, so I reached into my drawer for an aspirin.

I folded the Xerox that Sam handed me, tucked it into my shirt as I went to close up for the night. I had just thrown the bolt on the door lock when Nolan Brody appeared on the other side of the glass door. He was wearing a navy sports jacket, club tie, and a starched button-collared shirt. I unlocked the door and stepped out onto the sidewalk.

"This end of the county is getting out of hand," he said, throwing a casual glance toward the scene of the fire. "How long are you going to allow this to go on, Sheriff?"

"Who is this client you keep driving all the way down here to meet with?"

"That's privileged information."

"Actually, it's not," I said. "But I don't really care. I was engaging in polite conversation."

"I dropped by to remind you about the special council meeting this coming Tuesday."

He slid his hands into the pockets of his slacks and rocked back on the heels of his loafers, expecting some kind of reaction from me.

"Are you familiar with the story of Henry II and Thomas Becket?" I asked.

"I saw the movie," he said. "Are you comparing me to Richard Burton or Peter O'Toole?"

"I'm suggesting that it's wise to be cautious as to what you say, and to whom. Words can sometimes be misconstrued."

"I don't take your meaning," he said. "I think you're mumbling again."

"I was just locking up the office for the night," I said. "Is there anything else?"

"I want you to be aware that I'm putting forward a motion for a recall election regarding your position as sheriff."

"Have a pleasant weekend."

"I'll see you on Tuesday."

"You know, Nolan, we cowboys have a saying: When you're riding ahead of the herd, it's best to take a look back every now and then to make sure it's still behind you."

I went back inside and punched in Harper Emory's number on the phone.

"What the hell do you want now?" Emory asked after he recognized my voice.

"I don't ever want to hear about you having raised a hand to your wife again. If I do, Harper, you have my word that we will handle it the old-fashioned way. I want you to be crystal clear about that."

—◦◦◦—

THE LIGHT over the transom was flickering again and I made a note to myself to bring a ladder out on Monday so I could climb up and replace it. I made one last pass through the substation, turned out the lights, and left through the back door. There was one more stop I needed to make before I could go home and put this goddamned day behind me.

I left my truck parked in the back lot and walked through the elongated shadows and night noises of grackles and finches settling inside the limbs of alder trees that lined the empty street, testing the door locks on the darkened shops as I went along. I pushed through the door of the Cottonwood Blossom, and took my place at one of the stools along the bar. A thin layer of smoke floated beneath the rafters, and Dolly Parton was singing "Jolene" on the jukebox. It was still a bit early for the Friday night crowd, only a handful of tourists eating burgers and fries in a booth at the corner, and a swing band setting up on the stage beside the dance floor.

Lankard Downing looked as choleric and consumptive as he always did, wearing his usual unironed cotton shirt and black trousers with a white apron tied around his waist. He was reading the newspaper and smoking a cigarette, leaning on one elbow along the back bar.

"You on the clock?" Lankard asked as he stubbed out his smoke. "You still got your badge and your gun on."

I don't wear a uniform, but I do keep my badge clipped to a tooled leather gun belt with brass cartridges tucked into the loops. My three-quarter jacket had snagged on the butt of my Colt Trooper, exposing the whole rig, and I saw Downing's gaze slide over the room.

"Ain't great for business," he said. "You saddling up at the bar with your weaponry hanging there in front of God and everybody."

I unclipped the badge from my belt and adjusted the hang of my coat to conceal my revolver.

"Oly draft?" Downing asked without waiting for my answer.

The mug he handed me smelled like a goldfish bowl, but I sipped at the cold beer anyway.

"I hear they're gonna try and recall you," he said.

"That made it into the paper already?"

"Oh, hell no. I only read that rag for the classified ads."

"I want to talk to you about last night."

I pulled the Xerox copy of the mugshots from my pocket and slid it across the bar top toward Downing.

"You seen these guys in here, Lankard?"

He glanced at it and slid it right back.

"Yesterday. They were sitting over there at the Pong table making a racket," he said. "Giggling like little girls."

"What time was this?"

"Early. Ten, or ten thirty, probably. They left not too long afterward."

"Did you hear what they were talking about?"

He shook his head.

"No, but they sure as hell weren't working out quantum equations."

"When did you close for the night?"

"I called you a little bit after two A.M.," he said. He ran a hand along the hollows of his cheeks as he thought about it, stared at the oscillating fan bolted to the scantling. "That was right after I phoned the fire department . . . I guess I was outside the door, there, about five minutes before that. I could see the fire burning already. It hadn't got too big yet, but it was fixin' to start roarin'. You could smell it all the way up the block."

"You didn't see anybody outside? Nobody at all?"

"Not a soul."

I picked up my mug from the bar and swiveled in my seat. I noticed Leon Quinn slumped in a chair in the corner, his chin resting on his chest, fast asleep.

"How about Leon? Was he in here last night?"

"Probably," Downing said.

"You don't remember?"

Lankard Downing made a dismissive gesture and began wiping the bar top with a towel.

"Leon don't make much of an impression on me no more, Dawson. Unless he's trying to bust up my furniture."

"You have any idea what time he left the bar?"

"I don't keep track. Quinn and I have a new arrangement: He hands me a ten-dollar bill when he walks in, and I tell him when it's all used up. Sometimes, when he's feeling flush, he hands me another fin. Sometimes he just leaves. Keeps things a lot simpler for both of us."

I turned and studied Leon again.

"Was he this drunk yesterday?"

A dour expression split Downing's face.

"Leon ain't drunk yet, Sheriff. He's just studying the insides of his eyelids. If he was drunk, he'd be dancing or singing or raising up some kind of hell."

"But you didn't see him leave the bar last night?"

"No, sir, I did not."

I stood and withdrew two singles from my wallet, placed them on the bar beside my empty beer mug.

"Do me a favor and call me if either of those two men come back in here again, will you, Lankard?"

"You're still talking about Elvis and the bald-headed refrigerator?"

Something by Hank Snow came up on the box. I nodded and turned for the door.

"Sheriff Dawson," Downing called out as I was walking away. "Are those kids going to be okay, do you think?"

"What kids are you referring to?"

"The ones who used to play music out there on the street. Ain't seen them in days."

"I honestly don't know, Lankard. Don't know too much at all right at the moment."

"I kinda miss 'em," he said. "Funny what you get used to."

―⧥―

LOUD STRAINS of country music were drifting out of the bunkhouse by the time I got back to the ranch. I could hear the men laughing and whooping it up, readying themselves for a Friday night on the town. The smell of a wood fire permeated the stillness of the evening, silver smoke and orange embers floating into the sky between the main house and the horse barn. I broke into a jog and circled back around the house to investigate.

I couldn't hear the words, but Snoose Corcoran was gesticulating wildly and hollering something at Caleb Wheeler. I stopped running and watched as Snoose slammed the door of his flatbed and fishtailed out of the drive and onto the dirt service road that led to his place. Caleb watched Corcoran's dust cloud paint a stripe on the sky for a few seconds, then returned his attention to the glow inside the burn barrel.

"What's the matter with Snoose?" I asked as I came up beside Caleb.

"Aw, he was just showin' off his jawboning talents."

Caleb's face looked flush in the heat of the firelight. The wind had tailed off to nothing and the day's heat was rising from the soil.

"Seemed to me like there might be more to it than that."

"Snoose ought not to be talking to folks after he's been spending the afternoon with a bottle."

"Has he got something on his mind?"

Caleb poked at the fire with the broken end of a rake handle.

"Snoose wants us to keep our bull out of the judging at the show. He's of the opinion that we'll win—which we probably will—and that'll drive down the auction price of his stock."

"He's in a bad way, Caleb."

He tossed the rake handle aside and threw a broken tree limb onto the embers. He wiped his nose with the cuff of his shirt and looked at me.

"Him and everybody else," he said. "Take a look around. We don't get no more rain than the next man, and the next man ain't seen a drizzle since last April. The pastures are dryin' up everywhere, Ty."

The fire took hold of the limb and reflected in the whites of his eyes.

"The hell of it is," Caleb continued, "Snoose said it was the least we could do."

I slid the flats of my hands into my pockets and watched the pulse of the cinders in the barrel.

"Did you hear what I just said?" Caleb said.

"I heard you."

"The ungrateful sonofabitch."

"How's the kid working out?" I asked, to change the subject. I didn't have the heart for the argument Caleb was spoiling for.

"Genetics aside, that youngster might actually make a decent cowboy one day."

A bullfrog croaked somewhere in the darkness and sounded like a rusted door hinge. I heard a truck engine turn over on the far side of the bunkhouse and listened as it faded away.

"Sounds like the fellas are winding up for a big night," I said.

"There's a dance of some kind down at Lankard's place."

"You going with 'em, Caleb?"

He answered by throwing a splintered board into the fire.

I left Caleb to stew by himself, and walked in the direction of the music that still twanged inside the bunkhouse. Taj Caldwell, Tom Jenkins, Griffin, and Powell were the only ones left, the others having already departed. Caldwell was combing his hair in front of a mirror he'd hung from a string on the wall, and Sam Griffin was showing Tom Jenkins how to tie some kind of knot in a length of hemp rope. Jordan Powell was dressed in a shiny red snap-button shirt with white piping, white roses embroidered on the yoke. He was sitting on the edge of his bed and shining his boots with a rag.

"You're all spraddled out," I said.

Powell looked up from his work and grinned.

"I was just dudin' up to put in a good hop at the Blossom," he said. "Don't want to disappoint my fan club."

"Sorry to spoil your plans."

He stopped his work mid-shine, and the smile fell away from his face.

"What's that supposed to mean, Captain?"

"I need you to set up on the Rainbow Ranch."

"What? Like a stakeout?"

"Exactly like a stakeout."

Jordan's boot slipped from his hand and onto the floor. He threw a look toward Sam and Tom Jenkins.

"Why not send Griffin," he said.

Sam lifted his eyes from the knot he was tying, and smiled at Powell.

"I swear, the man takes a bullet just one little time, and he gets special treatment?" Powell persisted. "He ain't been shot this year, so far."

"Neither have you," I said. "Not yet. Besides, Griffin's been on shift all day long. Step lively, deputy. I need you in position out there before it gets full dark."

I drew a rough map on the back of an envelope and showed him what I thought to be the best vantage point.

"There's only one road in and out," I said. "So position yourself here, and keep track of anyone coming or going from either the commune or Harper Emory's place."

"All weekend long?"

I nodded.

"And keep a special eye out for aircraft, you read me?"

"What kind of aircraft?"

"C'mon, Powell," I said. "How many kinds of aircraft are there?"

"I was just asking."

"Feigning ineptitude won't make this assignment disappear."

CHAPTER TWENTY-ONE

MILA KINSLOW

(Excerpted from interview #MC1803/D)

THINGS REALLY STARTED getting sad after the sand-wich shop got wrecked and the record store burned down. I heard something about one of our guys being inside when it got torched, but nobody talked about it, so I didn't know which one, or what happened to him. After Sweet Pete and the other guys got sent out on sojourn, the vibe around the ranch got really weird.

"We need to drop some truth bombs in the shit stream," Scary Larry said one night at the bonfire. Deva and the other goon who worked down at the hangar smiled and nodded their heads like they knew what he was talking about. I had no idea myself, and I could tell the other girls didn't either. All we knew was that we wanted to keep our distance from those guys.

We had started to call the other goon Mac Nasty cause of the way he tried to grope us all the time. He smelled like moldy peanut shells and motor oil, and the skin under his fingernails was always dirty. He had this weird shaped ear where he said a piece got bitten off one time when he'd been in a fight, which I believed because he was straight-up mean. Scary Larry, though, was just plain nuts. He had a wall-eye that made him look even crazier than he probably was, but he was tall, and thick around the chest, and loaded to the gills most of the time.

In the beginning, when Pete and I first got to the ranch, nobody really paid much attention to those guys. Once in a while, a plane would fly in at night and fly out a couple hours later. The hangar was pretty much off-limits to everybody except Deva Ravi and those two, but as far as I could tell, nobody really paid it much attention anyway. We all had our own jobs and shit to do, so whatever went on down there was someone else's movie, you know?

One time, Deva asked me and Aurora to go and meet the plane when it came in. What he really wanted was for us to fuck the pilot while they serviced the plane. We did it, which was okay, but then Deva's goons decided they wanted a turn too. It was the first and last time that ever happened. That's all I'm saying about that.

⁂

YOU'D THINK that we would have all been happy when we heard that Saigon had fallen, and that maybe the war would finally end. The squares in Washington said they were going to end the draft, but they kept issuing draft numbers anyway, so even though the whole lottery trip wasn't happening at the moment, nobody my age really believed a word the politicians said. The way we saw it, the lottery thing was probably a setup of some kind. There was even a rumor about giving amnesty to draft dodgers and deserters, but we knew for sure that that was bullshit. Deva said it was The Man trying to trick those poor guys into coming back out into the open so that the Feds could toss them all in jail.

⁂

"YOU KNOW why the dinosaurs died off?" Deva Ravi said to us one night. "Because the cavemen ate their eggs."

I remember that his eyes looked like they were totally on fire, like he was radioactive. Scary Larry had started wearing that big hunting knife—in a sheaf or sheath or whatever you call it—on a belt around his waist. Had it with him all the time. He was all lit up too.

"See, the cavemen got tired of being stomped on all the time," Deva said. "So they got smart, and snuck into the dinosaurs' nests when they were out hunting and ate all of their eggs. Pretty soon, no more dinosaurs, right?"

We all kinda nodded, because his point sort of made sense, even if we had no idea what he was getting at.

"If we want to send a message to the Straights who want to kill us all and send us off to war, we gotta eat their eggs, man," Mac Nasty said. "You dig what Deva's saying?"

None of us really believed that Deva wanted to actually hurt anybody's kids, at least I didn't. I liked it a lot better when we used to sing songs and pass around a bomber joint, and talk about the stars and phases of the moon.

I missed Sweet Pete and the other guys, too, and it felt as though Deva had begun to move from seeking higher consciousness to no consciousness at all. He was operating the community by committee now, but the problem was, the committee members all lived inside his head.

CHAPTER TWENTY-TWO

JESSE AND I had spent the weekend at the coast, taking a long drive to a small seaside hotel near Depoe Bay. It was my attempt to make amends for the anniversary dinner at the Gold Hotel that had been tainted by the intrusion of Carl Spinell.

On our second day, after breakfast, we took a stroll along a quiet avenue lined with tourist shops and restaurants, and hanging baskets filled with flowers fixed to wrought iron lampposts. It was good to be reminded that colors still existed beyond those of rolling hills of dry brown grass, waterless creeks, and hay bales.

I came across a narrow path that led down from a walkway where a hawser had been strung between stout pilings as a handrail, a boundary along the edge of a steep cliff carved out of the stone by centuries of wind and tides. It took some time to pick our way downward, between the rocks and boulders where succulents and wildflowers had taken root inside the cracks. A cypress tree cast shade across the point at which the foot trail opened onto a secluded beach, where we leaned against the gnarled cypress and removed our shoes and socks. We wandered aimlessly along the tide line, our fingers hooked inside our shoes, the water cold and darkening our rolled-up pant legs, watching the pelicans glide their wingtips across the breakers.

A tangle of driftwood sat among the smooth rocks of an alluvial fan, where the snowmelt from the mountains had its final meeting with the sea. I went off to inspect it while Jesse took a seat on a shelf of dry sand. By the time I returned to sit beside her, her attention had been subsumed by something beyond the horizon. The wind tugged at her hair in such a way that it revealed the smooth planes of her face, the angle of her jawline, and the tiny dimples that had formed along the corners of her mouth. She must have felt the weight of my gaze, and turned toward me and smiled without inhibition.

"What are you thinking?" she asked.

"About our second date."

"That awful Mexican place in Santa Monica?"

"Yes. And our walk along the pier afterward."

"What about it?"

I wrapped my arms around my knees and closed my eyes.

"You told me you weren't looking for a knight to rescue you; you were looking for a man to stand and fight beside."

She laughed and I opened my eyes so I could watch her.

"That's some corny stuff," she said. "I can't believe you remember that."

"I fell in love with you that night."

She leaned in and kissed me on the cheek.

"A moment of nostalgia?" she asked.

"Gratitude."

She stood and dusted off her backside. I watched her walk toward the water, then bend into a crouch to observe a hermit crab skitter from the foam. She scooped her hands into the loose sand and let it sift between her fingers. Then she came back and showed me the bits of broken mollusk shells and colored beads of sea glass nested in her palms.

"What's really on your mind, Ty?"

I looked away and rubbed my eyes with my thumb and forefinger.

"You don't need my problems in your head," I said.

Jesse never wore much makeup. Never had to. But her cheeks and that place behind her ears suddenly flushed pink.

"Don't you dare treat me like a victim," she said, and cast the pellets of sea glass into the ocean one by one.

Jesse was right. She had lived up to her promise to me despite my silences. She carried the weight of her concerns so very differently than I. She looked out toward the clouds like the answers she was seeking were hidden in the wind.

"Harper Emory lost a son in Vietnam," I said. "I'm pretty sure his wife still hears his voice. She's nearly catatonic, but I believe Emory physically abuses her sometimes. Neither she nor Bryan, their younger son, will speak against him."

Jesse weaved her fingers inside of mine and brought them to her lips. Her breath felt warm against my skin.

"The man who calls himself Deva Ravi has those hippie kids under his power; they act like captives, and they don't seem to know it. He's up to something but I don't know what it is. If one or more of them actually did assault Harper Emory, I don't believe it had anything to do with stolen livestock."

I fell silent for a moment and Jesse gently squeezed my hand.

"Don't stop," she whispered.

"Nolan Brody holds to the opinion that sweeping the whole commune out of the county will turn back the clock. He seems to think that ending a revolution is the same thing as restoring the old order. He's dead wrong about that. All it does is transfer superiority to a new one.

"Brody's asking for a recall vote on me this Tuesday night," I said.

"We don't have to stay here, Ty."

"I want to."

She gave me a half smile and looked away.

"What are you supposed to do when someone hits you with a brick?" she asked.

"I don't know, but it's too late to duck."

CHAPTER TWENTY-THREE

I WAS SEATED at my desk inside the substation before the sun came up. Outside the window, a camp of brown Myotis dipped in from the dark and fed upon the flying insects that swarmed inside the light beneath the street lamps.

Shortly after dawn, Jordan Powell walked in through the back door and shrugged off his windbreaker. His eyes were rimmed in red and he wore the haunted, over-caffeinated expression of a man who had spent a sleepless night out on the wire, and he smelled of potato chips and unwashed laundry.

"Sam came out to spell me," he said. "So I tailed a couple of them girls when they drove in from the commune."

"Did they see you?"

His expression remained intentionally inscrutable. He was a good soldier and he did not like to disappoint.

"Of course not, Captain."

"You kept a log of who came in and out?"

"I would've, but I didn't need to. Didn't see one single soul all weekend long. At least, not until this morning, like I just said."

"Not even from Harper Emory's place?"

"No, sir," he said, and rested one of his haunches on the corner of his desk.

I cut my eyes out toward the street and studied the pale blue light behind the ridges of the mountain.

"And no aircraft of any kind either," he said, his tone shot through with disappointment, believing he had let me down. "Seemed to me like you might have been expecting something. Want to tell me what it was?"

"I don't know what I was expecting. For all I know, the whole story's a crock of crap. Every time I ask someone about it, all I hear is crickets."

"All due respect, how much longer do you think you want to keep up this surveillance? Not to complain, but I'm getting tired of pissing in a soda bottle. Might help if we knew what we were after."

"If I knew, I'd tell you," I said, and it came out sounding harsher than I had intended. I was frustrated, but it wasn't Jordan's fault. "I thought something—anything—might shake itself out over the weekend. Goddamn it."

I had known my share of alcoholics over the years. Some went to meetings and some did not. Each one had described to me the marble-eyed raven that visited them at one time or another, roosted on their bedposts through the endless hours of the night, waiting, staring, while they knuckled-out a dry drunk or wrestled with their consciences over some nameless remorse. Something about the rudderless nature of this present situation put me in mind of that, and left me feeling guilty that I had put my deputies through all that discomfort for a steaming pile of fly-blown nothing, while I had spent the weekend at the beach with Jesse.

"Grab yourself a shower and a change of clothes," I said. "I'm going to Rowan Boyle's for a bite. Come along with me."

"Much obliged, Captain, but I think I'd rather catch a few winks at my desk if you don't mind."

The street was mostly empty at this hour, the atmosphere was motionless and cool. The geometric fascias of frontier architecture etched themselves against the sky, and my footsteps echoed on the boards along an old section of the colonnade still inset with iron posts where teams of horses had once been tied. The morning smelled of ozone, and flashes of heat lightning flared along the peaks. These were the

conditions that struck fear into the hearts of dry land farm-
ers, when the air around you came alive with static electricity
while tufts of wild rye and brome made a sound like kindling
twigs beneath your boots.

⸻

THE MORNING regulars at Rowan Boyle's diner occupied their usual places. The rhythmic hum and hush and
natter of a dozen idle conversations filled the empty spaces
of a room already fusty with the smells of toasted bread and
sausage. I took a seat along the counter and nodded to Boyle
through the pass-through, where he leaned across the surface
of the griddle flipping fried eggs and pancakes. A copy of the
morning paper lay abandoned on the swivel seat beside me. I
ordered a cup of coffee and skimmed the curling pages while
I waited for my breakfast, taking in the sounds of normalcy,
of flatware raking speckled china dishware heaped with fried
potatoes, eggs, and slabs of ham and buttered toast, of cups
and saucers banging on the surfaces of laminated tabletops,
and punctuated by the ringing of the service bell.

The stories in the paper were full of talk about a gap
between the generations, yet we adults had a tendency to
speak of younger people as though they are no different
than we had been at their age. Maybe we had grown blind or
complacent, perhaps both, when looking through their eyes;
failing to register their lives using the same prism that they
did. The histories I was taught in school had been replete
with hope and triumph, but I myself had participated in an
armed conflict that the leaders we had entrusted with our
government had never had the courage or commitment to
declare for what it was. The soldiers in my war had bled and
frozen and starved and died and fought the damned thing
to a stalemate. We had since elected a new cadre of oligarchs
and egotists who appeared to treat their obligations to our
children with the same indifference they had shown to us,
yet we somehow expected the younger generation to be willing to endure it as we had. Nor did we want to recognize

the kids who ran away from home, who contracted sexu-
ally transmitted diseases or had abortions before they ever
graduated from high school, or got themselves strung out on
smack or speed because we wouldn't take the time to have a
simple conversation at the dinner table. We raised our voices
in alarm about the feral nature of our children, unwilling to
see them as we had created them, because to do so would
have forced us to examine our own culpability. It was easier
instead to react with bewilderment and outrage, wondering
how a man like Deva Ravi could have shown up in our town.

I blew the steam off my coffee and glanced outside
the window. The sky was fading to light blue and a gathering breeze was blowing shriveled leaves down the center
of the street. The phone beside the cash register rang and
I watched Lurline's expression falter as she listened to the
caller. She nodded several times, then cupped the receiver
to her shoulder. She saw me looking at her and she pointed
to the phone.

"Sheriff," she said. "It's for you."

THE TASTE at the back of my throat was exactly like
that of burnt copper. It was the bitter tang of unbridled rage.
Some men speak of seeing red, or bursting into uncontrol-
lable fits of violence of which they later hold no recollection.

That is not how it is for me.

When I get angry, truly gut-twistingly angry, I get a tin-
gling sensation at the back of my throat and a taste that is
exactly like scorched copper. My vision spins down like an
aperture and I am temporarily deaf to all but the sound of
my own pulse pounding in my temples and the searing white
heat that shoots up my spinal column to my brain stem. It
bypasses all the folds and creases and lobes that are responsible for reason or reflection, tactile sensation or even fear,
and lodges squarely in that place behind my eyes where physical reactions and mental focus fuse together, regulated by

that singular part of the human mind that is purely reptilian in nature.

Dr. Abel Brawley was a fixture in Meridian. He had been the town's sole medical doctor back when I was born, and even after all these years, remained the most beloved. He had delivered more babies, set more broken bones, and stitched up the muscle tissue of more cowboys and kids than he could count since he had moved to Meriwether County, when he was known to accept fresh eggs or garden vegetables as payment if a family couldn't pay.

He had coached little league baseball for two decades, though he and his wife had never had a child of their own. Abel and Ruth Brawley had been honored as Grand Marshals for the Rodeo Parade on three separate occasions, and he had volunteered as the chief medic for that event for as far back as I could recall, with Ruth acting as his nurse, accountant, and receptionist all the while. They were members of my church, and had been my family's doctor since I had been a kid myself. Decades later he had handed me the scissors to sever the cord the day Cricket was born.

Doc Brawley and Miss Ruth had come to their second-story walk-up office, directly across the street from tiny Pioneer Park, six days a week for nearly forty-eight years without complaint or misstep. At nearly eighty years of age, Doc Brawley could still greet almost everyone in town by name if he saw them on the street.

Not one of those folks would have recognized him as I saw him now.

—— ∞ ——

IT WAS two full hours after Jordan Powell and I arrived, before the team from the Criminal Investigation Unit showed up to the scene. While Powell taped off the front entry to Doc Brawley's office building to mark it as a crime scene, the first call I had made was to Captain Rose at the State Police in Salem. While my deputies and I had the capacity to handle the basics of forensics, like taking photos or lifting prints off a doorknob, for anything much more complex than that I call in the experts for technical support. The ground rules had changed since my granddad's day, and enforcement of the law was no longer about what you know to be the truth about a crime, it is now only about what you can prove in court.

After finishing that call, I tasked Powell with the documentation of the scene as we had found it, while I led Miss Ruthie to the anteroom to ask her a few questions and to wait for the staties and the coroner to arrive. I held a chair out for her and waited as she sat, then took a seat beside her and held her hand. The pale blue of her eyes had gone cloudy, her features fragile and birdlike, with thin lips and tiny teeth much like a child's.

"Doctor had insomnia," she told me. "And when he couldn't sleep, he'd just get up and come in to the office."

For as long as I had known Ruth Brawley, she had always referred to her husband in that manner.

"Did he do that very often?"

Her eyes flickered and slid away from me, beyond my shoulder where Powell was snapping photos inside the exam room. She flinched visibly with every flash emitted by the camera.

"Doctor did it all the time."

Since my arrival, she had moved beyond hysteria and had lapsed into a glazed state of abstraction. She searched my face for reassurance and I watched her drift away again when I could offer her so little of it. Her husband's body lay shattered on the floor not thirty feet from where we sat.

I stood and shut the door between the waiting area and the space where Powell worked, stepped over to the water cooler, and brought a cup to her. Her skin was pallid, moist from the stillness of the heat trapped inside the room, her face latticed with fine wrinkles like the obverse of a fallen leaf.

"When I came in a little after six this morning," she said. "I found him in there on the floor."

"Did you touch his body, or anything in the room, Miss Ruthie? Anything at all?"

She shook her head, and her focus shifted inward, fingers flexing, seeking purchase in the folds of the knitted cardigan she wore.

"I didn't have to," she said softly. "I'm a nurse. I could see that there was nothing I could do for him."

I heard the footfalls of the crime scene techs echo in the stairwell. I gently squeezed Miss Ruthie's hand and went to meet them at the door. There were three of them in dark-colored jackets emblazoned with the emblem of the state police, each carrying hinged leather satchels and wearing the clinical expressions of men who had seen it all, men who earn their paychecks extracting secrets from the dead. I led them through the doorway and introduced them to my deputy, then came back out and used the office phone to call my wife.

∞∞∞

CAPTAIN CHRISTOPHER Rose arrived as I was walking Miss Ruthie down the stairwell to the street. He nodded to me briefly as we passed him on the landing, Miss Ruthie's fingers digging deep into the crook of my arm. Her posture had grown stiff, her demeanor monotone and blank, taking her refuge in some distant place reserved for the casualties of violence and the prorogation of grief.

Jesse waited behind the wheel of our station wagon, idling at the curb outside, the sun visor casting a shadow across her eyes. I could tell that she'd been crying, but she showed me a small smile to let me know she was okay. Wind whipped the ends of the yellow crime scene tape that had been looped around the trunks of trees along the sidewalk, tied onto the balustrade behind me. I led Miss Ruthie to the passenger side and got her buckled in, then came around to Jesse's door and spoke softly through the open window.

"Call Pastor Dunn," I said. "As soon as you get time."

"I already did. Don't worry, Ty. Miss Ruthie won't be left alone."

I kissed Jesse on the cheek and waited on the sidewalk as they disappeared around the corner.

<hr>

"THIS IS some special kind of shit show," Captain Rose said as I stepped into the confines of the exam room. Jordan Powell had moved over to the doctor's file room to give the techs some space to work, and he shot a questioning look at me as I passed by.

"Go get that film processed, Powell," I ordered through the open door. "Then head back to the office and start writing. Every detail, every sound and smell. I want everything in that report while it's still fresh in mind."

"Roger that."

"One more thing: Not one word of this to anyone, you read me?"

"Understood, sir," was all he said, and he was gone.

Rose studied my face for a long moment before he spoke to me.

"You've got that look, Ty," he said.

"What look?"

"Like you got dry powder in your head and somebody torched your fuse."

Rose squatted on his haunches beside Doc Brawley's body, tossed a pair of rubber gloves to me, and gestured at the blood that had been smeared across the walls.

"You ever had a scene like this before, Dawson?"

"Not since Korea."

"Check this out," he said, and directed one of the techs to turn Doc Brawley's body on its side. "Exit wounds. Two of them. Looks like a .38: one through the lung, and one straight through the heart. Your victim bled out right here on this spot."

It was hard for me to reconcile that the body I was looking at had once been a younger man, and built like a lumber wedge, though he had softened around the edges in old age. He had always been robust, if somewhat slower than he had been in his youth, but none of that was visible anymore.

"My guys'll find the spent slugs in here somewhere."

"And the stab wounds?" I asked.

"Thirty-one of them. Two separate blades. Post mortem, near as we can tell. Autopsy will confirm."

"Jesus."

"Then they crushed his face with that thing," Rose said.

He pointed toward a heavy piece of crystal on the floor, where it had been discarded. The object had been cut as though to imitate the facets of a diamond and was roughly the size of a softball, an award or trophy of some kind. It was crusted with dried blood and flecks of gristle; the one clean spot along its base, presumably where the killer had been clutching it, had been blackened by smudges of fingerprint dust.

Rose's knees cracked as he came out of his crouch. He cast his eyes around the room and shook his head.

It had once been an ordinary exam room: Linoleum tile floor, exam table covered with waxed paper, hospital scale, little stool on rubber casters, and posters depicting various components of human anatomy on every wall. Now nearly everything had been stained by viscous castoff, one wall smeared intentionally with a hand towel that had been drenched in Doc Brawley's blood.

"We figure they started to write something up there, then changed their minds," Rose said. "Overkill like this? This is Chuckie Manson-style shit right here."

"Maybe," I said. "Anything stolen?"

Rose shrugged.

"That cabinet's smashed in," he said. "Could have been drugs in there. They might have got off with a prescription pad or two. Does the doc keep cash in the office?"

"I'll look into it."

Captain Rose followed me into the outer office and peeled off his rubber gloves. I leaned against a waist-high counter that described a half circle around the nurse's station where Doc Brawley's patient files were maintained.

"Any decent prints so far?" I asked.

"Not yet."

"Does that strike you as odd? Overkill like that, and not a single fingerprint?"

"What are you saying, Ty?"

"I'm saying the crazed-hippie Manson deal is a little on-the-nose, don't you think?"

"I don't know what I think. But hippies can wear gloves just like anybody else."

I was about to comment when the door to the waiting room squeaked on its hinges. I saw a young woman in civilian clothes, maybe twenty-five or thirty, standing at the threshold carrying an oversized handbag strapped across her chest.

"You didn't see the hundred yards of yellow tape strung across the front door?" I asked.

"'Police Line, Do Not Cross,'" she said. "I saw it."

She spoke like a wiseass, but something in her eyes appeared to harbor apprehension, as though she had been expecting a reprimand from me.

"I assume you are a cop," I said.

"I'm with the *Salem Observer*."

"Then you need to leave."

"I'd like a word with you about the wave of violent crime that's broken out here in Meridian."

I pulled back my shirtsleeve and looked at my watch.

"It's more than a two-hour drive down from Salem," I said. "Care to tell me how you knew to come here so quickly?"

"Police scanner," she said.

From the corner of my eye, I saw the captain shake his head from side to side. "We didn't use the radio to dispatch my teams."

"Neither did we," I said. "I'll give you one last chance to tell the truth."

She reached into her bag and withdrew a Nikon camera.

"Any comment on the recall vote tomorrow night?" she asked.

"You need to get outside and stay behind the line," I said. "And if you snap a single photograph in here, I will arrest you, and confiscate your camera and your film."

She smiled, but she knew I wasn't lying.

"So no comment then, Sheriff Dawson?"

"Have a nice day."

IT WAS early evening by the time the crime scene techs finally packed up. I locked Doc Brawley's office door behind us and sealed it shut with red security tape. Captain Rose hung back as his team departed, followed me across the hall and down the stairwell to the street.

Rose leaned his bulk against the trunk of an ash tree that had been planted in a square of soil where the concrete had been cut out. He slid a comb through his hair and watched me peel the police tape off the doorway.

"What aren't you telling me?" he asked. "Does this have to do with the Polaroid and the prints you asked me to run for you?"

I wadded up the ball of tape and stuffed it into the pocket of my jacket.

"Most likely," I said.

"Step carefully, Ty."

"I can't arrest folks just because of my suspicions, but if I could, I know who I'd be talking to."

"Have you spoken to Rankin about any of this?"

"Mr. Reasonable Doubt? I've got nothing to take to him to file charges. No evidence, no witnesses."

Rose's eyes cut away from me and focused somewhere up the street.

"I'll give you that," he said. "I've seen more aggressive DAs in traffic court."

I reached into my pocket for a cigarette, but changed my mind. I took out my sunglasses instead.

"I need that ID, Chris."

He drew his car keys from his pocket and stepped out of the tree shade.

"I'm working on it," he said. "I'll get this scene's evidence processed right away, Ty. Looks to me like you could use a win."

It was an odd turn of a phrase, I thought, as I watched him walk off toward his car. In this line of work, I wasn't certain that there ever were any victors; the ultimate zero-sum endeavor. To get a win, someone first had to lose.

Somewhere out along the state road, the rumble of glass-pack mufflers reverberated on the asphalt, reminding me that this was the final week of school before the summer break. Across the street was Pioneer Park. At one time it had been the site of an assay office, built during a time before the Civil War, when failed prospectors flocked here from California gold fields, following the rumor of rich veins of copper and silver in these mountains. The boom, such as it was, that came into this valley served only to enrich the promoters of the mining claims and the tent merchants who sold tools and canned goods to the dreamers. It did prove out to be good land for livestock, though, and those who had retained the means, the guts, and the flexibility of spirit had found their home. A stone obelisk fitted with an engraved bronze plaque stood between a pair of benches a short distance from the bandstand. It was all that remained to mark the memory of that time. The plaque wept green patina on the stone, and I wondered if anybody even read the words inscribed there anymore. When I was in grade school, our teacher made us memorize that inscription.

I moved slowly up the street to where I'd parked my truck. The setting sun felt warm across my back. I spotted Jordan Powell driving up the street, his forearm resting on the open window frame. He pulled over to the curb and waited for me, his pickup blanketed in dirt and dust from staking out the commune and the Emory place.

"You okay, Sheriff?"

"I'm fine."

"You want a ride?"

"Just heading to my truck."

Powell hesitated for a moment, chewing his lip as he glanced into his rearview mirror.

"Something on your mind, son?" I asked.

"You believe in God, right, sir?"

"I do."

"Even after what we seen today?"

I changed my mind about that cigarette, slid the pack out of my pocket, and lit up. I inhaled deeply and took a moment to watch the smoke swirl away before I answered.

"You fought in Vietnam, didn't you, Jordan?"

"Yes, sir."

"Then you know the devil ain't an atheist."

He grinned.

"I guess I never thought of it that way."

"I got a question for you," I said.

"Sure thing."

"How's the new kid working out?"

"Snoose's nephew?"

I nodded and leaned a hand against his truck bed.

"Old Caleb being too hard on him?" I asked.

"No, sir, I don't believe so."

"Only wanted to make sure that Caleb's rough opinions of the Corcorans don't cloud his judgment about the kid, is all."

Powell took off his hat, scratched his head, turned in his seat, and leaned a little farther out the window.

"The kid says he wants to be a top hand someday," he said. "Just callin' yourself a cowboy don't make you one. You know that better than anybody, Mr. Dawson."

I flattened my hand and slapped the truck bed twice, letting Powell know that he was free to go. As he began to pull away, I thought of something else.

"One more thing," I said.

"Sir?"

"We've got one shot at this investigation, Jordan," he said, "and we've got to keep the crime scene details to ourselves. If we go off half-cocked, or screw this up in any way, whoever did all this will end up sipping daiquiris in Aruba."

He gave my words a few seconds' thought.

"I won't let you down," he said. "And neither will Sam Griffin."

"I know you won't."

CHAPTER TWENTY-FOUR

THE NEXT MORNING, I watched a shiny, maroon-colored Buick pulling an Airstream travel trailer come up my driveway. I put down Jordan Powell's crime scene report which I had just finished reading for the third time, and stepped onto the porch. A lithe, attractive brunette climbed out of the Buick and followed a tall man with straw-colored hair and a ruddy complexion up the front steps of my house. He wore an expensive pair of Clubmaster dark glasses, the sleeves of his button-collared shirt rolled up on his forearms, and he was carrying a small wooden crate piled high with fresh-picked fruit.

"Picked these up at a roadside stand a few miles back," he said. "Couldn't resist."

Since most of the work Bill Kiefer and I conducted involved livestock operations and related property matters, most of our dealings were handled by phone. It was unusual for me to see him face to face more than once or twice a year.

"Looking good, Ty," he smiled.

"Lawyers aren't supposed to lie, are they?"

"I was referring to the ranch."

"That makes more sense," I said.

"Sorry to barge in unannounced," his wife, Kristen, said. "We spent a long weekend at the lake, and we thought it would be fun to stop in on our way home."

I relieved Bill of the crate and welcomed them inside, removed the fruit, and placed it in a basket on the kitchen counter.

"What is that wonderful smell?" Kristen asked.

"You don't have to say that," I said. "Cricket has become enamored with the nuts and seeds and greenery she buys at the health food store. She brings it to a boil on the stove and calls it oatmeal."

"Dad," she said, and leaned into a hug from Kristen Kiefer. "He's going to die from all the processed corporate poison he eats."

Jesse was gathering the coffee cups and saucers she reserved for guests, and Kiefer stepped up beside me and inclined his head in the direction of the gallery.

"May I have a word?" he asked.

I took a seat in one of the willow chairs at the far end of the porch, where the dogwoods cast their shade. Kiefer leaned his weight against the railing and focused beyond my shoulder where Taj Caldwell and Tom Jenkins had just begun to break another colt to saddle.

"What's on your mind, Bill?"

"I brought the file you were asking about. I tried to call you at the station, but kept missing you."

"Things have gotten a little rugged around here," I said.

"I heard," he said. "You know, I drove past that parcel you asked about on the way here."

"That's a fair piece out of your way."

"I figured it might help to see it."

He slid off his sunglasses, hooking an earpiece onto the pocket of his shirt. His attention remained locked on the two cowboys at the snubbing post, but his brow was furrowed and his eyes squeezed into slits.

"Did it?" I asked.

"Did it what?"

"Did it help to get a look at the property?"

He turned away from the corral and looked at me.

"Not particularly. It's dry as hell down there."

"It gets that way in that part of the county," I said. "You mention Oregon and everybody thinks that all it does is rain."

"Looks like a pincushion, all the water wells."

"It's rough country. Most of 'em are dry."

"Maybe that explains it then," he said.

"Explains what?"

"You asked about the chain of title," he said. "I've got the file in my car—I'll leave it with you—but the current owner is Ambervalia Corporation. They operate agricultural properties, hold water and mineral stakes all over the west."

"Okay," I said.

"That piece down south used to comprise a full section. Six hundred forty acres. They leased half of it to Harper Emory some time ago."

"Any idea what the terms are?"

"Fifty-five-year land lease, including underground appurtenances."

"And what about the other half?"

"There's nothing in the public record about the other half."

Taj Caldwell let out a whoop from down below. Inside a cloud of red dirt, the colt had started hopping, cat-backed, and kicking his heels. Caldwell threw a loop around its neck and calmed it into a corner while Tom Jenkins gingerly picked himself out of the dirt and dusted off his chaps.

"You think the kids out at the commune might be squatters?" I asked.

Kiefer shrugged.

"Maybe," he said. "But it would be odd. Squatters' rights are squirrelly, and an outfit like Ambervalia is sophisticated. They wouldn't allow a bunch of hippies to waltz in and lay claim to their property."

"Have you got a phone number for the owner?"

"It's in the file. I can follow up with them if you need me to."

"I'd rather do it."

Kiefer stood and stretched the muscles in his arms, took a few steps into the filtered light beneath the trees, and swept his gaze across the pastures and outbuildings.

"I meant what I said earlier," he said. "The place looks good. New barn?"

"The other one burned to the ground."

"Jesus. You never mentioned it."

"Long story."

He slipped his hands into his khaki slacks and heaved a sigh.

"I'm sorry, Ty. I wish I could have been more help."

"Let's go inside and get you a cup of coffee and a bite to eat," I said. "You've got a long drive ahead of you yet."

<hr />

I WAS delayed at the intersection where Founders Street meets the state road by a caravan of teenage kids in pickup trucks, project ragtops, and customized hot rods that gleamed like penny candy, following a line of eighteen-wheelers headed toward the fairgrounds. The truck beds and cargo bays were stacked up with temporary stock pens and fencing for the rodeo, and garishly decorated wooden panels that were soon to be assembled into food booths, rides, and game attractions on the carnival midway.

All weekend long, people will come from as far away as Portland and Salem, most of them blue-collar families and tough-looking kids who drank malt liquor skinned in paper bags. By and large, they meant no harm, just blowing off some summer steam, or making out in back seats, spending Eisenhower silver dollars that had been squirreled away in jelly jars and cigar boxes all year long. This weekend they would pretend that the future was the same for them as for everyone else, and would make believe they were content, like the world that existed for them outside the fairgrounds was not a place that inflicted hardship onto the victims of its low expectations.

"Captain Rose at CID identified two .38 slugs buried in Doc Brawley's wall," Sam Griffin announced when I finally stepped into the substation. "The stab wounds were inflicted as he lay bleeding out on the floor. The damage to his face was postmortem."

"Did they locate the shell casings?" I asked.

"No, sir."

"Then the killer either picked up after himself, or used a revolver."

"Appears that way."

I sat down in my chair and bucked my hat off my forehead with a knuckle. I picked up a pencil and bounced the eraser off my desk while I stared out the front window.

"Where's Powell?" I asked.

"Out on patrol."

An old Chevrolet pickup hauling a tandem horse trailer threw a shadow across the glass as it drove by. The circuit riders were beginning to arrive.

"Deva Ravi told me that all the men from the commune are out roaming around the wilderness on some kind of 'sojourn,'" I said.

"What's that supposed to mean?"

"Hell if I know. But I want to talk with every one of them that you can find. Assuming you can find them at all. That goes double for Carl Spinell and the two jackoffs he's got working with him."

"You want us to arrest them? For what?"

I shook my head and banged the pencil on my desk so hard it broke.

"No," I said. "Don't cuff anybody unless he's brandishing a firearm or staggering around in blood-spattered clothes, you hear? Especially Spinell and the idiots. Just bring 'em in so we can have a chat. If we arrest them without cause, my guess is they'll bring in a whole clown car full of lawyers and we'll never get another word out of 'em. Deva Ravi might look like a crazy man, but he's not a fool. That also goes double for Carl Spinell."

"Roger that," Griffin said.

"See if you can raise Powell on the radio," I said and swiveled my chair around to look Griffin in the face. "Pass along what I just told you, then saddle up, too, and get out there."

I thumbed through the file Bill Kiefer had dropped off with me, and located the page that listed the contact information for Ambervalia Corporation. The only phone number listed was for their agent for service of process, a number with a central California area code. A man picked up after the third ring.

"Tanner," was all he said.

"I'm calling with regard to Ambervalia Corporation."

"And you are?"

I told him who I was, and the reason for my call. When I was finished, the silence on the other end was so complete I thought he had hung up.

"Y'all have been misinformed with respect to my official duties," he said.

His tone reflected the unctuous accent and cadence of a small-time card cheat who dealt badugi out of the back room of a west Texas blind pig. He was breathing heavily, through his mouth, in the manner of a man for whom walking from the parking lot to his office door would represent a busy day. Speaking to him put me in mind of the depraved and licentious gun bulls or prison wardens from the Jim Crow south.

"Can you repeat that?" I said.

"Let me put this a different way," he said. "I don't answer questions about my client's business. If you need to serve a summons or have some other legal document to deliver, I can provide you with a post office box address. I don't believe that I can make it any clearer. Y'all have a pleasant afternoon."

———

THE TOWN of Lewiston was nestled into a tapered stretch of river flats between two ranges of sheer, rugged stone peaks. When the wind blew just right in the winter, it would whip through the narrows at velocities that could knock a grown man off his feet and drive rain and hailstones with a force that felt as though he'd been fired upon with a shotgun. In the summer, however, the prevailing breezes were impeded by the mountains and on certain days, by the time early evening came down, the stillness and humidity seemed enough to deny a man his breath.

This was one of those evenings.

I turned into the pea-gravel parking lot at the Grange Hall and took a spot as near the exit as possible, since it was not my intention to stay a moment longer than necessary. A pair of young children played on the swing set in the grass field where the mud puddles and dandelions of spring had withered and dried and turned back into hardpan. One of the children waved at me as I walked up the stairs, so I tipped the brim of my Stetson as I pulled open the door to the hall.

The atmosphere inside was stagnant and cramped, and didn't seem to have a temperature so much as a viscosity. I didn't have to stop off to pay homage to the family photo this time either; I could feel the eyes of my dad and grandfather following me from the moment I opened the door.

The conversational clatter resonated like the twitter of high-country bats as I moved from the foyer into the main hall, where several dozen men and women had taken their seats in the rows of the gallery and fanned themselves with hats or folded sheets of paper. I felt Nolan Brody staring as I shook hands with the other members of the council, acknowledging him with a brief nod as I took my appointed position at the far end of the table.

Before Brody could gavel the meeting to order, I raised my arms and called out for the crowd to be quiet.

"As you know, we lost a fine man and a fine friend of the community yesterday," I said. "I don't think there's anyone here who did not have a great fondness for Doc Brawley, and I'm no exception."

In my peripheral vision, I could see Brody thumbing the plunger of the retractable pen he had clenched inside his fist, his lips stitched into a thin line.

"I wanted to let you know that I won't be staying for the meeting tonight," I continued. "I merely came here to ask for your patience and your help while we set about finding whomever is responsible for his death."

A smattering of applause was cut short by Nolan Brody's interruption.

"You going to finally get after those hippies, Sheriff?" he asked.

He smiled as though he was recalling a private joke.

"Your fixation on those young people is both bothersome and unhealthy, Nolan," I said.

"And your inattention to the threat that they pose has proven to be dangerous to everyone in this county."

The room went silent, but for the rattle of the ceiling fan paddles rotating high overhead, which only seemed to recirculate the cloying heat and the body odor and tobacco smoke trapped inside.

"Doc Brawley was a friend to every soul in this room," I said. "And I aim to get to the bottom of all this. You people gave me this job, and I take it damned seriously. But this man seated here—Nolan Brody—intends to seek your approval tonight so he can circulate a petition to have me recalled as your sheriff. If enough of this county's voters sign it, then I guess we'll go ahead and have that recall vote."

A muted rumble passed through the crowd. Brody glared at me over the rims of his tortoiseshell reading glasses, making it clear that his objective had not been as widely and publicly known as he had given me cause to believe.

"I didn't come here to defend myself," I continued. "You all put me in this job, and you've got the right to choose somebody else to do it if you want to. I simply urge you to be cautious. Mr. Brody has ginned up a lot of agitation about what's going on around here lately. He's probably going to tell you that the agents of change are among us and they have to be stopped. But those hippie kids aren't Vikings hell-bent on pillage and rape. And they probably aren't Jonas Salk or Mother Teresa either."

"Are you about finished?" Brody interrupted. He wore an expression like a stray thought had just drifted into his sightline and suddenly disappeared.

"I've said it before, but it merits repeating: The sheriff's office doesn't exist to do one side's bidding," I said. "I work for everyone. We all lost a good friend in Doc Brawley, and you have my word that I will find the sonofabitch who killed him."

I plucked my hat off the table.

"Have yourselves a fine meeting," I said.

THE SUNSET burned red behind the haze along the western skyline as I drove home. A lightning strike had touched off a grass fire two counties away, and the smoke that it had propagated unrolled across the troposphere like a dirty bandage.

I cranked up the air-conditioning inside the truck and watched my headlights illuminate the lines separating the lanes. The drive tonight seemed much longer than it ever had before, the monotony interrupted only when I passed through a mile-long cloud of winged insects that spattered against my windshield like blood blisters.

The truck's lights raked across the broad side of the horse barn as I pulled in and parked behind my house. I stepped out of the cab and focused my eyes in the dusk and noticed Tom Jenkins pushing a wheelbarrow full of manure between the barn doors. I passed through the mud room, hung my jacket and holster on the rack, then went to the refrigerator and pulled out two bottles of Hires Root Beer and popped them open with a church key from the drawer.

"I'll be right back," I said to Jesse.

I pushed my way out through the screen door and headed toward the barn. I took a seat on a low rock wall that was just beyond the pale rectangle of incandescent light that spilled from inside and checked my watch. Tom's shadow stretched out before him as he stepped into the dark to haul another load.

"It's nearly nine o'clock," I said.

I could see that I had startled him, and he was trying to make out my face as his eyes adjusted to the unaccustomed dark.

"Yes, sir."

"Did Mr. Wheeler ask you to do that?" I asked.

"No, sir," he said. "It just looked like it needed doing."

"Why don't you let loose of that pushcart and take a load off for a minute."

I handed one of the bottles to him and I watched him drink down half of it in one grateful pull. His hat was hanging on a fencepost, the sides of his soggy hair still misshapen and indented by its crown. Patches of sweat soaked his shirt, and his shirttails billowed where they had worked loose from his faded jeans.

"Where'd the earring go?" I asked.

The corners of his mouth curled up into what might have been a grin, then he shook his head and looked off toward the bunkhouse.

"I don't wear that thing no more."

I heard Wyatt's paws galloping fast along the path from the house toward me. He skidded to a stop, wagging his tail, dancing and shuffling between my boots until I finally gave in and scratched him behind his ears. He chuffed a low bark deep in his throat and rolled onto his side in the dirt.

"You doing all right, Tom?"

"I'm okay, I guess."

"You entered in any of the events at the rodeo this weekend?"

"I like team roping, but all the fellas are paired-up already."

"How about calf roping? That's a one-man deal."

He scuffed his boot soles in the dust and stared at the little rows he'd carved there, then he hooked a thumb inside a belt loop and squinted at the barn lights.

"Maybe," he said. "I don't know. Rufe Zachary over on the Lazy Y Cross has been braggin' that he's won that thing three years in a row."

"I operate on the assumption that the people who boast the loudest tend to be the least competent. If I was you, I'd give it a run."

"I'll study on it," he said.

"Well, don't study too long or you'll miss your chance."

He upended the root beer bottle, emptied it, and ran a shirt sleeve across his mouth.

"Yes, sir," he said. "If everything goes right, I expect I'll sign up for something."

He stood up and placed the root beer bottle on the flat rock he'd been sitting on.

"Listen," I said. "When you're born, you don't always get the family you want; you get the one you've got. When it's your turn to raise up a family, you get to make it what you dreamed of. It's up to you."

I gave him a quick pat on the shoulder, picked up his empty bottle, and started back toward the house.

"By the way," I said.

"Sir?"

"Everything never goes right."

CHAPTER TWENTY-FIVE

I PHONED BILL Kiefer at his office first thing the next morning.

"I called the number in the file you gave me for Ambervalia Corporation and got exactly nowhere," I said.

"What did they tell you?"

"Absolutely nothing. Their attorney sounded like a penitentiary screw from *Cool Hand Luke.*"

"I don't know what else I can do, Ty."

"I had a thought when I was pacing around the living room with my dog at two o'clock this morning."

"I'd laugh, but I suspect you're not kidding."

"Would a land lease appear in the public record?"

Kiefer was silent for several seconds, only the drone of Portland city traffic murmuring over the line.

"Maybe," he said finally. "It depends how long the lease term is, and even then, it will depend on whether either party elected to record it. Not everybody does."

"Can you look into it for me?"

"Of course. But it's the same situation as last time around. It could take a little while."

I hung up the phone and dialed the number for the department's answering service. The only message had come in at 3:36 A.M. It was an ICU nurse at the county hospital calling to let me know that the burn victim who had been rescued from inside the record store had died as a result of

191

his injuries. I called back right away and asked for the attending physician, but was told that she was no longer on call. I was transferred instead to the duty nurse in Intensive Care.

Half an hour later I pulled into a parking space reserved for law enforcement and emergency vehicles outside the rear entrance to the hospital. It was situated on a knoll at an oxbow in the river, where the water flowed slowly, and cutthroat trout made dimples on the surface where they fed in the slicks that formed behind snags in the channel. The lawn and landscaping were neat, well manicured, and orderly, and I had since developed an opinion that the unimaginative geometry that was the outward appearance of Meriwether County Hospital was a clever mask, or maybe even a deception, compensation for the pain and the chaos that went on behind its windows and walls.

I followed a man through the glass doors that he held open for me as a courtesy. The temperature inside was not much cooler than outdoors, and the monotone drone of announcements being broadcast through overhead speakers, together with the antiseptic odors drifting through the hallways, triggered a sense of claustrophobia in me as I made my way up three flights of stairs to the ICU.

A harried-looking nurse stood beside a bank of file cabinets inside the nurses' station, flipping through the pages of some type of report that had been fastened to a clipboard. She looked up at me and adjusted her uniform.

"Sheriff Dawson," she said. "You're here about the burn victim?"

"Yes, ma'am."

"He was transferred to the morgue some time ago."

"I figured," I said. "But before I headed down there, I wanted to see if you could give me a list of any visitors or phone calls he may have received."

"That shouldn't take long," she said. "There weren't any."

She returned her attention to her clipboard, her white blouse stippled with perspiration.

"None? The whole time he was here?"

"Not one."

"Were you able to get an ID on him?"

"No, Sheriff, I'm sorry. You saw the condition he was in. The poor young thing's face was relatively undamaged, but the burns he sustained on the rest of his body had been so severe that the skin slid off his hands like rubber gloves. He never did regain consciousness, and we obviously weren't able to collect any fingerprints."

I had seen more than my share of burn victims in Korea, men who had been baked alive inside of tanks and armored transport vehicles by incendiary devices. I had no desire to see another. Not ever. But that wasn't a choice that was available to me.

"Is there someone on duty in the morgue that I can speak with when I get there?"

"I'll call down and let them know you're on your way," she said.

I rode the elevator to the subbasement where an unexpectedly perky female attendant wearing operating scrubs and surgical cap stood waiting for me as the doors slid open. Without preamble, she smiled and offered me her hand.

"I'm Laura Bursack," she said. "You're here to see the John Doe?"

I introduced myself and confirmed that that was what I was there for, and asked her if she would mind providing me with photos of the victim.

We passed through a pair of oversized doors inset with wire glass, and into a largely empty room in which a single row of stainless steel operating tables stood in a line. Fluorescent overhead lights hummed, threading the silence and reflecting blue light on the metal refrigerated drawers where the remains of the dead are contained. John Doe had been laid on his back atop one of the autopsy tables, his naked body resembling a sculpture, the insinuation of a human being, composed solely of molten tallow and rendered in shades of pink, purple, and black.

I watched as Laura shot half a dozen photos of the victim's face, torso, and extremities with an instant camera she had retrieved from a desk drawer in her office.

"What is that mark on his chest?" I asked, referring to a V-shaped scar that resembled sutures.

"A piece of jewelry, a necklace, is my guess," she said. "Not uncommon with burn victims like this one. When the metal becomes superheated, it sears into the skin, like a hot wire placed on a stick of butter. The ICU doc couldn't extract it without causing massive tissue damage, so they left it temporarily. If John Doe had survived, they would have gone in for it later."

"Will you please tag and bag it—and anything else you find—when you finish here? I'll have somebody come and pick them up."

"Of course. Anything else?"

"This man had no other belongings when he was brought in?"

"I'll double check the intake file in my office," she said, and was gone.

She moved with the assurance of a dancer, the energy level of a finch in the wild, and the personal demeanor of the captain of a high school pep squad. I made a mental note to add Laura Bursack to the growing list of anomalies I associated with this building.

"No, Sheriff," she said when she returned. "No personal effects. Only what was left of the clothes he had been wearing."

"Please bag them, too, if you don't mind."

A few minutes later, I climbed into my truck. Something about seeing that young man filled me with a sorrow so profound that I felt as though I was wearing it, and the white heat of my rage threatened to sear a hole behind my forehead. I had borne witness to death on the battlefield, and on the streets of my homeland as well. I had seen the final moment of loneliness and confusion extant in the expressions of the victims of accidents, and found little difference from those whose lives had been ended with malice and intention. Those experiences had left me with the unyielding conviction that no one deserves to die alone.

I let the air blow through the open windows of the cab as I drove the narrow lane that would deliver me back to the state road. I waited at the railroad crossing near the slough where a crossbuck sign with clanging bells and red flashing lights warned me of an oncoming train. Across the right-of-way, a dog barked from where he had been tied to a pole in the backyard of one of the tiny shotgun houses clad in peeled tarpaper siding that made up the grim and joyless purgatory of a neighborhood that the locals referred to as Little Hollywood. I idled there for a long time after the warning bells and red lights had been silenced and died away, until the rumble of steel wheels disappeared inside the slow, hot wind. Somewhere behind me, deep in the stands of old growth, a woodpecker hammered the tree bark and sounded like the winding mechanism of an antique mantel clock.

<hr/>

I RANG the doorbell and pushed open the screen door at Ruth Brawley's house.

"Hello, Tyler," Miss Ruthie said as I stepped inside.

"Miss Ruthie," I replied and took off my hat.

She was standing at the sink, running cold water over a charred baking pan. A cloud of steam that smelled of charcoal and scorched cheese rose to the low ceiling.

"I burned a casserole," she said. "I'm knee deep in the darn things."

Miss Ruthie pressed her thin lips into the shape of a smile and opened the refrigerator door to show me its contents.

"People keep bringing me food," she said. "Can I get you something to eat? Or maybe a nice glass of cold lemonade."

"Lemonade would be fine, ma'am."

I cracked some ice cubes from a metal tray I took out of the freezer and dropped them into a pair of service station give-away glasses stenciled with the images of sliced fruit. She arranged the glasses on a serving tray and I followed her into the living room. Chintz curtains had been drawn across the windows, the only illumination emanating from the torchiere lamp on the side table, its leaded glass shades marbling one half of Miss Ruthie's face in pink and green light.

"What brings you here to visit me, Tyler?"

Her tone and manner were very much the same as when I had last seen her driving away with Jesse, stoic and removed and shell-shocked all at once.

"I wanted to look in on you is all."

"That's very kind of you," she said. "But I'm fine."

"Plus I thought of a couple of questions that I need to ask you."

"What kinds of questions?"

"Did the doctor ever keep cash or narcotics in the office, Miss Ruthie?"

She shook her head, "Oh, no, dear. We have very little cash in the office. Most people write checks these days, you know."

"What about drugs? Is there a storage cabinet of some kind?"

She dismissed the question outright.

"Oh, heavens, no. The only drugs Doctor keeps in the office are penicillin and maybe some topical anesthetics for sutures. Anything else, you'd have to get from the pharmacist."

I couldn't help but notice the present-tense reference to her late husband.

My eyes roved the contents of the bookshelves and the walls. The Brawleys' furnishings were practical and modest, the artwork having been selected for color rather than content, I imagined. The books on the shelves were primarily classics, and a set of finely bound works by the great ancient philosophers was bracketed by hand-carved bookends that bore a design that looked familiar to me.

She cocked her head sideways and I saw that her attention had been drawn by the lamplight that reflected off a cheval mirror tucked into the corner of the room.

"Some people say I should hold you accountable for what happened to my husband," she said. "They think you should have run those young people out of town a long time ago."

I placed my lemonade glass on a coaster and watched her eyes move off the mirror. Her voice had taken on a monotone quality and she seemed to be directing her comments to a point high on the wall behind me.

"But Doctor wouldn't have liked it if you had, I can tell you," she said. "You know, he loved those kids."

For a moment I wasn't sure that I had heard her correctly, then I remembered where I had first seen the design on those carvings on the bookshelf.

"Your husband provided medical treatment to the members of the commune?" I ventured.

"Only to a few of the boys. They never paid us anything, but the big fellow with the strange hairdo gave us those book-ends you keep staring at."

I stood up from my chair and carried my empty glass into the kitchen.

"Thank you for your time, Miss Ruthie," I said. "I'm sure Jesse will come by and see you tomorrow."

"There's no need for her to do that," she said, and smiled. "I get so many visitors lately."

"Yes, ma'am," I said and opened the door. "She'll likely come anyway. Jesse's very fond of you."

She shielded her eyes with one fragile hand and blinked into the sunlight as she waved me good-bye with the other.

"Take a bottle of milk with you, Tyler," she said. "The delivery man left me too much this morning."

CHAPTER TWENTY-SIX

I PICKED UP one of the photos that had been taken of John Doe at the morgue, and added it to the stack I had collected of Carl Spinell and his two colleagues, Ducktail and Bullet Head the ex-con. I slid them into the pocket of my shirt, locked the door behind me, and headed down the sidewalk toward Mother Nature's Sandwich Shop.

The place was done up in tongue-and-groove paneling from wall to wall, adorned with shelves displaying makeshift artwork made from driftwood, and posters with idealized images of pine forests and mushrooms and sylvan waterfalls that seemed to vibrate inside their black-light display frames. Three teenage local girls sat near the window awaiting their lunch orders, smiling and bobbing their heads along with the rock music that blared out from inexpensive stereo speakers that had been braced between the ceiling and the rafters. The afternoon sunlight reflected off their faces as they laughed together in anticipation of an uncomplicated summer afternoon.

I recognized the girl standing behind the order window as the sylph with the heart-shaped face and gold curls who had first welcomed us to the Rainbow Ranch the day of the field trip. I leaned an elbow on the ledge and searched my memory for her name.

"Late lunch, Sheriff?" she asked, smiling.

"Your name is Dawn, right?"

"You remembered."

She withdrew a pencil from where she had tucked it behind her ear and tapped absently on a blank order pad. Behind her, one of the other girls I'd seen at the commune, but whose name I didn't recall, was busy piling tuna salad, sliced cucumbers, and other greenery on top of inch-thick slices of brown bread.

"I have some bad news for you, Dawn," I said. "You lost a friend today."

"Excuse me?" she said.

I dragged one of the photos from my pocket and placed it on the counter.

"This young man died early this morning," I said. "Smoke inhalation and third-degree burns over three-quarters of his body."

"I don't want to see that."

"He needs you to, Dawn. Nobody ever came to visit him. Not a soul the whole time he was in the hospital."

I studied her expression, watched the flicker in her eyes as she looked at the photograph. An involuntary shiver wracked her body and she pushed the image toward me with her pencil.

"I was a soldier once," I said. "One thing I learned is that you never let someone you care about wake up alone in a hospital bed. That's exactly how this young man died. Alone. He deserves a name, at the very least, Dawn. Tell me who this is."

Dawn threw a glance beyond my shoulder toward the girls who sat waiting beside the window. Then she locked eyes with me and shook her head, no.

"I know that you recognize him," I said. "I can see it in your face."

"Please leave me alone," she repeated.

"Who is this man, Dawn?"

"I told you I don't know. Take it away."

A new song burst through the speakers and I felt my pulse pound behind my temples.

"Can you please turn that down?"

Dawn reached into a cabinet beside her and twisted the dial on a stereo receiver. When she looked up again, I saw that all the color had drained from her face. The girl making the sandwiches stopped her work, joined Dawn at the counter, and glared hard at me.

"Are you always this angry, Sheriff?" the girl asked.

"Lately? Every goddamned day."

The wordless moments stretched between us as we waited one another out.

"How about you?" I asked the sandwich girl. "You want to take a look?"

"Leave us alone," she said and returned her attention to the cutting board.

I fanned the rest of the photos across the countertop, the ones of Spinell and his two associates. Dawn looked as though she was about to be ill.

"How about these guys?" I asked. "Have you seen them before?"

"I don't think so."

"You don't think so?"

"No, I don't think I have seen them."

Dawn's workmate came to her rescue again. This time she shouldered Dawn off to one side and leaned across the counter, her face only inches away from mine, her eyes wet and glassy with anger.

"What is the Rainbow Ranch's relationship with Doc Brawley?" I pressed.

"You need to leave, Sheriff," the girl said. "You need to leave now."

In the absence of the music, the teenagers at the table near the window had begun to stare at us. I took a step back from the counter and drew a deep breath.

"I know you don't believe me," I said, more quietly now. "But I can help you if you'll let me."

"It's you who needs help, Sheriff."

She pulled away and dismissed me with a shake of her head, pursed her lips, and studied me with an aspect that had spent all of its rage and now overflowed with something resembling pity.

"Why are the words 'I'm scared' so difficult for men to say?" she asked.

I collected the photos from the ledge and slipped them back into my pocket. When I looked up, Dawn had withdrawn completely, leaning silently on the worktable behind her and staring at the floor between her sandals.

"You tell Deva Ravi to come see me at my office tomorrow," I said to the second girl. "I want him there first thing in the morning."

She tipped her head and gazed at me with an expression so vacant I could not even guess at its meaning.

"The Deva never leaves the compound."

"You tell Deva Ravi what I said," I repeated. "If I have to drive all the way out to your place to drag him back here, I swear to God I will lock him in a cage and toss the key in the river. That is what you kids would call a stone fact."

⸺◈⸺

WHEN I returned to the substation, Jordan Powell was sitting on the corner of the table in the interview room talking with a barefooted young man wearing dungarees and a long-sleeved cotton shirt over a T-shirt with the words Blue Cheer scrolled in neon lettering across the front. His stringy hair was sopping wet, his clothing spotted with dampness where the moisture had soaked through.

"I found this lovin' sunshine brother under the trestle bridge," Jordan Powell said to me when I walked into the room. "He's been living in a lean-to in the gully."

"Why's he all wet?"

"He was nekkid as a newborn, washing his danglies in the river when I found him."

"Am I under arrest?" the hippie asked me.

He looked as though his head was balanced on a swivel, squinting back and forth between Powell and me while he twisted a loop of braided leather between his fingers. He behaved as if a grounding wire had pulled loose inside his skull.

"Not if you level with me," I said.

"About what?"

"Everything I'm about to ask you, starting with your name."

"They call me Corncob."

Powell laughed aloud and walked out of the room, pulling the door closed behind him. The kid's face was long and narrow, almost equine, with wide-set eyes and a sharply pointed nose and the worst case of buck teeth I had ever seen.

"I was referring to your real name," I said. "The one that your momma gave you."

"Steve."

"Is our entire conversation going to be like this?"

"Like what?"

I snapped my fingers about three inches from his nose.

"Focus," I said. "What's your last name, Steve?"

"Beck. Steve Beck."

"How long have you lived at Rainbow Ranch?"

"About a year, maybe a little longer."

"How many of you live out there?"

He shrugged and bit his bottom lip.

"There were about thirty of us when I first got there. But a bunch of 'em booked it out. There's probably only fifteen or so of us left. And that was before Deva told all the guys to boogie on down the road."

"Why'd they leave?"

"What?"

"Goddamn it, Steve. You've got to keep up with me, son. Why did everybody leave, where did they go?"

"I don't know, man," he said, and combed a hand through his hair. "I mean, I don't know where they went, but I figure I know why."

"Tell me."

He hooked an index finger into the collar of his T-shirt and tugged at the fabric.

"It started getting real uptight, you know? Deva and his two pet freaks were acting totally bizarre. The rest of us were mellow, but those dudes were eating mandrakes and black beauties by the handful and they started copping some very heavy attitudes."

He looked away from me and began to chew a hangnail on his thumb.

"Did you ever meet Doc Brawley?"

"Who?"

"The man who was murdered here two days ago."

He shook his head and pushed himself back from the table.

"I don't know anything about that kind of shit, man."

I studied his expression for signs of deception and detected none. I switched up on my line of inquiry again to keep him off the beam. It is much more difficult to fabricate a lie when you don't know where the questions might be headed.

"Why did Deva send the men away from the commune?"

"The sojourn? I don't know. He says it's like some kind of ritual, but I think it's cause he wants all the chicks to himself. Like I said, he and the freaks started to get very weird and paranoid."

"About what?"

He pinched his lower lip between his fingers and turned his attention to the floor tiles.

"I'm not digging this scene at all, man," he said. "I don't want to talk about this shit anymore."

I leaned back in my chair and slipped a pack of cigarettes from my shirt. I shook one out and offered it to Steve. The expression on his face was wary, but he finally took it and drew deeply when I lit it for him. We sat in silence for several seconds while he watched the silver smoke rise from the tip.

"Tell me about the airplanes, Steve."

His head whipped around and he locked eyes with me for a moment before he crushed the barely smoked cigarette into the ashtray, and the color drained from his face.

"No, no, no," he said. "I don't know nothing about that."

"I'm guessing you do. You look like somebody just walked across your grave."

"No, man," he said. "Nobody out there knows nothing about planes. Nobody's allowed anywhere near them except for Deva and the freaks. And a couple of the chicks, of course, right?"

"Why not?"

"I told you I don't know, man. It's not my bag."

"Gimme names, Steve."

"Who? The freaks?"

"Sure," I said. "And Deva Ravi."

Steve rocked forward on his chair and began twisting the leather braid again. He looked to me as if he were about to throw up, so I nudged the trashcan closer to him with the toe of my boot.

"We just call 'em Scary Larry and Mac Nasty. I have no idea what their real names are, and I don't want to know."

"And Deva? Do you know his real name?"

"I super don't want to know that."

"Do you think they'd do harm to you?"

He looked at me from the corner of his eye and squeezed out a laugh.

"I saw what they did to T-wolf, man."

I was about to ask him what he meant when I heard the phone ring on the other side of the wall. A few seconds later, the door to the interview room flew open.

"We've gotta go, Sheriff," Jordan Powell said.

"What's up?"

"Shots fired at the motel."

"The Cayuse?"

Powell nodded and strapped his gun belt around his waist.

"Guess we're finished here," I said to Steve. "For now."

"Okay," he answered, but made no effort to leave.

"Can I trust you to come back in here tomorrow morning so we can finish our chat?"

"You want me to leave now?"

"Most people prefer to leave on their own," I said. "Besides, I can't let you stay here all by yourself, can I? Come back at noon. Deva Ravi should be gone by then."

Steve stood and began rocking his head from side to side, his eyes darting in a kind of panic, failing to find purchase as he pressed himself into the corner of the room.

"What did you just say?" Steve asked. "You're gonna be talking to Deva Ravi?"

"First thing in the morning."

"Aw, shit, man," he said. He began chewing at the loose skin on his thumb again. "He's gonna know I talked to you. He's gonna think I told you stuff."

"I won't mention anything about you," I said. "You have my word on that. Now you have to get out of here, Steve. My deputy and I have got to go."

"Deva Ravi's gonna *know*, man. You gotta let me stay in here, at least until it's dark. You can't let 'em see me."

The terror in his eyes appeared genuine, at least it appeared extremely real to him. I was no closer to knowing what they were up to at the Rainbow Ranch, but I suspected that something had gone sideways and the utopia these kids thought they'd found had devolved into the forced perspective creation of a narcissist: an image tattooed onto the collective consciousness of the very people who had freely bound over their trust.

"If you can't leave me here alone, then lock me in a cell 'til you come back," Steve begged. "It's okay with me, I swear to God."

I didn't have time to argue with him anymore, and in truth, I felt more than a little sorry for him. I grabbed a couple cans of orange soda from the refrigerator, took a bag of jerky from the cabinet, and handed all of it to Steve.

"Jordan!" I hollered through the open doorway. "Run this guy upstairs. He wants to be locked up until we get back."

CHAPTER TWENTY-SEVEN

CONSTRUCTION OF INTERSTATE 5 was completed in this part of the state almost ten years ago, in 1966. It had been carved through the mountains by heavy machinery, over a route that had been known to earlier generations as the Siskiyou Trail, itself a Native American footpath that had been traveled for hundreds of years, linking the Pacific Northwest with the central valley of what is now called California.

When the interstate finally arrived, rural roadmaps had to be redrawn, as the service stations and diners and small businesses that had sprung up out of a culture of mobility were either forced to relocate or die.

The Cayuse Motel is one of the tombstones.

What had once been a thriving motel and Flying-A service station situated along the state route had long since been left in isolated disrepair, a sun-faded pink stucco relic whose rooms were most often rented to sundowners, deadbeats, and malingerers of a variety that most people wouldn't allow to drink out of their garden hose. It was a single-story structure in the shape of an L, the short end of which comprised an office and apartment for the manager, with the guest rooms laid out on the long end.

The low sun of the late afternoon glared hard into my eyes as I turned off the paved road and onto the loose gravel that defined the parking lot. Jordan Powell pulled his pickup beside mine in the meager shade of a portico and waited inside his cab while I had a word with the manager.

The door to his apartment/office was dead-bolted shut, so I pounded the frame with the ball of my fist.

"Sheriff's office," I shouted.

I heard the mechanical snap of the lock on the jalousie windows. I turned and recognized the unshaven, skeletal face of the manager peering at me from between slats of pebbled glass.

"It's just the two of you?" the manager asked, cutting his eyes in Powell's direction.

"Yes. Me and my deputy."

"I haven't heard no more shooting since I phoned you," he said. "Three shots from what sounded like a big gun. Bam-bam-bam. Just like that."

"You didn't see anybody? Hear anyone drive away?"

He squinted at me through the gap in the glass.

"When I hear gunshots, I lock the door and get my ass under the desk. I can't hear nothing 'cept my own heart pounding in my ears. I've been robbed before, you know."

"Where'd the shooting come from? Which room?"

"The very last one, there on the end. It's the only one that's occupied right now."

The manager backed away from his window and disappeared into the dark of his dwelling. Powell and I unshipped our weapons, pressed our backs to the concrete block wall and he followed me as I crabbed sideways along the open corridor, our guns angled upward toward the cantilevered roof. Powell's eyes swept the parking lot as we made the slow creep down the hall, taking turns covering one another when we would stoop into a crouch and duck walk underneath the guest room windows that looked out across the oil-stained gravel, beyond the road and into the shadows of the fern forest.

A trickle of sweat snaked down my spine as we reached the last room, the door hanging at a strange angle, broken off its hinges. The smell of spent gunpowder lingered in the stillness and it seemed that even the birds had fallen silent inside the dense growth across the road.

"This is Sheriff Dawson," I called out. "Put your weapons down and place your hands on your head. Come out here ass-first, and do it slow."

There was no sound but the hum of a swamp cooler that had been installed on the roof overhead. I called out my instructions again, louder this time, waited through a full thirty seconds of silence before I nodded in Jordan's direction.

I charged in first, sliding quickly past the door jamb, the hammer of my Colt Trooper cocked and ready. Powell moved into a flanking position on the opposite side of the doorway, and I nearly tripped over a body as I rushed in to make the first sweep of the room.

The right quarter of the victim's head had been completely eradicated, everything above his orbital socket reduced to fragments of fibrous matter and vapor by the blast of what had obviously been a shotgun. He had been shot point blank as he pressed his eye to the peephole in the door. A second shell had exploded the deadbolt and knocked the door off its hinges. The second victim was positioned like a ragdoll, legs splayed out before him, his back against the wall, a hole the size of a grapefruit in the space once occupied by his heart and lungs.

I recognized both bodies. The one without a face was the man I had referred to as Bullet Head. The other was Ducktail.

The crowded space inside the room smelled overwhelmingly of viscera and cordite, the susurration from a swarm of blowflies vibrating in the closeness. Three empty casings of twelve-gauge ammunition lay on the floor beside Ducktail, together with the remnants of a spank magazine he still clutched in one of his hands. His death mask expression was frozen with shock. His shaven-headed colleague, on the other hand, had never known what hit him, just a superheated orange flash of light as he pressed his fat cheek to the door.

"These are Carl Spinell's guys," I said.

The interior showed no obvious sign of having been ran-
sacked, only the expected domestic clutter of two low-life
recidivists sharing a twenty-dollar motel room. The curtains
had been drawn across the room's only window, and the
gooseneck lamp on the scarred desktop provided the only
light, apart from the black-and-white television that flickered
unfocused images of the network news, the sound having
been turned all the way down. A cheap suitcase was latched
and laid neatly on the floor inside the closet, a pair of blue
jeans and a couple of shirts hanging from wire hangers on
the rod. In the opposite corner, rumpled clothing spilled out
of an army-issue ditty bag that had been propped against the
wall next to the bedside table.

"This looks like a hit," Powell said. "A blitz attack."

I holstered my Colt and waved a fly out of my face as I
headed outside for some air.

"Well, if it was supposed to be a gunfight," I said, "these
guys sure as hell weren't very good at it."

<hr />

THREE HOURS later, after the coroner had finished his
business, I sent Powell to Salem to deliver the weapons we'd
collected to CID, one of which had been a .38-caliber revolver
that I wanted tested against the slug that had been dug out
of Doc Brawley's wall. The pair of plastic evidence bags that
sat beside me on my passenger seat contained the wallets
and identification belonging to the two victims. I intended to
run them through the system when I got back to the office,
though there was no hurry for these two anymore.

I drove north on the winding two-lane that traced the
course of the river through several miles of dense forest,
where the water flowed from the mouth of a steep rift and
sword ferns had taken root in the fissures of the sheer canyon
walls. I rolled down my window and the air felt ten degrees
cooler beside the riverbed. The colors of the day were waning
into dusk and the river appeared black as ink.

The acrid taste of the crime scene lingered in my mouth, and I seemed powerless to keep it from replaying in my mind's eye: The chaos is so sudden that there is no time for the gathering of senses. There are no words, no bargaining or mercy, only the final explosions that reduce the right quadrant of Bullet Head's skull to high-velocity spatter, and rearrange Ducktail's cardiopulmonary system into cranberry-colored meat.

The entire operation couldn't have taken longer than a minute from the first shot to the last, and I judged Jordan Powell's initial assessment of a blitz assassination to have been right on the money. While I couldn't muster much heartache over the loss of two deviant trolls, it seemed to me that the nature of the larger picture was changing. What I had initially believed to be an escalation of retaliatory acts that had begun with Harper Emory's alleged assault may have metastasized to the point that someone had decided to simply pull the chain and hose out the bowl.

It was nearly dark when I turned off the road and met Sam Griffin at Duke's, a drive-in burger place on the southern edge of town. I locked the evidence bags in my glove box and crossed the lot toward where Sam occupied one of the picnic tables beneath the eave reading a newspaper. I could feel the day's heat leeching from the pavement and up through the soles of my boots, the smells of grilled onions and burger grease billowing out of the roof vent.

"Been waiting long?" I asked.

"Naw. Just finished my shift," he said and tossed the folded paper into a rubbish barrel.

I walked to the window and ordered three cheeseburgers with fries, and popped the caps off two bottles of grape soda that I dug out from the ice in the cooler. I slid onto the bench opposite Griffin, handed him one of the soda bottles, and pushed the cardboard box containing his order across the table to him.

"What went down at the motel?" Griffin asked as he unfolded the oil-spotted paper from his burger.

"Somebody used a shotgun to take Carl Spinell's two morons off the board."

Sam looked into the middle distance and dipped a fry into a tiny paper cup brimming with ketchup and popped it into his mouth.

"You getting the impression there's more going on than a feud between a fake guru and a grumpy sheep rancher?" he asked.

"If it was ever about that at all," I said.

On the opposite end of the parking lot, high school kids had gathered in factions, clustered around wide-open doors of bathtub hot rods and the dropped tailgates of pickups whose radios spilled music into the evening. Their faces shone with perspiration and neon, animated by hot summer wind and hormones and the illusion of freedom that is the special province of youth, pushing away one more night's concerns over the draft, or a job, or the day that they might be compelled to bear witness to the blood of angels.

"You gonna eat that?" Griffin asked.

"What?"

Griffin pressed a napkin to his mouth and pointed at the burger growing cold in the box on the table beside my elbow.

"Powell located one of the Rainbow Ranch boys under a bridge," I said. "The kid was scared as hell, practically begged to be kept in lockup until nightfall. I wanted to make sure he had something to eat before I turn him loose. The burger's for him."

Griffin squinted, wadded his empty food wrappers, and arched a free throw into the garbage can.

"What's he got to be scared about?"

"It appears that Deva Ravi inspires more than just otherworldly devotion."

My reply had been glib, and in retrospect, I was ashamed that I had so badly underestimated the depth of the young man's terror. Because when I returned to the substation half an hour later, I found Steve Beck—the bucktoothed kid who had been nicknamed Corncob by his friends—hanging by the neck from one of the steel bars in his cell.

He had fashioned a noose from long pieces of fabric he had torn off his shirt and twisted into a makeshift rope. He had looped one end around a pig-metal stanchion, the other around his throat, and strangled himself to death. He must have done it shortly after Powell and I had left, because by the time I walked up the stairs to deliver his hamburger and release him, Steve Beck had been dead for at least a couple of hours, his face swollen to the color and texture of an eggplant, and his eyes bulged out as though golf balls had been pushed into the sockets.

CHAPTER TWENTY-EIGHT

"I THOUGHT I heard voices out here," Caleb said. "Little early in the day, ain't it?"

He was standing in the open doorway of the barn, a steaming stoneware mug of coffee in one hand, watching me run the curry comb across Drambui's withers.

"Just talking to my horse," I said without looking up.

"That must be mighty boresome for him. I'm surprised he ain't kicked your teeth out yet."

I heard Caleb amble across the sawdust and sand and sit down on an upturned water bucket beside Drambuie's open stall. He leaned his back against the slats, stretched out his legs, and crossed them at the ankle. I glanced over my shoulder and saw him stroking his mustache and staring out the barn door into the dark.

"You can prob'ly guess what I'm gonna say to you right now," Caleb said.

I set the curry comb on the tack box and grabbed a wood-handled brush. I pressed my hat down tighter on my head and began to work the knots out of Drambuie's tail.

"You're going to say: 'You don't need to know everything. You only need to know where to find someone who does.' I'm working on it, Caleb."

"You think your horse might have some insights for you?"

"He's got more answers than I do at the moment."

Caleb squinted at me, and I saw a hint of melancholy creep into his eyes.

"Things have gone a little OK Corral out there, ain't they?" he said.

"I can't tell who's the Clantons and who's the Earps. Hard to know which way to aim."

Caleb sipped gingerly from his mug, reeled his long legs in, and leaned forward on the bucket. He rested his elbows on his knees and looked up into the rafters.

"There ain't always a difference," he said.

"That may be true," I said. "But I'm still left with the same two choices: Engage in the fight or surrender. I'm not willing to surrender."

Drambuie shifted his weight and nickered, low and guttural. He turned his head sideways as much as the chain and halter would allow, and looked at me with one unblinking eye. Caleb stood and scratched my horse behind his ear.

"Take a shade for a little while, Ty," Caleb said. "Join me for a mug. I'll grind up some beans."

"Up on your roof?"

"In my kitchen, wiseass."

"Maybe later. I gotta muck out Boo's stall."

"We pay hands to do that kinda work."

"I got two hands right here."

"Have it your way," Caleb said and dumped the last few drops out of his cup onto the barn floor. He halted in the doorway for a moment and turned to me.

"One thing though," he said.

"What's that?"

"Make sure you keep drinking upstream from the herd."

A couple hours later, I saw Cricket collecting eggs and throwing feed inside the chicken run as I pulled out of the driveway. When she saw me looking at her in my rearview mirror, she smiled, blew a kiss in my direction, and waved a peace sign at me. I threw one back at her and drove away, lowering the visor against the glare of the approaching sunrise.

THE IDs on the two shotgun victims at the Cayuse had been run through the system during the night. I picked up several pages of flimsy thermal paper off the tray of the Mag-nafax machine in the file room, sat down at my desk, and leafed through them.

The man I referred to as Bullet Head was actually named Magnus "Mo" Guidry. As I had correctly thought, he was a recent parolee from Lompoc where he had just completed a two-year bit for poaching bobcats, coyotes, and gray wolves. There had been a couple additional codefendants in that case, a two-time loser named Cort Scheer—a man I also knew, and had come to know as Ducktail—and a man named Carl Spinell. At the time the three of them had been arrested, they had been in the employ of a sheep rancher who had no tolerance for predators, whether federally pro-tected or not, and showed even less concern about the meth-ods Spinell and his men implemented in their eradication. The rancher, together with Spinell and Ducktail, got off with a fine, while Bullet Head had been left to take one for the team.

I was about to turn the page and read more about the late Cort "Ducktail" Scheer, when I saw a panel van pull up to the curb outside and park. I paper clipped the flimsy sheets and dropped them into a manila file folder as I watched Deva Ravi and one of his girls step out of the van and glide across the sidewalk and through my office door.

He came in barefooted, wearing bell-bottom trousers and a chambray shirt he'd left unbuttoned to his navel, a neck-lace of multicolored ceramic beads looped around his neck. The girl followed three steps behind him and took up a mili-tant stance in front of my desk, arms folded across her chest, head tilted to one side.

"I can feel your damage, man," Deva Ravi said. "I can help you fix that."

"Knock that shit off," I said. "Remove your shades and have a seat."

Deva did as I asked and dropped his sunglasses on my desk as he sat down.

"Your life would be a great deal simpler if you had a phone," I said.

"Not a chance, man. I've got no interest in communicating with anyone but the universe and my people."

The girl nodded knowingly and moved toward the other chair.

"Not you," I said to her. "This is a private conversation."

"Deva Ravi wants me here," she said.

I cut my eyes to Deva Ravi. He was running his palm across the stubble of growth along the shaved sides of his scalp.

"Tell this girl to wait outside," I said.

"My name's Aurora," she spat. "You harassed us at the sandwich shop yesterday. Dawn was mindfucked for the rest of the day."

"That was a conversation between adults, Aurora, not harassment," I said. "Now I need you to step outside."

"I want a witness," Deva said. There was a cold severity in his tone and aspect that had not been present a moment earlier.

I shook my head.

"You want a witness, go to a tent revival," I said.

Something moved behind his eyes, and the coldness disappeared.

"Did you bring me down here to bust my balls about airplanes again?"

"I don't know," I said. "You got something you want to tell me?"

"No."

The crescent of a dimple dented Aurora's cheek as she smiled at Deva Ravi.

"This is the last time I'm going to say this nicely," I said. "Aurora, take it down the road."

She looked from me to Deva, and he gave her a little nod. Her face was stamped with hurt and insult, surprised that her spiritual mentor had not stood up for her. He touched her cheek with his fingertips and she visibly relaxed. I slid my chair away from my desk and took a sip of coffee that had gone cold. I watched her push past the door and sit down on the curb outside. She wrapped her arms around her knees and tilted her face toward the morning sun.

When I returned my attention to Deva Ravi, he grinned and winked at me. I was struck anew by the man's mercurial nature, unsure as to whether he was genuinely unbalanced or if he wore his various identities like costume props.

"I think we've reached a crossroads here, don't you?" I asked.

"I don't know what you're talking about."

"I wonder how many of your acolytes I'm going to end up having to bury."

"You need to work on your communication skills, Sheriff." He leaned back in his chair and crossed his legs, but I could see his eyeballs vibrating. "It might be at the root of all this hostility you're carrying around."

"You claim to be a spiritual man, but when two of your devoted followers die ugly, you do nothing at all. You speak of freedom, but you hide behind chained fences and barbed wire. One of those two believers committed suicide rather than confront you face to face."

"You're insulting my beliefs?"

"I don't give a damn if you're a Druid or Zoroastrian. But when you hurt people with whatever it is you teach, you earn the full and complete measure of my attention."

He shifted in his seat and squinted at me.

"You got questions for me, or not?"

"What is your real name?" I asked.

Deva shook his head and smiled.

"Try again," he said.

"Who owns the Rainbow Ranch?"

"I don't understand how the answer to that holds any relevance."

"Your understanding of my methodology is at the very bottom of a long list of things that I don't give a shit about."

"Nevertheless I decline to discuss that."

"My questions aren't going to get any easier."

"Let's give another one a try and see how it goes."

"Who are the men your people call 'Scary Larry' and 'Mac Nasty'?"

His facial muscles ticked ever so slightly, and his eyes glowed like the horns of Texas cattle in an electrical storm. I waited for the thunder, but it never came.

"Ask me what you really brought me here to ask me," he said.

"You and Harper Emory appear to be engaged in a race to the bottom. I'm here to tell you that the one who gets there second wins."

"That didn't sound like a question."

"Who killed Doc Brawley?"

"How the hell would I know something like that?"

"You knew the man," I said.

He held his silence for a long moment before he looked at me and shrugged.

"He treated a few of my guys," Deva said. "Doc Brawley was a friend."

"A *friend?*"

"Turns out there actually are a handful of people over thirty who can be trusted."

"Trusted with what?" I asked.

He leaned his head back and shifted his focus to the ceiling, whether considering the content of my question, or the consequences of its answer, I could not tell. The manic shifts of tension that had defined his behavior since he came into my office dissipated momentarily.

"Are you familiar with the term 'Four-F'?" he asked finally.

There was probably not an American alive who had not acquired a working knowledge of the present military draft system.

"Indefinite deferral from being called up for the draft," I answered.

"If you have bad eyesight or flat feet or epilepsy or asthma or allergies . . ." he said.

I took a few seconds to digest what he was telling me.

"Doc Brawley would falsify diagnoses? In exchange for what?"

"Nothing," Deva said. "Doc was a believer in justice, man. He didn't dig Tricky Richard's endless bullshit war."

"He could have lost his license to practice medicine. He could have faced criminal charges."

"So what are you going to do, throw him in jail? It's a little late for that."

"Is that why you killed him? Did he threaten to stop? Or turn your people in?"

Deva Ravi peeled his eyes off the ceiling and drilled me with them.

"I told you, Sheriff, the dude was a friend."

"I don't believe you."

"Fuck you. You don't believe anybody."

"Here's what I believe: I believe two of your businesses were vandalized by someone who wanted to drive you out of here, and one of your followers burned to death in the process. The next thing I know, one of Meridian's favorite citizens is shot with a .38 revolver, then stabbed, and beaten to a bloody pulp in the wee hours of the morning inside his own office. And last night, two recidivist assholes who might or might not work for Harper Emory, wind up with their shit decorating the walls of a rundown motel; and to top it off, another one of your stardust brothers strangled himself in my jail cell—a cell he *demanded* to be locked up in. I've got bodies stacking up like cordwood in this county, and I'd like for you to explain your involvement."

Deva turned and looked out the front window, where the shops along the street were just beginning to unlock their doors for business. Aurora had moved into the shade of a poplar tree, and was pulling the petals off a dandelion one by one.

"Am I under arrest, Sheriff?" he asked when he turned back around.

"Not yet."

He unfolded himself from his chair, picked up his sunglasses from my desk, and slipped them on.

"It's too bad about the old man," he said.

Later I would revisit that remark in my mind from time to time, the strangeness of his tone as he said those words. It was as though he was speaking the languages of regret and loss, but had no understanding of them, an accidental traveler through a place where he held no currency or passport, nor a ticket home.

———

I WAS locking up the office so I could grab some lunch when the phone rang.

"You were right," Bill Kiefer said. "There's a ground lease on the Rainbow Ranch property."

"Leased to whom?"

"Ambervalia Corporation is leasing to a company called Galanis United."

"Who the hell is that?"

A siren wailed somewhere outside his office window and spun across the line at me.

"I'm lucky to have found this thing at all," he said. "It's a one-page Lease Recital. Names of the lessor and lessee, legal description of the property, and the lease term. It's all I've got."

I thanked him and decided to skip lunch. If I wanted to birddog information on Galanis United, I could either make the two-plus-hour drive to the public library up in Lewiston on a Friday afternoon, or take my chances at the local high school on the last day before summer vacation. I opted for the latter.

As before, I checked in at the front office, and was given directions to the library. I passed through halls lined with metal lockers and littered with discarded notebook paper and the scraps of printed posters that had been stripped from the walls. I stepped outdoors into the breezeway that led to the library, and the smells of cut grass, barberry, and heather floating on the dry breeze struck me with a vertiginous sense of déjà vu. I wondered which of the lives belonging to the voices I now heard behind the doors and open classroom windows would be stilled, or scarred, or giving birth, or moving away, or billeted to some distant foreign outpost by this same time next year.

A car horn blasted from the parking lot and startled me back into the present. I shook off my morose distraction and continued along the concrete walkway.

Ten minutes later, I was squeezed into a study carrel along the back wall of the research section of the Meridian High School library being instructed on the use of the microfiche machine. My eyes burned from whatever spray the librarian had used to cement her hair in place.

It took more than an hour of parsing through microfilm copies of the local papers to find mention of Galanis United, the publication of a legal notice. I was about to rewind the reel when I felt a gentle tap on my shoulder.

"I saw you through the window," Molly Meadows said. She spoke softly, though we were the only people in the room.

"I beg your pardon?"

A flush of pink showed in the hollow of her throat and she glanced away.

"I saw you walking down the hallway," she said. "Past my classroom. They said I'd probably find you here."

"I didn't want to drive all the way to Lewiston to use the county library if I didn't have to."

"I had a nice time at dinner with you and your wife at Mr. Brody's the other night."

"You must be thinking of a different occasion than the one that I attended."

"Your wife, Jesse, is wonderful."

"She's my most popular attribute. She'll be at the rodeo this weekend."

"Oh, I don't know if I'll be going."

"Mandatory," I said. "Social event of the year in Meriwether County."

She didn't even attempt to fake a smile and I watched her, as she fidgeted with the pendant on the chain around her neck, wondering why she had come to seek me out. I waited through a few protracted seconds before I gave up.

"I'd better get back to it," I said.

"Oh, of course," she said. "I'm sorry to have interrupted you."

"It was nice to see you again, Miss Meadows."

The expression she showed me struck me as vaguely sad, and she hesitated for a moment before she moved toward the door.

"I know that Mr. Brody's pushing that recall petition."

"Politics," I said, but we both knew that was only part of the truth.

"He sent some people here to encourage the staff to sign it. I don't know if anybody did. I'm sorry."

"Don't be," I said. "I'll tell Jesse that you asked after her."

It was well after three o'clock by the time I threw in the towel. The school buses had all departed for their final rounds, and the last of the students had emptied out their lockers and headed off to celebrate. All I had to show for three hours of research was a headache that threatened to split my skull and the knowledge that Galanis United was a Nevada corporation that owned a couple of automobile dealerships, a string of drag speedways in California and Nevada, and an unspecified interest in Oregon timber. I was able to uncover nothing with regard to corporate shareholders, but the chairman of the board was a man named Minas Galanis who, I learned, was both kindly regarded for his involvement with several local Nevada charities, and pitied for the tragic loss of his son in combat overseas.

I walked back to the main administration office to use their phone, holding on to the hope that I could find a listing somewhere in Nevada for Galanis United, and that their company switchboard might still be operational on a Friday afternoon approaching happy hour. I struck out.

My eyelids felt like they had been scraped with sandpaper and I was about to climb into my truck when I felt the skin tighten on my scalp, and the sensation of a thousand pinpricks moving up my spine. I turned and jogged back to the school office and called Chris Rose's office at CID in Salem. He picked up on the second ring.

"Any word on those fingerprints I gave you?" I asked.

"From the Polaroid snapshot? It hasn't even been two weeks yet, Ty."

"I just thought of something, and I need you to give it a try for me."

CHAPTER TWENTY-NINE

FLAT PLANES OF sunlight slanted through breaches in the cloud cover the next morning and washed the mountain range in patches of golden light as I watched Caleb and young Tom Jenkins hazing our show bull, Julius, into the trailer. Across the way, between the bunkhouse and the barn, several of the hands had parked their personal truck-and-trailer rigs, and were busy loading their gear and their favorite horses from the remuda. Red dust floated over the corral, where the animals had begun to circle in agitation as my cowboys tossed their loops and snubbed their mounts, rushing to transport them to the county showgrounds in time to take part in the Grand Entry procession, where the "Star Spangled Banner" would be sung, and this year's Rodeo Queen would be introduced. If they played their cards right, they might work their ways up close enough to let the queen and her court get an early peek at them before the rough stock events landed them face-first in the dirt, cracking ribs and busting noses, and worse yet, tearing holes in their finery.

───⊗⊗⊗───

"THAT HORSE is snortin' like it's got rollers in its nose," Caleb said to me.

It was a little past nine in the morning, and we were leaning on the rodeo rail, watching the last couple of riders prepare to take their turns lacing up on the saddle broncs.

"He does look a little snuffy, doesn't he?" I said.

The rider nodded to the gate man, and the horse came out hopping, spun in a tight circle, and nearly buried his nose in the dirt.

"Who's the peeler?" I asked.

Caleb squinted, spat a stream of tobacco at the base of the post.

"They call him 'Bootjack,' though I don't know why," Caleb said. "He's a rough-string rider over at Steeple Fork."

The horse completely boiled over at that moment, humped his back, and came down with all four legs stiff as ramrods.

"That animal's likely to drive that cowboy's spine right through his hat," I said.

Caleb smiled and wiped a sleeve across his lips as the man they called Bootjack came unstuck and landed hard on his left shoulder. The crowd cheered and whistled when he picked himself out of the dust and waved his hat toward the bleachers. The grandstand announcer gave the ride time over the loudspeaker.

Sam Griffin wandered up beside us, leaned his elbows on the fence, and rested a boot on the bottom rung.

"I didn't see your name signed up on no contestant list," Caleb said to him.

Sam grinned and ran his palm across his thigh where he'd taken a line-of-duty bullet that had required months of physical therapy to get him up and walking without the assistance of crutches or a cane.

"I believe I'm still in the walk-trot category," Sam said. "Say, you seen Taj Caldwell around?"

"I ain't seen him since yesterday afternoon," Caleb said. "That sumbitch better damn well be here somewheres though. Him and Tucker are s'posed to represent us in the team roping. I swear to God, if he went tail-up, I'll have him digging postholes for a month."

Inside the arena, a couple of horsemen dragged the infield smooth with a section of chain-link fencing tied to a rope, while a third one controlled the dust and loose dirt with a water hose. The emcee announced a short break between events and I left Caleb and Sam to sort out our ranch's cowboy complications while I made my way around to recon the fairgrounds.

I had only been half joking when I had described this weekend to Miss Meadows as the social event of the year. For many residents of Meriwether County that is exactly what it was, and since the rodeo's official inception in 1889—when it was mostly used as an excuse for local ranchers and their hands to raise a little hell—it had grown to become an important stop on the professional circuit, and had begun to take on the trappings of a class reunion.

The midday sun hovered hot and white overhead. I took a handkerchief from my back pocket and wiped away a line of sweat beneath my hatband. The equine odors and grandstand commotion receded into the distance as I walked among the food and craft booths that had been set up on the lawn in the shade of old-growth willow trees that lined the edge of a manmade pond where paddle boats had been drawn up to the shore. Across the way, I thought I saw my daughter browsing inside a merchandise booth strung with hanging plant holders made of macramé, and table displays of pottery and handcrafted jewelry. The rest of the crowd seemed to be shunning that particular stall as they wandered the commercial bazaar. The air inside was heavy with the smell of patchouli incense as I ducked beneath the low canvas awning and stepped up to the table where Cricket was standing. She was lost in conversation with a pair of girls who had their backs turned to her, busy unloading items out of a cardboard packing box. Their dialogue continued unabated, until finally they finished whatever it was that they were doing, stood up, and turned to face us. In retrospect, I should not have been surprised to see that the two girls were Dawn and Aurora.

Cricket slipped an arm around my waist when I came up beside her. Dawn's face colored suddenly and her eyes flew open wide. Aurora trapped me in her glare, hunched her shoulders, and sunk her hands deep into the pockets of her cutoffs.

"Hey, Dad," Cricket said.

I kissed the top of my daughter's head and smiled politely at Dawn and Aurora, pointedly ignoring their displeasure and surprise at seeing me.

"The sheriff is your father?" Dawn asked. There had been a shift in her expression, which no longer displayed astonishment, but something more closely resembling panic.

"It's not something she tends to brag on," I said. "I didn't realize that you all knew each other."

"Dawn's a friend of mine," Cricket said. "From the sandwich shop. She's the one who showed me how to make the oatmeal you hate so much."

"How special," I said. "Thanks for that."

I touched my hat brim with two fingers and showed myself out, left Cricket to resume her conversation with the rainbow girls, and made my way across the lawn to one of the food booths for an ice cream cone. It was clear that I had just inadvertently dropped a turd into their punchbowl.

———

I MEANDERED for nearly an hour, eventually circling back toward the barn buildings where the rodeo contestants boarded their stock. The Diamond D occupied one entire section that Jesse bedecked every year with flags and banners in our traditional maroon and gold motif, and bearing the distinctive markings of our brand. I located Jesse in the horse stall we had designated as a makeshift cocktail bar and tack room, speaking in hushed tones to Tom Jenkins.

Tom had his back to me, so I couldn't hear him very clearly, but judging by the timbre of his voice, he was harboring second thoughts about his participation in the calf roping. I was aware that he had been the butt of a considerable amount of hazing from the other ranch hands, but even at the age of sixteen, a cowboy was expected to take it if he was ever to earn their respect. I also knew that if he failed to make a decent showing in the ring, he'd never hear the end of it. It was obvious Tom knew that, too, and the worry was wearing hard on him.

I was about to step inside when I heard Jesse begin to tell him the old Cherokee parable about the two wolves who live inside of each of us, constantly in battle for our spirit. One wolf represents the qualities of bravery, kindness, and integrity; the other, those of fear and greed and hatred.

"Your actions determine which one will win, Tom," she said.

"How?"

"By deciding which wolf you're going to feed."

I moved across the threshold as though I hadn't been listening, clapped Tom on the shoulder.

"I want to give something to you," I told Tom.

"Sir?"

"For the calf roping."

"I don't—"

I grabbed a pair of batwing chaps from a hook on the wall before he had a chance to try and tell me he was backing out, and handed them to Tom. I'd owned them for so long the leather felt as soft as a chamois in my hands.

"Put these on," I said. "I never scored out of the money when I wore 'em. They'll bring you luck."

He ran his fingers over the tooling on the belt, and looked at me with an expression that contained both doubt and gratitude.

"Thank you, sir," he said.

"You'd better jangle them spurs and saddle up," I said. "You don't have much time before they call your event."

He firmed his hat and headed outside, the glare of the afternoon sun casting his narrow frame in perfect silhouette inside the doorway when I called out to him.

"You clear your head of everything except that calf," I said. "Throw that string straight and true, you hear?"

He nodded and neither Jesse nor I said another word until the music from the steel rowels spinning inside the shanks strapped to his heels faded away around the corner of the barn. I took her hand in mine, pulled her close, and kissed her, soft and slow.

———— ∞ ————

CALEB, JESSE, and I stood along the rail while Paul Tucker and Sam Griffin joined us, watching from horseback a few yards away. The colored lights of the Ferris wheel pulsed and glowed beyond the crowded grandstands as the afternoon gave way to evening. I caught Tom Jenkins's eye from where he sat in his saddle, nervously working the loop on his pigging string. He gave me a brief nod and turned his horse away, walking him in a loose half-circle behind the chute and starting box.

"What kind of odds are you giving?" Tucker said to me.

"Sometimes you win, sometimes you learn," I said.

"That's Ty's way of saying he ain't laying no bets," Caleb said. "But I'll throw a wager or two. How about five bucks the kid places?"

"Done," Tucker said. "I believe that we're about to see that cupcake learn that there's a lot more to calf roping than sittin' in the saddle lettin' your feet hang down."

"Only a buzzard feeds on his friends," Griffin said.

"Why, thank you for your spiritual insight, Deacon," Tucker said. "I was wonderin' whether you'd opine on all the gamblin' taking place hereabouts."

Tucker was down ten dollars after the first two rounds, Tom Jenkins having placed in the top three both times. His rope work was true, and it was obvious he'd spent a good deal of time training with his horse. The kid had grit, and a bloody lip to match after he took a calf hoof to the mouth while he was dallying up in round two. The third and final round came down to the wire, with Jenkins faulting and coming up a full second short, and out of the purse, against three seasoned hands who had driven all the way from Wyoming.

We waited for him as he brushed himself off and ambled slowly in our direction. His face was filmed in dust, a rivulet of muddy sweat snaking out of his hatband. I shook his hand and saw that his knuckles were bleeding and the pocket of his shirt had nearly been torn off.

"I guess I used up all the luck in them chaps you loaned me," he said.

"You beat out a dozen men with a hell of a lot more experience than you have," I said. "It's only failure if you quit; when you keep going, it's called experience."

"You might want to share that bit of wisdom with your Uncle Snoose," Caleb added, and folded his five-dollar net winnings and slid the bill into his pocket.

CHAPTER THIRTY

THE WHITE AND purple hyacinth that Jesse nurtured in the greenhouse had come back into bloom, and the air in the kitchen was sweet with the fragrance of the cut stalks that she had arranged in a vase on the table. The three of us had just returned home from Sunday services and were changing our clothes for the remainder of the day.

After breakfast, we made the drive back to the fairgrounds, where Jesse and Cricket and I walked together across the dirt parking lot, weaved our way among the horse trailers and competitors' barns, and rounded the corner to ours. Caleb Wheeler was shouting and waving his arms as he stalked back and forth in front of the rest of the Diamond D hands. They were gathered in the shade of an eave that ran the length of our stable, where the horses' heads poked out from their stalls, ears cocked forward in curiosity.

"What's all this?" I asked.

"Goddamned Taj Caldwell called me not an hour ago, is what it is."

I scanned the faces of our cowboys, but perceived nothing that could help me decipher the meaning of Caleb's statement.

"Where did Taj call you from?" I asked.

"A bar."

Caleb stared at me, his face growing redder as he waited for me to catch up.

"The goddamned bar is in Phoenix," he said.

"Taj is supposed to be Tucker's heeler," I said, finally registering the problem.

"Diamond D ain't never scratched a team roping event. Not ever. I swear I'm gonna skin that sonofabitch when he gets back."

I cut my eyes sideways at Jesse and Cricket for a moment, then considered the rest of our cowboys.

"Tucker," I said, "what do you figure on doing?"

Paul Tucker tugged on the end of a hay stem he'd been chewing, narrowed his eyes as he looked off into the glare.

"I s'pose I see it this way," he answered. "Griffin is still gimpy, and Powell can't throw a loop down a well. All due respect, Mr. Dawson, sir, you ain't tossed a catch-rope in a while . . ."

Tucker halted and roved his gaze across the men in the shade and considered what he was going to say next.

"Out with it, you coward," Caleb said.

"You ain't a young maverick no more, Boss," Tucker said.

"There it is," Caleb said, and spat a wad of tobacco juice that landed three inches from the toe of Tucker's boot.

Tucker shifted the hay stem to the opposite corner of his mouth and his eyes landed on Tom Jenkins.

"I guess that leaves the kid," he shrugged. "Even I can't ride two horses with one ass."

———

I WAS making my way to the stock tent, where a blue ribbon awarded to a stud horse or bull could mean tens of thousands of dollars in breeding fees. While the rodeo and midway were largely entertaining diversions, what went on in the stock tent could mean the difference between saving and losing a ranch when times were lean as they had been for the past couple of years.

The footpath to the stockyard passed through the fun zone, where the trash barrels had begun to overflow with empty beer bottles and spent plastic cups. In the distance, the voice of the event announcer resonated like a stannic and discordant chirrup. The breeze blew hot, and smelled of popcorn, hot dogs, and funnel cakes, while strings of multi-colored triangular flags snapped and popped above my head.

I could sense someone coming up from behind me more rapidly than I was comfortable with, and when I turned to see who it was, I nearly ran headlong into Harper Emory.

"I need to speak with you, Dawson," he panted.

His face appeared flushed from both heat and exertion, but it was clear that he no longer required the use of his cane.

"Walk and talk," I said. "I'm on my way to the pens."

I began to move on through the noise that rose from the lines of onlookers mobbing the game booths when Emory tugged on my shirtsleeve.

"Not here," he said, and pulled up short.

Emory's voice came out in a hoarse whisper, his attention locked onto something behind me, the folds of his eyes twitching as if insects were feeding under his skin. He took a step backward and looked as though he wished he could vanish into my shadow.

"Tomorrow morning," he said. "At your office."

I watched as he skittered away, losing himself inside the milling crowd as swiftly as he had appeared. I removed the sunglasses I was wearing and wiped the dust off before resuming my course toward the stock tent. I hadn't made it three strides before I recognized what Harper Emory had been looking at over my shoulder, the thing that had stopped him in his tracks and sent him scuttling off in the other direction.

A low frequency electrical hum droned from an amplifier where a guitar player occupied a makeshift stage inside the beer garden, where red-faced men tipped long-necked bottles, sweated through the fabric of their shirts, and tapped fingers on shaded table tops underneath striped umbrellas. Carl Spinell was sitting at a table by himself, wearing a gray snap-button shirt and black jeans, paring the nails on his fingers with a pocket knife. His hat was pushed back off his forehead, his legs stretched out and encroaching into the pedestrian walkway, the sun glinting off the tooled silver decorations on the toes of his boots.

"I see you're looking covetously at my hoof covers," Spinell said to me.

"I don't know where you went to school, but I don't believe they taught you the proper definition of 'covetous'."

"You don't like my brand new Luccheses?" he asked without lifting his eyes off his manicure.

"If you're the bouncer at a Tijuana whorehouse."

He sliced away some loose skin on his thumb.

"I never have believed in economizing on footwear."

"You've been a difficult man to draw a bead on," I said, changing the subject. "I've been looking for you."

Carl Spinell drew himself out of his slouch and stared at me, admiring his own reflection in the lenses of my shades.

"Just enjoying a grin over a cold beverage or two."

"That puts you one up on most of the folks around here. They haven't had much to smile about since you arrived."

"Aw, Sheriff," he said, his drawling delivery like needles in my ears. "You can't be placing the blame on me for the misfortune that's befallen this unfortunate town. It's become downright dangerous around here."

"I suspect more than a little responsibility for that lands at your doorstep, and that of your two dead amigos."

"Quite a shock about them two, I admit," he said, and folded the knife blade into the handle and slid the whole thing into the pocket of his pressed jeans. "Who would've guessed that they were fairies, am I right? Prison does strange things to some folks. Speaking of which, did my eyes deceive me, or did I just see you conversing with Harper Emory?"

"You need to express yourself more plainly, Mr. Spinell. I don't believe I understand the connection."

"I shouldn't presume to tell you how to do your job, Sheriff."

"I need you to come in to my office and give a formal statement," I said. "Tomorrow works for me."

Deep lines radiated from the corners of his eyes when he smiled.

"I don't believe that I wish to say anything further to you in the absence of legal counsel," he said, and made a grand pantomime of surprise when Nolan Brody stepped up to the table carrying two frosted beer bottles, their necks covered with inverted plastic cups.

"Why, I'll be damned," Spinell enthused. "Here's my attorney now."

———∞∞∞———

WHEN I returned to our temporary stables an hour later, I was still seething with anger that a man like Carl Spinell had been invited into Meriwether County to track his shit across our town. I wandered around looking for anybody from the Diamond D, but it was quiet. I finally located Tom Jenkins out back, in an open patch of hardpan practicing heel roping on a wood peg he had driven into the ground. I watched him catch the peg and draw up tight on it. His eye was good, and his reactions quick. I knew it would do me some good to clear my head of Spinell, Brody, and Emory, if only for a short while.

"You nervous?" I asked.

I saw that the scabs he'd earned in the ring the day before had broken open, but he didn't seem to notice or care that fresh blood was running down the fingers of his left hand.

"I'm all right, I s'pose."

"You tell your uncle how you did with the calf-roping yesterday?"

"No, sir."

His tone of voice betrayed no hint of carping or self-pity. In fact, I was somewhat puzzled in that it betrayed no emotion whatsoever.

"Did you tell Snoose you're gonna represent us in the team roping? I imagine he'd want to see that."

"I doubt that, sir," he said.

Tom pulled the rope slack through the honda and rolled the lasso, then slapped it hard against the side welt of his boot. He trained his focus on his target, but it was clear that his attention had drifted away.

"I reckon I'll go and talk to him," I said. "You happen to know where he's set up his stable?"

"He didn't rent a stable this year," Tom said, and turned his eyes away. "Last time I saw him he was out near the feed lot drinking Wild Turkey out of a paper bag. He's been sleeping in the stock trailer that he used to haul the breed bull over here."

Tom lined up his twine and turned it loose again. He overthrew his target by at least a foot. It was the first miss I had seen since I'd begun watching him.

"Why don't you fall off and rest your feet a minute," I said.

His hat was pulled down low and I could not see his eyes inside the shadow of the brim when he turned to face me.

"With respect, I ain't got a lotta time before the ropin'," he said. "Them boys'll tan my hide if we lose because'a me."

"We ain't gonna lose because'a you," I said. "I've watched you throw. I've never seen you hot-rope a horse or steer, not even once. You're a natural. Now set down here with me a minute."

He took off his hat and squinted in the harsh sunlight, stepped into the shade, and sat down on a hay bale across from me. I went into the tack room, grabbed a cold bottle of soda from the ice chest, popped the top, and handed it to him.

"You given any thought to what you're gonna do when the summer's over, Tom? You figuring on going back to California to live with your momma?"

"I don't imagine there's much for me down in California no more," he said and tipped the bottle to his lips.

"We got high schools here in Oregon, too, you know," I said.

He tried not to let me see him smile as he leaned forward and studied the topsoil.

"I only got one more year before I graduate," he said.

"Old Snoose could surely use a decent hand, Tom. That ranch could be yours one day, if you were of a mind to work it. Your uncle doesn't have anybody else."

Something lit behind his eyes and flickered out, like he could not afford to allow himself more than a moment's worth of hope.

"I don't know whether he can hold out that long," he said. "It seems like my uncle's busting apart at the seams."

Tom placed his empty pop bottle on the ground beside the hay bale and ambled back out into the sun. He spun his line in a slow circle over his head, steadied his aim, and turned it loose. The rope flew straight and kicked up a tiny dust cloud as it caught the peg.

"Are you familiar with the American flag, son?" I asked. "It was the man on horseback who put most of them stars on it."

He pivoted on one foot and squinted in my direction, tried to locate my face inside the shade where I stood leaning against the wall.

"A man with land, water, and livestock is the freest man in the world," I went on. "This thing we do is a way of life, but it isn't going to stay this way forever."

"My uncle's property don't belong to me."

"You're a Corcoran, aren't you? If you want it, you've got to commit," I said. "If you don't, it'll disappear right out from under you. Opportunities die of neglect, not murder."

Tom Jenkins seemed to take notice of the blood on his knuckles for the first time. He drew a kerchief from his back pocket and wrapped his fingers in it while he considered what I had told him.

"I don't think it's as easy as that," he said.

"Are you asking me if it's simple, or if it's easy? That's two completely different things."

"Do you really think my uncle would consider it?"

"There hasn't been an abundance of hope lingering around here these days," I said. "I do believe it's been a helluva long time since your Uncle Snoose had much to look forward to. I don't know for sure, but that might apply to you as well."

CALEB WAS still furious with me for taking the Diamond D bull, Julius, out of the judging and stock auction. But I made him come along with me to locate Snoose anyway, on the likely chance that Snoose might be in a surly mood. Tom had been correct as to his uncle's whereabouts, and we found Snoose passed out on the floor of his split-tailgate cattle trailer, resting his head on a pile of dried straw, his crumpled hat drawn down to cover his eyes. I grabbed hold of his shoulder and shook him awake. He made a grumbling noise that reminded me of the sound an old dog makes and pushed his hat off his face, but he didn't appear overly surprised to see either Caleb or me standing there inside his trailer. He didn't seem particularly pleased either.

"What the hell do you fellas want? I don't recollect inviting y'all out here."

"It's time for you to pull on your boots and cowboy up, goddamn it," Caleb said.

Snoose's bloodshot eyes wandered from Caleb to me and back again.

"We get married or something when I wasn't payin' no attention?" Snoose asked. "Cause I don't recollect leaving you in charge of my doin's, Wheeler."

"I suggest you shut your mouth," Caleb said. "Most people never get to meet their own angel."

"I ain't never come palm-up to either one of you," he said.

Caleb shot a look in my direction that told me he was one more stray comment away from letting loose of his long-restrained frustration with Snoose Corcoran.

"Are you kidding me?" Caleb said, and spat a dollop of tobacco juice into the corner. "I'm surprised your paws ain't sunburned from all the daylight they've been exposed to at Ty Dawson's door."

Snoose's face turned red as he scrambled to push himself up off the floor.

"Relax," I said. "I've got a business proposition for you, Snoose."

"You'd be wise to hear Ty out," Caleb said. "If it was up to me, I'd let you sleep in this trailer 'til Christmas."

"Your nephew, Tom, is becoming a damned fine hand," I said. "He's even heeling in the team roping event for the Diamond D tonight. I want you to come and watch him."

Snoose smoothed a hand across his thinning hair. He sat up straight and reached for the paper bag he had propped against the wall, but Caleb kicked it over before Snoose could get a hand on it. The fumes of low-shelf whiskey burned my eyes inside the overheated stillness.

"You sonofabitch!" Snoose bellowed at Caleb. "I don't recollect askin' you to be my goddamned sponsor."

"You been doing a grand bit of recollectin' for a man who's had his head stoved in as much as you have," Caleb said. "You're staring at your last good chance right this very second and you can't even see it. You'd best hold your tongue and listen."

"You gonna hear me out, Snoose?" I asked. "Give me an honest consideration?"

I could see it in the set of his jaw. When he had been a younger man he would have tried to take both Caleb and me right then and there.

"I'm too drunk to fight or lie," he said, rested his head against the wall, and closed his eyes. "I ain't got the energy no more."

I turned away and stepped down from the trailer, lit a cigarette, and waited in the fresh air as Caleb followed me out. The late afternoon sun was dipping low against the crenellated mountain ridge and elongated the shadows at our feet.

"I'm tired of seeing decent people lose," I said.

"You get to an age where you start to insert the past where the present oughta be," Caleb said. "Do it long enough, people think you're crazy, but you ain't. It's just self-defense."

I took a long, last drag and flicked the cigarette, watched it land in a shower of sparks and roll along the caliche before I moved back inside the trailer.

"Help me drag Snoose to our stable," I said. "I'll get some coffee in him."

CHAPTER THIRTY-ONE

The DAWN DID not break that morning, nor did it announce its arrival with any color at all; the day merely began.

The atmosphere was unusually quiet, my cowboys having raised more than a little ruckus once all the work had been done and after placing second in the team roping event that they had all but written off. As a result, I was more than a little surprised to see Tom Jenkins shamble out of the bunkhouse at such an early hour.

"You look like you're re-herding your own sheep, son," I called out.

The first shafts of pale sunlight cut between the tall pine boughs and the chatter of goldfinches drifted out of the forest shrubs.

"Just getting a head start on the day, sir," he said.

"Thought you might've earned a couple extra winks after your big win," I said, and offered him my hand in congratulations.

He shook it and his face broke into an uncertain grin, then he looped his thumbs through his belt loops and looked into the overgrowth.

"I don't like to air out my feelings too loudly," he said. "I don't want to jinx nothin'."

"Winning never feels quite like you think it's going to, does it?"

He dug a furrow in the loose pine needles with his boot heel and nodded.

"No, sir. It don't."

He shifted his weight and began to turn away.

"Beats the hell out of losing though," I said.

Tom Jenkins's face broke into a full smile that began with his eyes and slowly migrated across his entire face.

"Yes, sir. It certainly does do that."

THE CLOCK TOWER down the street from the office was chiming nine when I phoned Chris Rose at CID in Salem.

"I'm telling you, it was damned odd," I said. "Harper Emory seemed genuinely scared when he laid eyes on Spinell. He nearly threw a shoe trying to get away."

"Carl Spinell is a criminal," Rose said. "And a sack of shit."

"There was more to it than that."

"Nobody's gonna blunt no nails hammerin' into that man's intellect."

"Which man are you referring to?"

"Pick one," he said, then laughed, and I heard him take a bite of something; my guess was a jelly doughnut. "But I was talking about Harper Emory."

"Regardless," I said. "It struck me as odd."

"Maybe Emory ain't afraid of Carl Spinell. Maybe he's afraid of being seen talking to *you*."

I waited while I heard him leaf through the pages of what sounded like a sizable report.

"We got ballistics on the .38 used in the Doc Brawley murder," he said. "It matches one of the weapons you recovered off the dead shitweasels from your motel. We matched one of their knife blades to the postmortem stab wounds as well."

He paused for effect. Through the open window in my office I could hear the steel wheels of the Southern Pacific echo between the canyon walls as it slowly climbed the grade.

"Cort Scheer, the dead hepcat—the guy you called Duck-tail?" Rose said. "He has a sheet that includes acts of arson."

"And the fingerprints off the Polaroid?"

"Slow down, pard. Did you hear what I just told you?"

"Yes, I heard you," I said. "I'll take it to the DA."

"Why don't you sound pleased?"

"Because my suspects are already dead," I said. "And they can't tell us why they murdered Abel Brawley, torched the record store, or who it was that ended up smoking their worthless asses."

"Two of those matters are now concluded, Ty. I usually celebrate when I can close a case. Don't complicate your life."

I pressed the handset to my ear and picked up the phone housing from my desk, the wall cord snaking behind me as I carried it to where I could talk while I looked out the window.

"It isn't complicated," I said. "When the facts change, I'll change my mind."

I heard him sigh and shut the file he'd been reading from.

"I'll send this stuff over to you," he said.

"What about the Polaroid?"

"When did we last talk about that?" he asked. "Friday afternoon? It's only Monday morning, Ty. I told you these things take time."

"Either you reach out to the lab or I will," I said.

"I have cultivated a civilized and respectful relationship with them over the years. Don't you go screwing that up for me."

"I'm out of time, Chris. I can feel it."

"I'll call 'em and get back to you."

I SCANNED the files on my desk and found the handwritten notes I'd made while at the high school library regarding Galanis United. I dialed the company's Nevada number, let it ring a dozen times, but no answer. I broke the connection

and stepped into the break room to refill my coffee, then
dialed the number again and achieved the same result.

I tried to ignore the inchoate rage that I felt rising inside
my chest, and rifled through my Rolodex until I landed on
the card bearing the name and number for Ambervalia Corporation. I immediately recognized the west Texas accent of
the man who answered when I'd called before.

"Who is Galanis United?" I asked him.

"I don't know. A Greek soccer team?"

"Your firm does business with—"

"Am I speaking to the sheriff of that pissant town in
Oregon?"

I chose not to answer, silently enduring several seconds of
labored breathing from a man who had turned complacency
and lethargy into a career path. Whatever the true nature of
his relationship or responsibilities for Ambervalia was anybody's guess.

"You've got to stop calling this number. I'm serious," he
said. "Why don't you save yourself the long-distance charges
and pester that lawyer who works for us up in your neck of
the woods."

"I don't think I heard you correctly, bubba," I said.

"Let me try and come at this a different way: If that ass-
hole up there wants to answer your questions, I guess it's up
to him. Beyond that, you leave me out of it from now on, you
hearing me correctly now?"

"Give me his name, and I'll do my best."

"And nobody calls me 'bubba'."

"Just give me the name."

I could hear the man wheeze as he rifled through his
desk drawers.

"It's in here somewhere," he said. "Yankee name. Niles?
Nevin? Nelson . . ."

"Nolan?"

"Sounds about right."

"Nolan Brody?"

"Bull's-eye."

—∞∞∞—

I TURNED off the county two-lane, and sped across the long, narrow entry to Nolan Brody's estate, my rear tires sliding sideways on the crushed rock. Brody's MGB convertible was parked at an angle between the fountain and the front door of his house, and I skidded to a stop just short of his bumper. I leaped down from the cab and left my truck running, took the portico stairs two at a time.

I badged Brody's manservant and pushed past him as he cracked open the front door, and left him staring after me as I stalked down the hallway in search of his boss. I finally located Brody in a large study I had not been invited into on my previous visit.

Like the rest of the house, the room was expensively furnished, but more masculine in that it was paneled in burnished mahogany from the floor all the way to the cathedral ceilings more than twenty feet overhead, where exposed beams were upheld by hand-carved corbels fashioned into the images of cherubim. An antique billiard table occupied the center of the floor, midway between a leather sofa and club chair setup and the mirror-backed bar that spanned the entire width of the room. In a dwelling whose sole purpose was to serve as a stage prop, this room reeked not only of cigar smoke, but of a flagrant masculinity so impudently out of character it seemed like some sort of mockery.

Nolan Brody was leaning on the bar, a pool cue in one hand and a smoldering Panatela in the other, watching Carl Spinell line up a shot.

"Hello, Sheriff," Brody said. "I didn't hear the doorbell. Did Manring show you in?"

Spinell glanced at me from beneath heavy brows, then returned his focus to the cue ball without a word.

"I let myself in," I said.

Spinell tapped the cue ball and sunk the five off two cushions. He smirked as he slid around the side of the table to set up another shot.

"How very familiar of you," Brody said.

"Who is Ambervalia Corporation?" I asked.

"I don't know what you're talking about."

"How about Galanis United?"

"Never heard of them either."

Spinell snapped off another shot and came out of his crouch. I could see that he wasn't smirking anymore.

"That's all I needed from you," I said. "I'll see myself out."

"You won't stay for a game?"

Brody was doing his best to feign impassivity, but something flickered behind his eyes.

"Thanks just the same," I said. "But I only stopped by to see whether you'd lie straight to my face."

"You know, sometimes you can be a very difficult man to understand. I have no idea what to make of that statement."

"Try this one then, Nolan: You'd better hope the gallows burns down before I come back for you."

I COULD hear the tractor mowing the ryegrass in the North Pasture when I returned home that afternoon. The air smelled sweet and ripe with summer and freshly cut grama, and the magnolia tree was dropping its spent blossoms on an unfamiliar car parked in the drive.

I heard footsteps on the gravel as I gathered my belongings off the bench seat of my truck.

"Dad?" Cricket said. "I thought I heard someone in the driveway and I was hoping it was you."

"Where's your mom?"

"It's her volunteer day at the Thrift Shop."

Cricket's cheeks were flushed, and she kept glancing behind her, toward the back door to the mudroom that she'd left open.

"Whose car is that?" I asked. "Is everything okay?"

"I'm fine. It's Dawn's car."

"Dawn from the commune?"

"I found her sleeping in it right outside of our gates," she said. "She told me she pulled off the road by the dry wash and tried to hide it. She's really scared of something, but she won't tell me what it is."

I followed Cricket inside the house and found Dawn where she had wedged herself into the corner of our living room sofa. She was rocking slowly back and forth, arms encircling her knees, her bare feet drawn up tight beneath her. Her hair was wet, dampening the collar of a blouse that I recognized as my daughter's, and she smelled strongly of Cricket's shampoo. The girl's expression was a mask of complete desolation.

"I lied to you," Dawn said when she saw me come in.

"About the photos I showed you?"

She nodded.

"I knew Peter Troy. I called him 'Sweet Pete.' I think I might have even loved him once."

"We're talking about the victim from the fire?"

"I gave him the Saint Christopher necklace that caused the scar."

She turned her head toward the picture window that looked out over the office and corral.

"Those guys you showed me in those pictures," she said. "They did that to him."

"The bald one and the fifties greaser?"

She nodded.

"How do you know it was them?"

"I just do. They came around the shop a couple times and said things to me and the other girls."

I followed Dawn's empty gaze beyond the window. Caleb's horse was saddled, reins wrapped around the fence post, his lever-action Winchester tucked into a scabbard strapped along its withers. Predators had been picking off newborn calves over the past few days. When she turned her eyes back on me, they held equal parts fear and despondency.

"It started so beautiful out there," Dawn said. "When it all turned to shit, it happened so fast."

Cricket sat down beside her and gently laid a hand on her shoulder.

"I mean, if the people around town thought hippies could do all this horrible stuff," Dawn said, "what would the squares do to *me?* We all started thinking that way. Things were never the same again after the fire. It was like Deva just gave up."

She paused and closed her eyes. When she opened them again a few moments later, no words would come, though she tried, and she buried her face in the palms of her hands and wept.

"I wish you had said something to me, Dawn," I said.

Dawn dropped her hands from her face, watched the dust motes in the light from the window as she recovered her breath.

"Deva said he had it all in hand, but it was too late by then," she said. "They're going to come looking for me, you know."

"Deva Ravi?"

Something dark passed over her and she shook her head.

"Mac," she said. "Or Larry. Maybe even Aurora. I don't know. But if they find me, they're going to hurt me bad."

"Let my dad help you."

"You don't understand."

"Then tell it to me," I said. "All of it. Every detail. From the beginning. Can you do that?"

Dawn gauged me for several long seconds, then turned her eyes on Cricket. I saw her squeeze Dawn's hand again when she nodded her head.

I borrowed my daughter's cassette deck, and all three of us moved into the kitchen and seated ourselves at the breakfast table. Outside the window a scarlet hummingbird hovered beside the feeder and seemed to study our faces before darting away.

Cricket placed the tape deck at the center of the table and plugged in the mic. Dawn ran her tongue along her dry, cracked lips and stared at the machine.

"I'll get you a glass of water, and leave you with my dad," Cricket said, and stepped over to the sink.

"No, no," Dawn said. "Please stay."

I pressed the *Record* button and tested the sound.

"Can we begin with your legal name?" I asked.

"Mila Kinslow."

"My name is Sheriff Tyler Dawson of Meriwether County," I said. "The file reference for this interview is MC1803 stroke D. This is side one."

Dawn reached across the table, laid her palm on my daughter's wrist, and shut her eyes.

"Whenever you're ready, Mila," I said, using this unaccustomed name for the first time. I suspected that I would always think of her as Dawn. "Take your time."

Dawn's eyelids began to flutter, as though she was dreaming. She drew a deep breath and began to speak.

"I remember spending my sweet sixteenth birthday watching the lights flash on the Ferris wheel far below us, and the long line of cars idling outside those gates," she began softly. Her tone glided into its native southern cadence and her posture and affect became almost childlike. "We was sitting on the porch of the old house, Momma and me . . ."

CHAPTER THIRTY-TWO

IT WAS LATE afternoon by the time Dawn completed her story, but the summer sun still rode high over the mountains. I got up to stretch my legs and stepped out on the porch. Caleb was just returning from his varmint hunt, pushing his horse across the runnel in the direction of the paddock.

Cricket and Dawn stepped out to join me a minute later carrying three cold bottles of root beer. Cricket stretched out in the willow chair, and Dawn cocked a hip against the wood rail, her face half-shadowed from the sunshine, and offered me the extra bottle she'd brought outdoors with her.

"Maybe your county's biggest problem isn't the way we look and live and dress," Dawn said to me. "You'd think y'all would get tired of making petty judgments."

I was about to respond when I saw the crimson blossom appear on the white blouse she was wearing, materializing out of nowhere a few inches below her collar bone. The piercing snap echo of the rifle shot followed a split second later.

CHAPTER THIRTY-THREE

CALEB WHEELER galloped at top speed toward my house the moment he heard the weapon's report. His boots were on the ground before the horse had skidded to a stop.

"This girl's been hit," I said.

Cricket sat speechless, unable to process what she had just witnessed.

"I've got this," Caleb said. "Take my horse."

The cough and sputter of a dirt bike came from somewhere beyond the woodshed near the tree line. The rider had choked it out in his panic to get it kick started, and the engine wouldn't catch.

"The keys are in the Jeep," I said to Caleb. "She can't wait for an ambulance."

Caleb wadded his neckerchief into a tight ball and applied pressure to Dawn's wound. It was percolating blood the color of black cherry, keeping time with her weakening pulse.

"Cricket," I said. "Call Jordan and have him meet me at the Rainbow Ranch. Tell Griffin to get over to the Emory place."

She gazed back at me with the empty-eyed expression of a forest animal.

"Cricket!" I shouted, and she returned to the moment.

I jumped down the stairs and leapt into the saddle, reined Caleb's mare in the direction where the motorcycle had just sprung to life. I rounded the far corner of the barn and vaulted the narrow creek where the water ran shallow and green along the edge of the pine forest. I knew he would be heading toward the dirt road that divided into a V about three-quarters of a mile farther up the track. One direction led to the county access, the other to Snoose Corcoran's ranch. As I drew closer I could see the dust the rider was kicking up, losing traction in the loose gravel. He threw a glance over his shoulder as his rear tire slid out beneath him, causing him to fishtail wildly as he neared the split in the road. His front wheel slammed into a rut and whiplashed the rider's head, drawing blood against the barrel of the rifle he had slung across his back.

I spurred the horse and gained enough ground that I was able to come up on his right flank, block and haze the bike toward the leftward road, as I would an Orejana maverick. He saw me in his peripheral vision, downshifted, and tacked away, toward the Corcoran place.

The knobbed tires of the dirt bike dislodged stones that pelted the horse and me like birdshot as we drew within ten yards of him. I groped along the pommel for the Winchester when I saw the bike and rider disappear into a cloud of sand and grit that resembled a small explosion. The engine screamed like a gut-shot boar and I had only a fraction of a second to recognize what had happened as I closed the gap between us. I spurred the horse into a last-moment jump over the wreckage, and skidded to a halt on the hardpan. I slid the lever-action from the scabbard as I hurdled from the saddle, sighted down the barrel as I stepped through the roiling dust, and came up on what remained of the motorcycle and its rider.

Before leaving his ranch for his weekend at the county fair, Snoose Corcoran had blocked his access road with a length of industrial gauge wire rope, and strung it with a No Trespassing sign. The rider had obviously not seen it in his haste, and the cable had neatly severed him in half just below the ribcage. His mouth was moving like a fish that had been left to die on a pier plank, his walleyed stare only beginning to exhibit recognition as to what had happened to him. His entrails sagged out of his torso, and the air smelled of engine oil, blood, and excrement.

I had no radio or other means of communication, and Corcoran's house was a good half mile farther up the road. Even had I been inclined, there was no chance that I could summon help in time. I offered not a single prayer as I stood and waited there beside him, looking down into his crooked eyes while he stared back into mine. Neither of us made a sound as he watched me watch him die.

———

SNOOSE CORCORAN drove out to investigate what had happened. I left him there to look after the body and to await the coroner's arrival while I galloped back to the Diamond D to swap Caleb's horse for my truck.

There was nobody at my ranch when I got there, and I hoped that Jordan Powell had received the message I had asked Cricket to pass along to him. My tires spun as I crossed the dry bottom of the runoff gulch and accelerated toward the county road.

I have spent the vast majority of my life out of doors. As both a rancher and a soldier, reading the terrain and environment has made the difference between survival and disaster.

There is such a condition as *too quiet*; when the ordinary sounds of birdcalls or the stir of wildlife along the forest floor, and the susurrus of insects suddenly fall silent, subsumed by wind and the rustle of tree branches. There is a dissonance inside of these silences that sets my nerve endings on edge, a disquieting outrider passing beyond the fringe of firelight.

That is how it was as I climbed out of the Bronco and swept my eyes across the empty landscape of the Rainbow Ranch. It seemed that even the breeze tendered no sound as

I touched my fingertips to the Colt Peacemaker strapped to my side, taking comfort in the texture of the bone-handled grip. I lifted the Winchester rifle off the back seat and racked a shell into the chamber. The mechanical rasp of the lever-action echoed inside the oppressive stillness, and I was overcome with the sensation of being too hot and too cold all at once.

I stepped toward the main residence, pressed my back to the wall, and took a defensive posture as I crept sideways toward the front door. I waited outside for nearly a minute, listening for any sign of occupancy, but heard nothing. I wedged it open with the toe of my boot and leveled the barrel of the Winchester into the breach. The fragrance of sandalwood still lingered in the air, but it was clear that the building had been vacated.

I made a reconnaissance of the dining hall and the Deva's residence next door, and found each deserted. There was no sound or evidence of livestock, and discarded hand tools and farm implements lay where they had been last used, as though the occupants had been plucked out of their daily routines and dematerialized.

─────

I DISCOVERED the first two bodies inside a surplus army tent near the communal bonfire pit. A girl I judged to be in her early twenties lay naked, sprawled across a tick mattress, a perfect bloodless circle blown through the center of her forehead. Her auburn hair was fanned across a similarly naked man a few years older than she. Two high-caliber projectiles had defaced a tattoo on his chest that once had borne the winged image of an air force unit mascot.

I located three more dead girls inside a spring house near the edge of the pine forest. It appeared as though these three had been herded there, to huddle in a corner where they held fast to one another even in death. Each one had been executed with a single round to her heart.

I stepped out from the stench of death and stillness and humidity inside the spring house, blinking hard against the late afternoon light. I leaped the width of the stream and angled toward the large metal building at the far edge of the property that Dawn had variously described to me as either an airplane hangar or mechanic's shed. The building had been off limits to us when we had toured the commune with the high school, so I clung to the edge of the tree line as I approached it, knowing nothing of the layout, or whether the murderer of all these kids was holed-up inside.

A line of sweat slid down my forehead and burned my eyes. I brushed it away with a shirtsleeve and wondered where the hell Jordan Powell was, or if Cricket, in the haze of her shock, had simply failed to phone him. I had no time to waste, so I was left with no alternative but to move in on the hangar alone. I drew a deep lungful of air and moved out from the shadows of the old growth and made a beeline for the nearest corner of the shed.

I pressed my back against the warm steel of the building, stilled my breathing while I listened for signs of activity within. I thought I heard noises from somewhere inside, but I wasn't certain, so I inched my way forward, hesitating every few steps to take advantage of whatever cover I could find.

I could hear voices more clearly then, one male and one female. I couldn't make out the words, but their tone was unmistakably agitated, rushed, and short of breath from some sort of manual labor. I waited several seconds, then took a chance and peered around the corner, trying to take in the entire picture in one brief glance.

What I did manage to see was a small plane, a four-seat Cessna Skyhawk, parked at an angle facing outward through the sliding doors in the direction of the cut-grass landing strip, its tail section lost in shadow where it rested on the floor of the hangar. In the dimness of the yawning span of beams and trusses, I could make out Deva Ravi and Aurora manhandling what looked to me like ammo boxes and canvas ditty bags into the rear hold of the aircraft. The rearmost portion of the building was cast so deep in shadow I could not distinguish anything more detailed than the vague shapes of motor vehicles in various states of repair, and a workbench that was littered with automotive tools. I had risked exposure long enough, so I withdrew, cocked my rifle, and made one final inventory of my limited options.

I gave myself a mental ten-count, then swung around the corner of the building and planted my feet wide, pressed my cheek against the stock of the .30-.30 and locked the sight onto the center of Deva Ravi's chest. I kept Aurora in my peripheral vision and waited a beat before I spoke.

"Your friend Larry won't be joining you," I said.

The reverberation of my voice echoed in the rafters and caught Deva and the girl midstride, arms strained by their loads. They dropped the boxes they had been carrying and faced me, chests heaving, neither of them in possession of a weapon that I could see.

I had no way of knowing what was about to happen in the next few moments, but it would play out, unbidden, in my subconscious for a long, long time to come.

Years ago, as the captain in charge of an MP unit in Korea, I had been ordered to arrest a young second lieutenant who was believed to have committed atrocities during a night raid on a tiny rural village. He surrendered to me without resistance, but awaited his court-martial in a state of moral antipathy so profound that it might as well have been tattooed on his skin. I watched him disappear from the inside out as he paced his cell each day, the feral illumination behind his eyes retreating into preterition. I saw him for the last time shortly before they shipped him to the states for incarceration. I cannot say with any certainty that he had gone insane, only that he had become hollow. He gave no outward sign of guilt or regret, or even malevolence; what remained was, simply an empty hole where a human being once had been.

This was the same expression that I read on the face of the man who stepped out from behind the tail section of the Cessna, an army issue Colt 1911 automatic clutched inside his fists.

"Put the rifle down," he called out to me.

No emotion resonated in his tone or bearing, no recognizable content whatsoever.

"Let me guess," I said. "You're the one they call Mac Nasty."

"You must have shit for brains coming out here by yourself, Sheriff."

He sidestepped from the shadows into the open, never once taking his sights off me, and took a position behind Aurora. I glanced at Deva Ravi, who feigned an expression of neutrality that was meant to mask the depth of his humiliation at having somehow surrendered his authority to this man. Deva had speculated on his version of the great mysteries and come up orphaned and bereft.

"You'll leave here in cuffs, or you'll leave in a bag," I said. "Your choice."

"I don't think so, Sheriff. Put down your rifle, or I will empty this girl's brain on her blouse."

He took a step forward and angled the barrel of his weapon only inches from the side of Aurora's skull.

"Pig," she said.

"Shut the fuck up," he said to Aurora. To me, he said, "Last chance. Put it on the ground."

The evening shadows vanished all at once as the sun slid behind the mountain. The sheen of Aurora's perspiration glowed gold as she dampened her dry lips and stared at me with hatred and contempt.

He took one step closer to the girl.

I gently thumbed the hammer and uncocked my Winchester, crouched very slowly so I could place it on the floor beside my feet. I splayed my open hands at waist height in a demonstration of compliance, and I watched his gaze slip off my face and land upon the Colt Peacemaker tucked inside the holster at my hip.

He pressed his lips together and something rippled through his eyes. That singular, impossible instant expanded into a slow-motion photogravure as I watched the rough skin on his knuckles turn white against the grip of his automatic. The roar of his .45 resonated like thunder, the muzzle flash a momentary blinding light, as the side of Aurora's head disappeared inside a puff of pinkish haze. He never took his eyes off me.

"That one's on you," he said.

His pupils had reduced to pinpricks in the center of his irises, and he angled the pistol on me then.

"Do you hear that?" Deva asked.

Deva cocked his head upward and listened. I heard it too. "A car's coming."

The man with the automatic kept his gaze locked on me, but I was well aware that human nature can be a sonofabitch, as predictable as it is insistent. I sharpened my senses and waited for that clear, inevitable moment when I knew his attention would instinctively shift, when his eyes would cut away from me—if only for a fraction of a second—to visually confirm the auditory message that his ears were sending him.

Tick.

The muscles of his jaw distended as he clenched his teeth, and his pulse throbbed inside the vein that stood out on his temple.

Tick.

The drone of the auto engine drew nearer, flared briefly, and went silent. A car door opened then slammed shut.

Tick.

His eyes flicked sideways, toward the intrusion.

The Colt Peacemaker cleared my holster before he had time to process what was happening, and the first of my 200 grain rounds shattered the bone and sinew of his elbow and drove through his torso. Reflexively his grip constricted inside the automatic's trigger guard, and he squeezed off a round that split the air so close to me that I could feel its heat. His knees began to buckle, but he held fast to his weapon, discharging two, three wild shots in succession as I hit him with two more in the chest. The force of impact lifted him off his feet and I heard the hollow thud of his skull grazing the stabilizer as he fell to the concrete.

The hangar seemed like a vacuum in the aftermath, the atmosphere inside heavy with silver smoke and the odor of spent powder. I moved swiftly toward Deva Ravi, keeping him in the Peacemaker's sights as he lay curled up in a ball on the concrete floor with his head wrapped in his arms.

Jordan Powell breached the building with his service weapon outstretched before him in a perfect Weaver stance. He sighted down the barrel of his revolver as he swept the scene, slowly backing in my direction.

"You all right?" he called out over his shoulder.

"I'm good."

I dragged Deva Ravi off his belly and onto his knees, then patted him down for weapons.

Powell made a quick pass through the recesses of the room, clearing it, then checked Aurora and the dead pilot for any sign of a pulse.

"Sweet Jesus," Jordan said.

"Where the hell have you been?" I asked.

"I was all the way up in Lewiston. Got here as fast as I could," he said, stepping around the back end of the plane. "Looks like they was fixin' to change the tail numbers."

Deva Ravi winced as I cuffed him and dragged him to his feet. He glanced outside, through the opening between the doors, across the landing field where the wind dented the dry grass.

"You think the world is one thing, but it turns out to be something else," Deva said. I was unclear as to whether he was talking to me or to himself.

"You speaking in some sort of code?"

"That guy would have killed both Aurora and me," Deva said to me. "You know that, right?"

"You're not the victim here," I said. "You forgot to leave yourself a way out. The con's over, Willie."

Deva dipped his chin and glared at me over the rims of his dark glasses, eyes twitching in their sockets.

"I'm not the grifter, Sheriff," he said.

"You already know who this fella is?" Jordan asked.

"I believe I do," I said. "I take it Captain Rose phoned you about the fingerprints while I was out?"

Powell nodded absently, removed the sunglasses from Deva's face and studied his features.

"I don't see it," Powell said.

"Never was much of a family resemblance as I recall," I said. "Of course, this one was off the grid for a few years before he ever came back home."

"Still . . ."

"William Barker Emory," I said. "You are under arrest for more shit than I can possibly recite."

—⚬⚭⚬—

I TOLD Powell to lock the former Deva Ravi in one of our holding cells until I had time to interview him. Once that was done, he was to get in touch with CID in Salem and send a team of criminalists out to the Rainbow Ranch to process the massacre.

I watched the taillights of Powell's vehicle disappear around the corner beyond the gates, and ducked my head inside my Bronco and keyed the radio. I had expected it to function better out in the open country than it did practically anywhere else in Meriwether County, but I was mistaken. After several failed attempts to raise Sam Griffin for a status report, I threw off and lit a cigarette. I had no fondness for standing idle, particularly when I had a deputy operating solo in a situation that had apparently jumped the rails, but I couldn't leave this scene unattended without putting the ultimate prosecution of the case at risk.

The sky was violet with afterglow as I leaned against the fender and felt my hands begin to tremble from adrenaline release. I drew deeply and exhaled, watching the smoke tear away on the breeze. Somewhere beyond my sightline I could hear the ginning of what had once been a simple windmill, but from here on out would function as a cenotaph.

Half an hour later, I turned the whole place over to the crime scene guys from the State Police and sped out past the shattered chain gate of the Rainbow Ranch.

CHAPTER THIRTY-FOUR

ALL THE LIGHTS had been switched on inside the Emory household, and it glowed like a navigational beacon standing alone against the black expanse of moonless rangeland. The jangle of the bellwether and the bleating of the flock echoed from the pasture as I switched off the ignition and climbed out of the Bronco.

Bryan Emory was seated on the porch stairs, his eyes rimmed in red as he watched me unfasten the garden gate latch and pass through. Sam Griffin stood beside the front door just a few feet away, his thumbs tucked in the belt loops of his jeans.

"How'd you smash up your truck?" Bryan asked me.

He seemed completely disconnected, his voice a hoarse and faded monotone, the question itself a non sequitur.

"Busting through your neighbor's gate," I said. "What's happening here?"

"You need to step inside with me, Sheriff," Griffin said.

Bryan made no attempt to accompany Griffin and me, but stood and moved into the garden instead. He hesitated for a moment, stooped, and picked up a handful of gravel and began pitching the stones one at a time into the shadows.

Once inside, I saw Harlan Emory's wife sitting in a chair beside a gooseneck lamp in the corner of the parlor. She was stitching a floral pattern onto a needlepoint canvas, her features as impassive and opaque as a department store

264

mannequin. Her brow was furrowed in concentration and it sounded as though she was humming some sort of tune under her breath. She glanced up momentarily, seemed to register my presence without alarm, and returned her attention to her work.

"Follow me," Sam said, and moved down a long hallway whose walls were decorated with early century samplers and old family portraits framed in bubble glass. A door stood wide open at the far end of the hall, and Sam halted just short of the threshold, gesturing for me to enter first.

Harper Emory's eyes were thrown open wide, his face locked in a mask of shock and fury as he sagged sideways in his desk chair, his blood stippling the draperies that had been drawn across his office window. He clutched a .38-caliber Smith & Wesson revolver in his right hand, the top drawer of his desk yanked off its sliders, as though he had withdrawn the weapon in a rush. I leaned in close and examined the cylinder, saw that there were no bullets chambered there.

"His gun's not loaded," I said.

"No, it isn't," Sam said. "But this guy's was."

He inclined his chin toward the body of Carl Spinell sprawled on the floor beside the desk, his clothing soaked through from the discharge of buckshot that had completely pulverized his center mass. A pump-action ten-gauge shotgun was propped neatly beside the office door. Spinell's pistol lay some distance away.

"I already notified the staties," Sam said.

I nodded.

"This'll be their third scene today in Meriwether County," I said.

"Say that again," Sam said, but I ignored it.

"What the hell happened here?" I asked.

"Better if you hear it from the kid."

Outside, Bryan Emory had moved to one of the chairs beside a small table at the far end of the porch, the same spot where I had first been introduced to Carl Spinell.

Bryan's face was in silhouette in the light from the house, and I could see the resemblance to his mother.

"I heard them shouting in Dad's office," Bryan said.

His chin rested inside the palm of his hand, his elbow propped on the table.

"What were they shouting about?"

His eyes locked on mine for a long moment before he spoke.

"Your name came up," he said.

"They were shouting about me?"

"From what I could tell, Mr. Spinell was warning my father not to speak to you. Threatening him."

Sam pulled out a chair opposite Bryan and folded himself into it. He drew a breath and reached across the table and patted the boy on the forearm.

"Tell the sheriff what you told me," Sam prompted.

Bryan ran the back of his hand across his lips.

"It's my fault," he said finally. "I knew she was going to do it."

His voice had dropped into a whisper.

"Your mother? Going to do what?"

"She was afraid that Dad was going to hurt her again. That he might hurt both of us again."

Upstairs, in the frame of an open casement window, a curtain twisted on the wind. Bryan turned and studied it for a long moment then leaned back in his chair.

"She took all the ammunition out of my father's guns," he said. "I knew what had happened in his office as soon as I heard the shot. He never had a chance against that man. He couldn't defend himself."

"So you shot Carl Spinell?"

Bryan Emory nodded.

"With my bird gun."

"Spinell would have come after you and your mother next," I said.

"It was my fault," he said again.

"It was an act of self-defense, Bryan."

He looked at me and I could tell that he wished he could believe me but could not.

"I was talking about unloading my dad's guns," he said.

"I know you were," I said. "So was I."

"Why did he make her do that? Why did he have to be such a bastard sometimes?"

"Betrayal never comes from your enemies, son."

—⁂—

I STOPPED at the office before going home that night. Jordan Powell had been dozing upstairs, his boots propped on the desk, while William Emory paced inside his ten-by-ten jail cell. Powell pushed the brim of his hat off the bridge of his nose when he recognized the sound of my footfalls on the landing.

"Everything okay?" I asked.

"Rowan Boyle brought some chow over from the diner a bit ago."

I stood outside the flatiron bars of the holding cell, wondering how a man like Harper Emory and his family had ended up this way.

"Don't leave him by himself," I said to Powell. "Make sure somebody's with him at all times."

"Yes, sir."

"Give me your belt," I said to the man inside the cage. "And your shoes."

He shook his head and blinked at me, his face uninhabited by emotion.

It is said that the human soul possesses weight, and that its loss can be measured scientifically at the moment of a person's death. I don't know whether that is true or not, but if it is, I could see in his expression that the man who had once referred to himself as Deva Ravi had already surrendered his, and I wondered whether redemption could exist for such a man as this.

"I'm not going to kill myself," he said.

I did not reply, only waited for him to do as I had asked of him. He stepped toward the door where I was standing, handed me his belt, and kicked his shoes across the floor to me between the bars.

"No," I said finally. "You're probably right. People like you don't kill themselves. It's the ones who place their trust in you who wind up dead."

CHAPTER THIRTY-FIVE

WILLIAM BARKER EMORY sat cross-legged on his fold-down cot, staring beyond his cell bars out the wire-glass window as he ignored me and the questions I was asking. I had relieved Jordan Powell at about five o'clock that morning and sent him home. I was not expecting any other visitors for at least a couple hours.

"Your father's dead, Willie—"

"I told you to stop calling me that."

"Your brother could have been shot trying to protect your mom. He's a teenage kid, and had to kill a man. Had to shoot him in the back. Bryan has to live with that."

He shrugged.

"The universe thrusts life upon us," he said. "Everybody has to grow up sometime."

"Blood doesn't always wash off, Willie."

I admit to having grown frustrated by his ongoing display of hippie insouciance and cynicism, but he had inadvertently tapped into my well of rage with that remark.

"I think you've let other people pay your dues long enough," I said. "It's time for you and me to take a walk."

I unlocked the cell door and stepped inside with him. I dragged him off his bed, cuffed his hands behind his back, and frog marched him across the room to the landing at the top of the steep set of stairs that led down to the main office.

"Let me explain something to you, William: We're all alone in this building right now. Nod if you understand what I'm telling you."

He looked blankly at me for a moment, then reclaimed the middle distance with his focus.

"I'm giving you one final chance to speak to me like a man," I said. "Or you are very likely to fall victim to one hell of a gravity storm."

"WE HAD always had a plan to bug-out if we had to," William "Deva" Emory said. "It was inevitable at some point, man."

We were entering our third hour together in the interrogation room downstairs, the tape reels spinning as I listened to him describe his return to Meriwether County for ten days' leave from the army, in between completion of his training and his scheduled combat deployment to Vietnam back in the spring of 1967. His father, Harper Emory, had always considered himself both a simple farmer and a patriotic man, but the incompetence and ignorance of the politicians in their execution of this Indochinese boondoggle had driven him to conclude that he was no longer willing to offer up the life of his eldest son to the insatiable gods of war.

Not long before young William's return, Harper had met the man who held the ground lease on the property next door. The man's name was Minas Galanis, and the content of their conversation would end up shaping events that ultimately delivered a violent end to the lives of more than a dozen people in my county almost a decade later.

In early January of '67, Minas Galanis received the notification that no military family wishes to accept. He had lost a son to sniper fire beside the Thi Tinh River while on a mission code-named Operation Cedar Falls. By spring that same year, the grief suffered by Minas Galanis had metastasized to seething hatred for all things concerning Vietnam, and he made those feelings known to Harper Emory in no uncertain terms.

The two men hatched a plan to use the Galanis property as a covert staging area for the transport of deserters from the US military to safety in Canada, where desertion—a crime whose punishments ranged from years of federal prison time all the way to execution—was not an extraditable offense. The two men saw their cause as noble, a waypoint on an Underground Railroad of sorts for young Americans unwilling to engage in combat overseas.

The future Deva Ravi was spirited away to the Yukon Territory where he labored for nearly two years, first as a lumberjack and later as an oil field roughneck. The army's investigation had been cursory at best, and since William hadn't deserted as a consequence of a separate crime, the case was placed on a permanent back burner.

Harper Emory fabricated the fiction that his son had been killed while serving overseas to dispel any local curiosity regarding his eldest son's whereabouts. For his part, William used the absence to reinvent himself. By the time he returned to Meriwether County in 1969, no one was looking for him, and even if they had been, nobody ever would have recognized him. The transformation, both physical and otherwise, was complete.

The unforeseeable and unintended consequences, though, had fallen first on William's mother, who had always been somewhat fragile and deemed to be a weak link in the scheme. Harper Emory believed that she could never have been trusted with the truth about her son, and the fiction of his death shattered her heart, her spirit, and finally her sanity.

"So we always had a bug-out plan," William said. "How was I supposed to know that Mac and Larry would go apeshit?"

"It escaped your notice that your people referred to them as 'Mac Nasty' and 'Scary Larry'?"

"Mac used to be a recon pilot. They were my mechanics, man. We had to have facilities for the aircraft, you know, to get them in and out and refueled quick."

"You complicated your own universe by about a thousandfold," I said. "You stacked up at least five murders, and that's just at the Rainbow Ranch."

"I didn't have anything to do with that. We were just supposed to split."

"Not buying it, bud," I said. "You'd think that after six years faking your own divinity, you'd be a better actor."

He laid his head down on the table and looked at his reflection in the two-way mirror.

"Let's go through it again," I said.

"Cut me a fucking break, man."

"This time, let's start with you telling me why—after everything you set up—your father dropped a dime on you, and raised such a public commotion about the commune."

———

IT TOOK me three days to follow the threads of the story William Emory eventually laid out. Half of that time had been spent in Portland, where Bill Kiefer helped me slog through the tall weeds, through the years' worth of court filings and legal minutiae, in order to stitch the whole scheme together. By the time I returned home to Meridian, I had collected the evidence I needed to make one more arrest.

A blade of silver sun shone through a rent in the cloud cover the morning Sam Griffin and I drove to the home of Nolan Brody. We spoke very little on the way up the valley, each of us contemplating avarice, and that its nature knows neither social nor geographical boundaries. It is endemic in the psychological makeup of certain people, like the carriers of a rogue gene.

Sam Griffin stood beside me on Brody's landing, the palm of his hand resting on the grip of his sidearm as we waited for the butler to respond to the doorbell.

"May I help you?" he asked as he pulled open the door.

"You might want to start collecting your references," I said as I brushed past him and edged toward Brody's study.

Nolan was seated at his desk, scribbling notes on a legal pad, as I stepped in. He startled from his work, blinked uncomprehendingly for a moment before his features hardened into an expression of insolence and antipathy.

It was an expression I had witnessed often, most recently when he spoke about the need to extricate the seasonal sundowners and roustabouts who sometimes gathered beyond the far edge of town, near the old grain silos and the disused railroad spur. In the late afternoons, they would come together in small groups of three, four, or five, smoking cigarettes and passing pint bottles of cheap liquor, making jokes about the disasters they had brought upon themselves as they stood beside a flaming oil barrel, their skin shining with alcohol and perspiration and regrets that had no external origin. To Nolan Brody, these men were unworthy of forbearance or empathy, the cramped travel trailer that they shared, thick with trapped heat and body odor, nothing more than an eyesore and a public nuisance.

His gaze moved from my face and landed on Sam.

"Oh, good," he deadpanned. "*The Mod Squad* has arrived."

"You missed your opportunity to skip town," I said.

Brody slid the cap onto his fountain pen and placed it on the desk blotter.

"Why would I do that?"

"William Emory gave you up on your extortion scheme."

One corner of his mouth notched upward into the pretense of a smile.

"I have no idea who you're talking about," he said.

"You pissed your shirttails this time, Nolan."

"Forty percent of a watermelon is better than 100 percent of a grape."

"Except that it wasn't your melon patch," Sam said.

We cuffed and stuffed Nolan Brody into the back seat of Sam Griffin's cruiser and booked him in at the Meridian substation. Jordan Powell had transported William Emory to county lockup, so that I could have a few hours alone with Brody. I wanted him to know what he was facing.

I guided Brody into the interview room, unhooked his cuffs, and parked him in the same chair that had been occupied by the former Deva Ravi only seventy-two hours before. Sam Griffin followed Brody and me inside, closed the door behind him, and remained standing in the corner of the room, arms crossed on his chest.

"I want a lawyer," were the first words out of Brody's mouth once he was inside.

"In a minute," I said. "You won't need a lawyer to help you hear what I have to say to you."

I recited the basic architecture of what I had uncovered, how Nolan Brody had represented both sides of the real estate transaction between Ambervalia Corporation and Harper Emory in the lease of a portion of its holdings to Emory, and had done exactly the same thing in a similar transaction between Ambervalia and Galanis United on the property next door.

"That's not illegal," Brody said.

"No, it's not," I said.

However, what Brody did after that traversed the line between piss-poor ethical behavior and outright fraud. As the owner of the property, Ambervalia paid for a geological survey, which was intended to identify potential water aquifers, and to take soil samples to determine mineral content. As Ambervalia's attorney, Nolan Brody was to oversee this due-diligence operation.

When the geological report came back, however, it became clear that while water might be scarce, there was an unusually high concentration of rare earth metals in the soil samples. A little research on Nolan Brody's part revealed that despite the name, rare earth metals are not particularly rare. What *was* rare, however, was that these materials are usually widely dispersed and as a result, not economically exploitable; such was not the case on the Ambervalia holdings. At well over one thousand acres combined, the potential value of the property as a mining operation was staggering.

"I want a lawyer," Brody said again.

He cleared his throat and threw a glance toward the door.

"Try to relax, Nolan. We're just two guys talking."

Recognizing his opportunity, Brody bribed the geological engineer to omit certain facts regarding the rare earth minerals from his report before sending it along to Ambervalia. Meanwhile, Nolan Brody was taking steps to purchase the entire parcel from Ambervalia. Ambervalia politely refused his overture and moved forward with the leases to both Harper Emory and Galanis United.

But Nolan Brody was not about to simply give up and walk away. Because Brody had acted as legal counsel to all three parties, he believed himself to be acutely aware of each of their motivations, desires, and weaknesses. Further, he had no reservations about using that knowledge to his advantage. He made separate offers to Harper Emory and Galanis United to acquire their leasehold interests, but was rebuffed by both of them as well. In his mounting frustration, he made a second, considerably higher, offer to Ambervalia, but was again turned down.

"Do you ever miss the army, Dawson?" Brody interrupted.

He tilted back his head and lost himself inside the blue light of the ceiling fixtures for a moment.

"No," I said.

"You don't ever miss the order? The organization? The regimentation?"

"Never."

I waited for the fulgid glow to retreat from his features before I let him hear the rest of what I knew.

Infuriated by the rejections from Ambervalia, Harper Emory, and Galanis, Brody saw no choice but to foment discontent among the parties. The way he saw it, if he were able to inflame animosities among them, he could not only motivate the sale—in the extreme, it might even void the lease terms outright—at the very least, it would drive down Brody's purchase price.

He went to Harper Emory and strongly suggested that the commune that shared his property line represented a serious public threat, and that something should be done to throw them off. Harper and Galanis, of course, had an undisclosed agenda of their own, and Emory refused to act, which infuriated Nolan Brody all the more.

But Brody still had contacts in the JAG corps, and it didn't take much digging to discover that William Emory had not actually been killed in combat, but was listed as a deserter with intent to avoid hazardous duty. Though Brody had no proof of, nor did he genuinely believe, that there was any real connection between Harper Emory and the Rainbow Ranch, the threat to publicize the truth about his AWOL son had proved to be the only leverage he required.

In fact, I suspected that Nolan Brody was even more surprised than I when he learned who Deva Ravi was. I was proven to be correct when I saw the look on Brody's face after I told him.

"Lawyer," Brody said.

He leaned into the empty space before him, hunched his shoulders, and contemplated the floor tiles.

"I'm not finished yet," I said.

Facing the threat of the initiation of a renewed military investigation into the whereabouts of his son, Harper Emory acquiesced to Brody's blackmail, and faked a claim against the commune. Secretly and separately, and unbeknownst to Brody, Harper was encouraging his son to close up shop, explaining that the risk simply wasn't worth it anymore. But William was resistant, a true believer. To make matters worse, he had lost control of Mac and Larry. Which is when Brody grew impatient, with not only Harper Emory, but with the county sheriff as well, and proceeded to make two critical mistakes.

First, Brody brought in Carl Spinell to muscle both Harper and the Rainbow Ranch; and second, he allowed Spinell to hire two sadistic flunkies who subsequently jumped the tracks and committed not only vandalism on the hippies' sandwich shop and an act of first-degree arson on the record store, but perpetrated the vicious murder of Doc Brawley in the furtherance of Brody's scheme.

"You had Doc Brawley slaughtered just to set up Deva Ravi. Was that your idea, or did Carl Spinell improvise on your behalf?"

"Are you finished?" Brody asked.

He turned sideways in his chair and wouldn't meet my eyes as he removed a stick of gum from his pocket.

"For the time being," I said.

"I want my lawyer."

Thirty minutes later, Sam Griffin and Nolan Brody were on their way to the Salem lockup, where I knew that Captain Rose could keep an eye on Brody while he was in their custody. I didn't kid myself, however;. I knew Brody wouldn't remain inside for long. Turns out, it was even shorter than I had expected.

By sunset that same day, a judge released him on a seven-figure bond.

Five days after that, US Border Patrol bagged Brody on a fugitive warrant when he broke the terms of his bond, crossed state lines, and tried to enter Mexico at the San Ysidro border. He was wearing a fake mustache, theatrical makeup, and a ball cap at the time. That was the mug shot that ran in the Meriwether County newspaper that week.

I had that issue framed.

It hangs beside the door that leads into the interrogation room.

CHAPTER THIRTY-SIX

THE QUALITY OF the sunlight had begun to soften and the nascent signs of autumn were showing in the trees. The ryegrass had turned green again after the heat wave finally broke and the first decent rain we'd had since early spring fell across the lowland.

I was savoring an ice cold stubby of Olympia, sitting on the porch rail and studying a hawk feather that the wind had blown across the gallery when I heard Caleb Wheeler hollering at one of the cowboys in the workshop behind the barn. I could tell that he was warming to a double-barrel rant.

"How many times do I haveta tell you to leave this stuff alone?" Caleb shouted. "I'm goddamn tired of fixin' things."

"I only moved a few odds and ends around."

I recognized the second voice belonged to Taj Caldwell, who still had not fully recovered his standing after nearly two months of contrition. Caleb had been furious with Caldwell ever since his disappearing act before the rodeo.

"Well, cut it out!" Caleb said.

It went quiet for several seconds, and I thought the show might already be over, but I was wrong. Caleb was just gathering his steam.

"You see this thing on the peg board?" Caleb hollered.

"Yes, sir."

"Leave it alone."

"Okay."

"You see this deal hanging on the wall?"

"Yes."

"Leave it the hell alone too."

"I think I got it, Boss."

"You see this stray stuff on the workbench?"

I assume Taj Caldwell nodded.

"What do you think you should do with it?" Caleb asked.

"Leave it alone?"

"That's right. You leave it all the fuck alone!"

I was about to step back inside when I heard Tom Jenkins come around the corner of the house. He was wearing a clean snap-button shirt and pressed jeans, and a pair of brand new Dan Post D toes, his white straw hat pushed back on his head. He wore an expression that I had never seen on him before, and I was about to say something to him when Caleb stormed out of the shop door and up the path toward Tom and me.

"You ever wish folks would just leave things the way they are?" Caleb said to both of us and no one. Then he shook his head and stomped off in the direction of his cabin.

Taj Caldwell stepped outside a few seconds later, craning his neck beyond the door jamb to be sure that Caleb had really gone. He took off his hat and wiped his forearm across his brow and looked first at me, then turned his attention on Tom Jenkins.

"I see you're all gussied up," Taj said. "I'm runnin' a little late, on account of I had to straighten a couple things out with Mr. Wheeler."

Tom grinned and Caldwell started toward the bunkhouse. He was halfway to his destination when he stopped and executed an about-face.

"Hey, Silver," Taj shouted. "You and the fellas don't need to wait for me. I'll catch up."

"If you don't mind my asking," I said once Taj was gone, "what was that about?"

Tom rocked back on his undershot heels and shyly slid his hands into his pockets.

"The boys are throwing me a sendoff. I'm heading back to work my Uncle Snoose's spread."

"I heard something about that," I said. "But it's not what I was referring to."

He looked at me with puzzlement, not knowing what to say.

"He called you 'Silver'," I said.

"It's cause of the buckles me and Paul Tucker won in the team roping."

I handed Tom the hawk feather, and he tucked it into his hatband.

"It sounds as though you earned yourself a nickname," I said.

His eyes slid to the ground, but the smile that broke across his face shone like the facets of a gemstone.

———⬦———

THE NEXT day, Jesse surprised me at the office with a picnic lunch she'd packed inside a wicker basket. We took our time walking toward Pioneer Park, where we spread a blanket on the grass beneath a weeping willow on the river-bank and stretched out in its shade. Damselflies rippled the burnished surface of the flats along the shoreline.

We ate cheese sandwiches and sipped cola from straws tucked inside the necks of frosted bottles, listening to the tanagers and buntings in the trees as Jesse told me of the young doctor, newly arrived from Grants Pass, who had acquired Doc Brawley's practice. He had graciously inquired as to whether Ruth Brawley might be willing to stay on to help him run the office, and Jesse had offered to help Ruth get things reorganized. Ruth was still adjusting to her life alone, but Jesse and I were both at peace knowing that this job would help to keep her engaged with the people in town who loved her, and would occupy the long, empty hours of her new reality.

When we finished lunch, Jesse walked barefooted across the lawn and stood before the stone obelisk and engraved bronze plaque where the short history of our county's founding was inscribed. The sunlight filtered through the tree limbs and cast her face in gentle light, and I could see the tiny wrinkles form along the corners of her eyes as she began to smile.

"You once told me you had to memorize this," she said.

"Yes, ma'am, that's a fact. Third grade."

"Let's hear it, Ty Dawson."

The workings of the human mind have long amazed me, and it didn't take more than a few seconds to exhume those lines that had lain dormant in my memory for decades and to recite them for my wife. Her eyes shone with the dampness that frequently betrayed her sentimental spirit, and she kissed me on the cheek once I had finished.

"When is the last time you said those words aloud?" she asked.

"Third grade. Probably 1940 or '41."

Jesse cast her gaze toward the empty bandstand, daydreaming on a private thought.

"I don't remember Cricket having to memorize the words on that marker when she was in school," she said at last. I was uncertain whether she was speaking to me or to herself.

"They don't spend much time on that sort of thing anymore," I said.

"Maybe they should."

I looked at the green patina that wept down from the plaque, took Jesse's hand in mine, and drifted back to collect our picnic basket from our spot beside the river.

"Do you still love me like you did when we were young?" she asked.

"You know my favorite season has always been autumn."

───❧───

JORDAN POWELL had taped a handwritten message to my desk while I was out. It said to phone Bill Kiefer as soon as I got back. The scheduled trials for Nolan Brody and William Barker Emory, aka Deva Ravi, were still several months away, though I harbored little doubt they would stack maximum time once it was all said and done. I hadn't heard from the attorney since the petition to recall me as sheriff had been withdrawn. Having collected fewer than fifty signatures, the whole thing had died of disinterest and neglect. I didn't have any new ranch business of my own with Kiefer, either, so the message left me curious.

"Ambervalia Corporation has retained me," Kiefer said after the preliminaries. "I thought you'd want to know."

"What does Ambervalia want with you?"

"They reached a settlement with Bryan Emory and his mom. The Emorys agreed to vacate the land lease in exchange for a share of the mining operation."

If the mineral report that Brody had attempted to suppress proved to be correct, that share was likely to be worth a small fortune. Bryan had been swiftly cleared of criminal charges stemming from the shooting of Carl Spinell, but a couple of other things concerned me.

"What are they supposed to do in the meantime?"

"Ambervalia has agreed to underwrite the cost of institutional care for Mrs. Emory, and to put Bryan through the college of his choosing, once he graduates high school."

"Living arrangements?"

"A monthly stipend for Bryan and his mother, and clear title to a nice three-bedroom house in Springfield, over near Eugene."

"That's some distance from Meriwether County," I said.

"That's what the Emorys wanted."

I couldn't say I blamed them one bit.

IT HAD taken several weeks for Dawn, née Mila Kinslow, to recover well enough from her wounds to be released from the hospital. She was ambulatory, but the damage that the bullet had caused to her left lung would leave her with a permanent reminder of the time she'd spent at Rainbow Ranch.

She and Cricket had grown close during Dawn's post-surgical recuperation, and my daughter brought Mila home to stay with us upon her discharge. It had only been for a few days, and some part of me felt that I owed her for her willingness to go on the record and help to bring down the hammer on what may very well have grown into a full-scale range war.

I thought it ironic that the two girls were out on the porch when I got home that evening, seated in positions almost exactly as they had been when Dawn had taken an assassin's bullet that had been intended to silence her forever. Through the window in the living room, I watched them laughing, the Tennessee mountain castoff and the college cowgirl, enjoying their last evening together. Dawn's friend Sandi, from Los Angeles, had been so pleased to hear from her that she agreed to drive up and take Dawn back to California where she could make another new beginning.

In spite of the differences in Dawn's and Cricket's lives, their laughter was a balm after a summer with so little to smile about. I took heart in their openness and absence of guile, but mostly I admired their strength.

I do not hold to some prelapsarian view of my upbringing; change is inevitable, whether through inattention, disdain, or design. The values and mores that I had been raised with were falling away, and I now somehow found myself entering an era in which people had grown more tolerant, but less self-confident, more socially equal, but less economically so. Bluntness substituted for subtlety, self-expression for courtesy, belligerence for dialogue, and sexuality for love. Nor could I identify the exact moment when desires had become rights, and the holding of elected office became a career path.

But these things never present themselves with clarity. Love and hate do not exist as two sides of a coin; rather, they coexist in an infinite ball that is as clear as the crystal on the table of a midway gypsy. Neither can we shrink from the choices we make. Like a drop of ink in a bucket of water, the drop disappears, but the water is irreparably affected.

I took off my hat and removed the band, one I had crafted decades ago with my own hand from leather and horsehair over weeks spent beside open range cook fires. I stepped out through the living room doorway and onto the porch, and gave it to Mila Kinslow, the girl whose name would always be Dawn to me.

"A keepsake," I said. "To remember us by."

She thanked me and smiled and slid it onto her head like a crown, like a Paiute princess.

"I don't have anything to give you in return," Dawn said.

"How about you and Cricket show me how to make that oatmeal she likes so much."

My daughter grinned, and the resemblance to her mother at that same age momentarily jolted me.

"You told me you hated it," Cricket said.

"I never really tried it. I told you that I hated the smell."

"And you want us to show you how to make it?"

I nodded and moved to go back indoors.

"Think of it as a cultural exchange," I said.

———— ⚬⚬⚬ ————

THE MORNING was mild, holding fast to the last remnants of Indian Summer. False dawn had begun to glow along the mountain ridge, though sunrise was still thirty minutes away. Dried folioles of dogwood littered the pathway that led down from my house and cleaved the predawn stillness as they crushed beneath my boots. It was the time of year when the leaves had only just begun to turn to shades of tamarind and gold, abandoning their branches until next spring. Any day now, autumn would sweep in without warning, carried on the frigid and blustery wind that would hold the valley in its grip from one end to the other until winter arrived to take her place. The rooftops and pasture grasses would crust with early morning frost, and our breath would become clouds of steam. It was the time of year that reminded me that yet another cycle had moved nearer to its end than its beginning.

Pale yellow light showed through the window of Caleb's kitchen, so I stepped up on the stoop and knocked with my free hand. He answered it a moment later, already dressed for the day but for his hat, which still rested on a coat hook beside the door, and the moccasins he wore in place of boots.

"I brought coffee," I said, showing him the thermos I carried.

"I've already made coffee."

"I thought we might climb the ladder and drink it on your roof."

Caleb looked at me through narrowed eyes that told me he was evaluating whether I was being sincere or poking fun at him.

"Autumn's coming," I said. "The frost'll be here any day, and we won't be doing any roof-sitting for a long damn while once it does."

He plucked his hat off the hook and fitted it on his head.

"I'll get my coat," he said.

We sat in silence, perched on the shingles, until the sun passed well above the mountains, the clouds like wisps fading from red to pink to white where the distant rain streaked the skyline. I could not shake the imagery a man named Blackwood had planted in my head: a world aptly symbolized by ouroboros, forever eating itself alive. But lately I had begun to hear the voices speaking to me inside the wind, a little louder and more frequent as I grew older.

"Where'd you slide off to?" Caleb asked.

I turned to look at him, the light and shadow of the rising sun accentuating the deep lines on his face. I had known this man all my life, the last living connection to my relatives and my family's history on this ranch. He had known all of them.

"I'm not exactly sure," I admitted. "I lost track of a few minutes, I suppose."

"Don't let that become a habit, son," he said. "There's precious few minutes as it is."

I have discovered that the space between the hours is far different when you're young. In more recent years, I have found that every tick of the clock seems to hit home with the impact of a trip-hammer.

Caleb stretched an arm across the space between us and gestured for me to refill his coffee mug. I did and topped mine off while I was at it, then screwed the thermos cap back in place.

"I'm not even forty-five years old," I said. "And sometimes, I swear to God, I already feel like an old man."

"Get used to it," he said. "Change ain't gonna come no slower just cause you don't cotton to it."

The schism between the old and the young is often blamed on a lack of understanding. I do not believe that is true. The difference lies not in the fact that the elders do not understand the young, but in the fact that they do. I took a sip of coffee and looked beyond the horse pasture, followed a V of geese as they cut across the sky.

"You remember what your grandpap used to say, don't you?" Caleb asked.

I waited for him to answer his own question.

"'Time's the one thing you can't hold onto, son. Might as well try to hang on to a fistful—'"

I smiled and looked away, down the slope toward the stand of aspen trees that lined the creek, where the fallen leaves had already piled up in heavy drifts along the bank and tree trunks showed the scars where they'd been marked by the high water of past seasons.

"Aw, hell," Caleb said. "Who'd I think I was talking to? You know how the saying goes."

ACKNOWLEDGMENTS

MY SINCERE GRATITUDE to two great friends who provided me with some invaluable insight and background for this book: The first is my pal Mark Simon, whose expertise with police protocols from back in the day is profoundly appreciated; and secondly, my longtime friend Edward Mishow, who helped me understand some of the finer intricacies of the legal profession. Thank you both for your generosity and your time.

As always, to my family, for their endless supply of enthusiasm, love, and reinforcement. Christina, Allegra, Britton, Christan, Nick, Ashton, and Kheler . . . *Aloha pau ole*!

Thank you, yet again, to a pair of true professionals (whom I have the distinct privilege of also numbering among my friends), my publishers, Martin and Judith Shepard, at The Permanent Press. And that goes for you, as well, Chris Knopf.

And finally, my deep appreciation to my incredibly talented copy editor, Barbara Anderson. And to cover artist and designer, Lon Kirschner—thanks again, amigo! You two are the best.

Until next time . . .